# SOPHIE AN...
## S...

by

## EVELYN CULBER

CHIMERA

Sophie and the Circle of Slavery published by
Chimera Publishing Ltd
PO Box 152
Waterlooville
Hants
PO8 9FS

Printed and bound in Great Britain by
Cox & Wyman Ltd, Reading.

# SOPHIE AND THE CIRCLE OF SLAVERY

## Evelyn Culber

This was the birching block, standing ominously near the furthest wall, and Sophie had cast several nervous glances in its direction, trying to work out exactly how it was used. Sister Tanya enlightened her.

'The traditional block, as used mainly in boys' schools, was a simple affair, consisting of a bit to kneel on and a higher part to support the upper body,' she explained. 'The naughty boy – and as girls' schools became more common – girl, would kneel down, thighs resting against the front of the upper part, lean forward and present his or her bare bottom to be whipped. Ours is much more flexible. Let me show you.'

Just call her Sophie.

Or, to be more precise, Slave Sophie.

She is content with her lot – and often very happy.

Nobody beat her over the head and dragged her off into slavery. She was not drugged or blackmailed and, if there was occasional persuasion on her journey, it was, under the circumstances, quite gentle.

She is twenty-five and pretty. Not outstandingly so, but certainly worth the many second looks discerning observers cast in her direction – especially when she is walking away from them. Her hair is a lovely and natural golden blonde, her complexion is classically English, her big eyes are blue/grey and her mouth full and soft. She is about 5' 5", with a neat rather than opulent bosom and a behind which more than compensates for any perceived mammary shortcomings.

Perhaps surprisingly to the uninitiated, she is far more striking now than she was a year ago when she first encountered the exciting and strange world she now inhabits with such satisfaction.

# Chapter One

Her first step was apparently totally innocuous. She had read Law at Oxford, qualified as a solicitor, and had successfully completed a six month trial with a large and busy firm in the West End of London. With a reasonable salary now assured and with the additional security of the interest from a Trust Fund set up by her late father, she could afford to rent a decent flat, and had been looking in vain for the right combination of comfort and privacy when a colleague pointed out an advertisement in an evening paper.

*Girl wanted to share pleasant house near Regents Park.*
*Must be prepared to do more than her fair share of housework*
*– Very reasonable rent in exchange.*

A naturally neat and tidy girl, the prospect of extra work did not worry her in the least, and the thought of living in a house rather than a flat more than compensated, so she lost no time in making contact.

She found her way to the address in good time, having given herself ample opportunity to look around the immediate neighbourhood, and was impressed. With Oxford Street within walking distance, the Park a great deal nearer, Marylebone Road far enough away to reduce the noise of the traffic to tolerable proportions, and some lovely houses for the seriously rich to walk past enviously, it suited her down to the ground.

The house itself was in a delightful mews. Sophie stood for a moment, studying the immaculate paintwork and discreet curtains, and it took her about two seconds to come to the conclusion that she desperately wanted to live there.

An hour later she was even more enthusiastic. The owner of the house had captivated her to such an extent that most of the details of the house had faded into insignificance.

Her name was Elspeth, and she was arguably the most beautiful woman Sophie had ever met. Her voice on the phone had been reassuring enough – low and warm, with a hint of Edinburgh in her intonation – and her physical presence had an even greater impact.

At that stage Sophie was still shy and surprisingly naïve. She had lost her virginity to a predatory rowing blue at Oxford, and the pain of the almost immediate ending of the relationship had convinced her that her natural caution was easily the safest course. So she buried herself in her work to such good effect that she had only just fallen short of getting a first class degree, despite her lack of real intellect.

So it was not surprising that her first impressions had concentrated on Elspeth's face, rather than her figure, other than noticing that she was tall, slender, but not fashionably scrawny. It was her eyes which had first attracted the young girl's attention, and not simply because they were the first feature she had focused on when the front door had been opened. They were dark brown, widely spaced, oval and clearly needed minimal make-up. Her eyelashes were long and almost perfect, so much so that Sophie at first assumed they must be false, only changing her mind when she had a chance to look more closely. Above all they had a penetrating quality and, whenever the two females looked directly at each other, Sophie felt a strange and almost disturbing feeling that her innermost thoughts were being studied analytically.

After Elspeth's eyes had made their initial impact, Sophie's attention had been drawn to her mouth, quickly noticing her hair on the way – short, dark and styled in that unfussy way which suggests a top hairdresser. Not quite jet black, but very nearly. The mouth was too full for sheer beauty, the subtle pink lipstick deliberately chosen to minimise its size but failing to reduce the impact, especially as the lips were curled upwards in a quizzically welcoming smile.

The two of them had looked at each other for several seconds on the doorstep, both appreciating the importance of the occasion and both in their different ways apparently satisfied, for Elspeth's smile had broadened, giving Sophie a brief flash of inevitably perfect teeth.

She had responded shyly and had been immediately taken with the hall, which was more spacious than the outside of the house had suggested and impeccably furnished, albeit quite sparsely.

The sitting room was much less sparse, although far from cluttered, and the same quiet good taste was reflected throughout the rest of the house.

Sophie's desire for acceptance grew with every minute.

As they sat in the tidy kitchen, enjoying a cup of real coffee, Elspeth outlined the sort of household duties she expected Sophie to carry out, and the young girl's eyes looked away, flickering round the room, vainly trying to hide her enthusiasm.

Elspeth smiled to herself and, as she automatically went through the requirements for polishing the silver and brass, she had already decided that Sophie was the one. She mentally listed her attributes:

Basically pretty, although her clothes, hair and make-up all seem to have been selected to make her look as unremarkable as possible.

In spite of her obvious intelligence, very shy and with little confidence in herself.

No real knowledge of art and antiques but seemed to have an instinctive appreciation of them, and therefore would probably treat the furniture and other precious things with proper care.

Sexually very immature; she had blushed rather sweetly at her first sight of the fairly graphic painting of a female nude in the sitting room, and then looked away – but had definitely sneaked a second glance.

Promising, very promising, Elspeth concluded as she gave the impression of thinking of any other chores she might have missed. There were of course quite a few, which were not for discussion until later.

'Well, what do you think, Sophie?' she asked after a thoughtful pause.

Sophie swallowed nervously, blushed again, looked around, lowered her eyes, saw that her hands were twisting spasmodically on her lap, planted them firmly on her thighs, and finally looked up at Elspeth's face.

'Er… I'd love to live here,' she said simply, and the shy smile with which she responded to Elspeth's obvious pleasure at her acceptance transformed her face.

After a brief discussion about what Sophie owned in the way of bed linen, towels etc., they agreed that she could move in on the following Saturday.

On the appointed hour, a time-expired mini cab rattled to a halt outside the front door and an hour later, Sophie's things had been put neatly away and the two of them settled down with a celebratory bottle of good champagne.

Sophie felt happier and more secure than she had since the death of her parents.

It was probably just as well that she couldn't read Elspeth's mind because, if she had somehow managed to 'see' what that elegant and lovely woman had in mind for her, she would have found it both terrifying and totally incomprehensible.

Luckily, she had inadvertently fallen into the hands of a real expert.

It was the first stage of her transformation.

The second came about five weeks later. Up until then, all her hopes and expectations had been more than satisfied. Elspeth was proving to be a perfect person to share with and the two of them soon slipped into a comfortable routine. Working days started with Sophie having to do no more than make sure that the living rooms were tidy and to get Elspeth's breakfast ready, before going to the office.

They took it in turns to do supper, but Sophie always did the washing-up and gave at least one of the main rooms a more thorough going over before settling down to enjoy the rest of the evening with Elspeth, either quietly reading or watching television.

Saturdays were taken up with more serious chores and Sophie soon noticed that the more efficient she got, the more work Elspeth piled on her. Not that she minded, because she was finding her new friend's company far more stimulating than the potentially dangerous allure of pubs and clubs.

And so, the fifth Saturday saw a happy young girl, dressed in her usual cleaning outfit of an old jumper and tight leggings, humming to herself as she carefully polished the various ornaments on the sitting room mantelpiece. Now that she was beginning to feel at home, she was no longer embarrassed by the painting of the naked girl right above her, nor of the two porcelain statuettes of nude dancers on the mantelpiece. She handled them as carefully as ever and simply accepted that they were beautiful.

Until that day.

As she dusted a delightful coloured glass figure of an elegant swan, her eyes drifted up to the painting, studying the model's face first of all and noting the calm, almost dreamy expression on her pretty face. Sophie was too unsophisticated to know that the pose and style were inspired by Boucher's classic *Mme O'Murphy*, and too naïve to appreciate the sexual subtleties of the painting. She only saw that the model seemed utterly at ease with her nudity, lying face down on a chaise longue, her right arm propped up on the raised end, her left elbow on the seat and her chin resting on her hands. Her legs were sprawled casually apart, the right one on a big cushion, the knee slightly crooked, so that the pink sole of her foot was visible.

Sophie's eyes drifted on to the soft, clearly relaxed bottom, smiled at the realisation that her cheeks were discernibly pinker than the sculptured plain of her back, and then she tried to imagine how she would have felt in the same position, with a handsome young artist capturing her wanton image for posterity. She shook her head at the thought and then carefully started polishing the lovely old clock in the middle, unaware that she had missed two ornaments.

An hour later she looked around the room with a nod of satisfaction. All the woodwork was gleaming, the brass shining, and it all should pass muster. The door opened and Elspeth glided in with her usual economic grace and began her tour of inspection, while Sophie stood calmly to one side.

Her thoughts were on a generous mug of proper Kenyan coffee, so she failed to spot Elspeth's increasingly disapproving expression as she inspected the mantelpiece, and was already basking in the expected compliments when she was jolted out of her complacency in a way which she found completely incomprehensible.

'This is filthy!' Elspeth's voice showed no signs of real anger, but there was enough soft menace in her tones to banish all thoughts of refreshment from Sophie's mind. She looked up to see her mentor holding a Venetian glass paperweight up to the light.

'Oh, I'm sorry, I'll do it right now,' she said briskly, and took a few paces towards the fireplace before an imperiously raised hand stopped her dead in her tracks.

'Let me just check the rest of the room,' came the ominous reply.

Three further failings were ruthlessly pointed out to the abashed girl before Elspeth moved up close enough to reach out with a forefinger, rest it under her chin, and exert enough pressure to lift a furiously blushing face.

'I'm a little disappointed in you, Sophie,' she said quietly.

'Yes, I understand,' Sophie stuttered. 'I really am sorry. I'll do them properly, right now.'

'That's right, you will – but not immediately. After I've spanked you.'

She did not know it, but Sophie was now facing the second and arguably the most crucial step in her development. Obviously the vast majority of girls in the London of the late 1990's would either have burst out laughing or have threatened to walk out. It was certainly on Sophie's mind to ask whether Elspeth was joking, but just one look at her face was quite enough to make it clear that she wasn't.

Her jaw sagged against the pressure of the retaining finger, her cheeks burned bright red, she felt slightly sick and completely at a loss. She had not, as far as she knew, ever been spanked in her life. Her tender bottom had never even been threatened – apart from one casually insulting swat by the Oxford blue as she got out bed.

Elspeth took pity on her. 'I know it sounds strange, pet, but it's the best way, honestly. It will clear the air. I won't be angry and disappointed in you any more, and you will feel much better. Promise.'

'All right,' Sophie whispered miserably, and resigned herself to what she could only see as an indescribably degrading experience.

Firmly but sympathetically, Elspeth ordered her to fetch one of the dining room chairs. She obeyed, and the activity helped to clear her mind a little, giving her just enough courage to try and discuss the matter. She didn't fancy her chances of success, but felt that she should make at least one attempt to stick up for herself.

She came back into the sitting room, holding the chair in front of her and paused, not quite sure what to do next. Elspeth was by the fireplace studying the pretty nude, her head cocked to one side, and Sophie felt even worse at the subtle reminder that her bottom was about to be brought into similar prominence. She cleared her throat.

Elspeth turned languidly and smiled at the red-faced girl,

noticing that the chair was shaking gently in her nervous grasp.

'Put it over there, dear, with the right side facing the window. That way there will be more light on the subject.'

In her confusion, Sophie did not see the gleam of eager anticipation in her tormentor's eyes, but had heard the unexpected endearment, and her planned protest suddenly seemed rather pathetic.

With the chair in the required spot she straightened up, swallowed convulsively, and finally summoned up the courage to say her piece.

'Er... Elspeth?'

'Yes, dear?' She turned away from the picture as she responded and, as Sophie saw the implacable determination in her expression, her desperately marshalled arguments on alternative punishments vanished into oblivion.

'Nothing,' she said forlornly, her face burning again with the additional humiliation of her easy submission.

With her heart thudding in her chest, her mouth dry, her palms moist and her bottom tingling with dread, she resigned herself to her fate.

For very different reasons, Elspeth was almost as worked up. She had anticipated far more verbal resistance from such an intelligent girl, and the way Sophie faced up to the prospect of a spanking came as a pleasant surprise. In fact, she was proving to be the most promising subject for a very long time.

First and foremost, the many surreptitious glances at her rear over the past few weeks had left her in no doubt that Sophie was blessed with the type of bottom Elspeth preferred; quite broad but curving out prettily from her back, adding a girlish pertness to the womanly breadth and, at the same time, deliciously mobile. Watching her walk away in those leggings was always a source of great pleasure.

Secondly, she was quite clearly pretty shattered at the prospect of having her bottom smacked. While Elspeth had often enjoyed dishing out mock spankings as a prelude to an

13

energetic bout of lovemaking, when her victim was reluctantly facing a genuine punishment the thrill was far more intense. To have a fit young girl in her power to the extent that she was prepared to allow herself to be bent over and suffer an embarrassing and painful punishment was enormously satisfying. Since Sophie had moved in, Elspeth had devoted all her skill and experience to establishing a firm but not harsh domination over her – and her efforts were about to bear fruit.

She moved slowly across to the chair, sat down and, ignoring the quaking Sophie, rolled up the sleeves of her silk blouse with pointed deliberation. Then she smoothed her skirt over each thigh in turn, before looking up into the girl's flushed and worried face.

'Bend over my lap, please Sophie,' she ordered, quite gently.

Her victim bent forward, then hesitated. Carefully looking at the floor to avoid eye contact, she opened her mouth, desperation at last giving her the courage to stick up for herself.

'Isn't there some other way of punishing me?' she whispered. 'This is awfully degrading.'

Elspeth felt even happier. Some resistance at last! 'That is half the point, my girl,' she replied, with the first touch of steel in her voice. 'The other half, of course, is that you end up with a sore bottom. Now stop arguing and get across my knee.'

Sophie wisely decided that she had pushed Elspeth as far as she dared, and then lowered herself awkwardly into position, ending up with her torso resting on the parted thighs and her knees almost on the floor. Her bottom was nicely bent but well to Elspeth's right – in reach but not properly in view.

'No, not like that,' Elspeth sighed, resting her hand on the fullest part of Sophie's cringing behind and applying enough pressure to communicate her desire to have it higher and further forward. The confused girl heaved herself up and eventually found herself in the traditional position, with her weight evenly distributed between hands, feet and middle.

In the following brief pause, as Elspeth looked greedily down at the well-defined bottom spread on her lap, Sophie glumly tried to make some sense of her situation. Her backside felt even more prominent than it had when she first bent over, and her bent angle meant that the blood flowed steadily to her head, exaggerating the sound of her pulse. She was not in the least bit happy, but her wits were so scattered that all she could think of was a fervent prayer that her ordeal would be relatively short-lived, encouraged by the wildly erroneous thought that smacking another female's bottom couldn't be exactly fun for Elspeth, so she was unlikely to drag the affair out any longer than necessary.

Naturally she was completely wrong and, if she had thought of peering up over her shoulder, she would have seen the light of battle in Elspeth's eyes.

She did get some hint of Elspeth's feelings when she felt a hand on the seat of her leggings. It rested on the crown of her right buttock for a moment, then the fingers pressed down. After a couple more squeezes, it moved to the upper slopes of the same cheek and the process was repeated. Sophie gulped and her face reddened again at the slow and blatantly sensual examination. She felt even more degraded as she lay there, helplessly allowing an intimate part of her body to be groped so freely. Once again she considered a plea for an alternative way, but decided that in her vulnerable position she would be far better advised not to aggravate Elspeth any further.

With her mind in such a whirl, it was not exactly surprising that an apparently inconsequential memory returned. Her rowing lover had been part of a group in her college, whose regular chant whenever they made a collective appearance had made them somewhat conspicuous:

'And they said that things couldn't get any worse –
But they *did* get worse,
*the very next day*!'

15

For a time it had become a popular catchphrase and had even been heard in the hallowed precincts of Balliol College, but she had forgotten it completely.

Until now.

Because things *did* suddenly get worse.

She felt Elspeth's fingers take a grip on the waistband of her leggings, and she caught her breath in dismay. The prominence of her bottom had been bad enough as it was, but the prospect of being made to expose her knickers was nothing less than appalling. Especially as they were not exactly new, had shrunk in numerous washes, and had ridden up obscenely into the deep cleft between her buttocks.

Once again she had to bite her tongue to restrain herself from protesting volubly at this last straw, but this time failed to choke back an anguished, 'Oh no!'

'Oh *yes*!' Elspeth snapped, and continued with the evil deed until the lightweight garment was rolled down and out of the way.

As Sophie struggled to get her breathing under some sort of control, Elspeth was looking down at her half-naked bottom with a great deal of pleasure. Everything had gone swimmingly. A pretty girl; a virgin spankee; enough resistance to add savour to the whole experience and, last but by no means least, a bottom which showed every sign of being a joy to spank.

The buttocks swelled delightfully up from the nicely curved thighs, with two charming, well-defined folds clearly marking the change from one to the other, and with skin which was white with just a hint of creaminess, flawlessly smooth and satiny. Her palm began to itch for the first touch but, with years of experience to season her innate sensuality, she knew that her pleasure would be enhanced if she took her time and satisfied each of her senses in turn.

Sight first. And the next move was obviously to get Sophie's plump bottom nice and bare. Her heart began to beat faster as she carefully reached down with both hands and took a firm grip of elastic waistband between each forefinger and thumb, pulled upwards to lift the tight band clear, and slowly drew the knickers down, her eyes gleaming brightly as they focused on the slowly emerging cleft, to her the key visual point of any bottom.

Ignoring the anguished squirm and the wail of dismay from her victim, she kept going until the pressure of Sophie's front against her thighs made further progress difficult.

'Lift up, dear,' she ordered gently. 'I want to get them right down to your knees.'

'Oh please, Elspeth, does it have to be on my bare bottom?'

'Of course it does,' she replied, with another hint of steely resolve in her voice.

With a choked sob, Sophie lifted her hips and her remaining protection slithered easily down to the required position.

Elspeth let her hands drop to her sides and contemplated Sophie's bare bottom at leisure, slightly relieved to find that her imagination had not let her down. Rather the opposite, in fact, as her new find proved to be even better reared than she had expected. Her buttocks were firmer than anticipated, and her classic English rose complexion was even more apparent on her lower cheeks than on her facial ones. The dividing cleft was unusually tight, and there wasn't the slightest hint of body hair peeping out at the junction of her thighs as a distraction from the rich array of smooth, white flesh.

No longer able to ignore the growing itch in her palms, Elspeth moved her right hand on to the nearer thigh and smoothed it upwards, lingered at the fold, and then stroked over both mounds, fairly briskly but without undue haste. Satisfied that Sophie's skin was as soft and smooth as it looked, she then tested the resilience of her naked flesh. She rested her hand on the top of the left cheek, the tips of her fingers briefly relishing the warmer and even softer skin in the cleft, and then pressed and squeezed, her eyes glued to the way the round buttock shifted under the pressure.

She repeated the process twice, moving down to the base

before treating the other side in the same way.

By this stage Sophie's nervousness and resentment were beginning to conquer the numbing shock which sapped her resistance at the beginning. As Elspeth's hand roamed, she moaned and pressed her front into Elspeth's thighs in an instinctive attempt to reduce the prominence and size of her bottom.

Elspeth realised that she was in danger of pushing Sophie too far so, slightly reluctantly, put her left hand on the small of her back, pressed down firmly, and started the spanking.

She was far too experienced to get carried away, even though Sophie's bottom was an absolute joy to deal with. Her flesh had a rare combination of firmness and softness; her skin reacted quickly and prettily to the smacks; her buttocks wobbled beautifully under the measured assault – springy rather than flabby. After the first dozen or so Elspeth tuned her senses to take note of Sophie's reactions, and found more signs of promise.

Surprisingly, the first spank had come as something of a relief for Sophie. She had resigned herself to the inevitability of a degrading punishment and had even submitted to having her knickers taken down with reasonably good grace, at least as far as she was concerned. But having her bare bottom felt by a member of her own sex had tested her submissiveness almost to the limit. She had felt at a complete loss. She had felt violated. Abused. She had heard her own muted protest through the pounding of her heartbeat and had begun to struggle, albeit very feebly. Then there had been that horrid ringing sound as Elspeth's hand had connected. She had felt her flesh shudder under the impact and the warm, stinging pain had taken her breath away. The spanks had kept coming, in fairly rapid succession, although Elspeth seemed to be able to judge her rhythm so well that the immediate pain of one impact had just begun to fade before the next one landed.

The she had begun to get used to it and, to her intense surprise, it was proving to be far more tolerable than she had feared. She relaxed over Elspeth's thighs and, with the first glimmer of understanding, came to the conclusion that she didn't hate Elspeth at all, and that being spanked like this was probably a far better incentive to improve her work than anything else. Gritting her teeth against the steadily mounting pain, she let the last shred of her resistance fade away and simply lay there, meekly submitting to being spanked.

Elspeth felt both the extra weight as Sophie slumped resignedly on her lap and the relaxation in her buttocks. Sensing that she had conclusively won the first round of her campaign, she smiled with satisfaction and decided to make some subtle changes in her approach. Until then she had delivered spanks which were basically punitive, although nowhere near as hard as she usually considered proper for a punishment.

Now that she could be fairly sure that Sophie had come to terms with the situation, she felt able to bring in a touch of the sensual. She relaxed her palm a little so that it matched the curves of the girl's buttocks, and instead of driving her hand into the flesh, swept it down in an arc so that it skimmed rather than flattened. The spanks sounded different, lacking the ringing tones of the previous ones, but there was ample compensation in the way Sophie's bottom wobbled even more dramatically.

The effects were twofold. Firstly, the pain was noticeably less. Secondly, the extra movement of the buttocks sent little stimulating messages to the most sensitive parts. Elspeth smiled happily when, after a dozen or so, Sophie's cries and moans took on a new quality.

After what seemed at least an hour, Elspeth announced that it was all over.

'Thank you,' Sophie gasped, as relief flooded through her and she clambered awkwardly to her feet, instinctively rubbing her throbbing bottom, gasping again as the heat of her skin seemed to burn her hands. She blinked away her tears and, as her vision cleared, she saw Elspeth was staring at her exposed front. With an apologetic squawk she scrabbled for her knickers and leggings, dragging them up with indecent haste and eventually managing to get everything more or less in place.

She stood there, trembling like an aspen, utterly miserable, feeling about six inches tall and at a complete loss. She dimly saw Elspeth stand up, then her hand was firmly gripped and she was led on unsteady legs to the sofa. For one horrible moment she felt sure she was going to get another spanking, and was about to scream at the injustice of it all, when she was guided onto the seat and Elspeth's arm was round her shoulders, drawing her head down to rest on a comforting shoulder.

She burst into a flood of tears.

Elspeth held the sobbing girl close, tempted to take her knickers down again to soothe her bottom properly, but decided that the maternal role would be more productive. She heard Sophie's choking attempts to pull herself together.

'Let it all out,' she advised gently, and her new friend gave in completely, ridding herself of several years' accumulated stress and tension.

For the rest of the day Elspeth was consideration personified. She helped Sophie with the rest of the chores, took her for a brisk walk in the park, and finally kissed her warmly on each cheek when the exhausted girl asked if she could have an early night.

After a good night's sleep, despite a number of vaguely disturbing dreams, Sophie set about Sunday's housework with new energy, determined to do everything possible to avoid another punishment. If she had been really pressed she might have admitted that being spanked wasn't anything like as painful as she had feared – but that was not the same as actually looking for another one!

To her intense relief, Elspeth's tour of inspection passed with only praise for her efforts and, with the house properly clean and gleaming, the pair settled down to relax. Gradually Sophie began to forget the events of the day before and to respond to the new sense of intimacy between them.

Although classical music had never played a big part in her life, she was more than happy to sit and listen to Beethoven's seventh, which Elspeth described as an excellent introduction. Restless at first, she began to find it increasingly absorbing, and during one slow passage, with the brass section's muted contribution underlining the more complex theme of the string section, felt unaccountably moved.

For the second time she was tired well before her usual bed time, and for the second time, Elspeth kissed her good night with something more than sisterly affection.

She did not fall asleep immediately, but lay for a while, taking stock.

She still felt a little ashamed of herself for the way she had spent so long crying on Elspeth's shoulder, and the fact that she had been treated far more like an intelligent adult than a wayward child ever since just added to her confusion.

In spite of all her efforts to divert herself, she failed to stop her thoughts drifting on to her spanking. Her head still told her that it was an inexcusably degrading way of punishing her for what was a pretty insignificant offence and yet, as she relived the experience, she found that she no longer saw it that way. Somehow, there had been an indefinable feeling of security in that bizarre position. It did not make any sense, but she could not deny it as she tossed restlessly in her comfortable bed. Even the thought of Elspeth's vision being filled with her upthrust bare bottom seemed less awful in retrospect than it had at the time.

She rolled onto her stomach, drawing her pyjama bottoms tight across her buttocks and sending the nerve-ends in those sensitive mounds flickering into life.

She remembered the strangely pleasant warmth after the

21

stinging pain had died away.

Her nostrils flared at the recollection of Elspeth's lovely scent and the softness of her hair on her cheek.

The soft imprint of Elspeth's lips on her face.

The comfort of her arms.

She rolled back onto her side and tried to clear her mind.

It didn't work, and she flung herself back onto her front.

Her pyjamas were even tighter and more restrictive.

Blushing, she pulled them down to her knees and the feeling of the cool air on her skin revived the full range of feelings and emotions she had experienced when Elspeth first bared her bottom. With a groan, she forced her right hand under her tummy, squeezed her plump, crisply haired mound, her middle finger instinctively delving into the wet heat of her tight slit, finding the stiff little button and, for the first time in ages, she brought herself to an amazingly strong climax, burying her face in the pillows to stifle her cries, and her wildly flailing legs sending her pyjama bottoms flying across the room.

She just managed to wriggle back under her duvet before she fell asleep.


At exactly the same moment Elspeth was lying on her back, completely naked, her raised knees widely parted, sensuously running a sophisticated vibrator around her neatly trimmed mound. Her eyes were closed, her tongue flickered over her lips, her breathing was still reasonably steady as she trailed the humming tip purposefully across both full lips, up and down the insides of her thighs, between her buttocks to her anus, and then up the slit to her clitoris.

Her free hand gripped her left buttock and began to squeeze rhythmically, matching the regular contractions of her muscles as the waves of pleasure built up.

Her mind was filled with the clearly remembered sight of Sophie's lovely bare bottom, quivering and reddening.

As her climax approached, the middle finger of her left hand slid into the tight warmth of the cleft between her pumping buttocks, nudged against her anus and, with the slick timing of long practice, thrust past the tense ring of muscle and into the clinging warmth within just as release flooded through her.

Both Sophie and Elspeth fell asleep at the same time, although the former's troubled mind resulted in a restless night, punctuated by disturbing dreams.

Elspeth, by contrast, had a contented smile on her face – which lasted until morning.

To Sophie's surprise, the following week saw her as happy as she could remember being for years. At work she began to realise that she was more decisive and self-assertive than before, and the occasional complimentary remarks from the two partners with whom she was most closely involved were much appreciated.

If she went to the office in the mornings with a lighter step, she hurried home in the evenings with even greater enthusiasm.

There was the lovely house to look forward to; the chance to bask in the warmth of Elspeth's personality, her extensive collection of classical music to explore, challenging and stimulating conversations, and good food and wine.

Elspeth was teaching her how to cook, and she was enjoying it. Her chores did not take up too much of her time and, with her new-found enthusiasm for life in general, were proving to be satisfying.

She was increasingly comfortable with the growing intimacy between Elspeth and herself. They always kissed each other good night, and even though it was only a quick peck on each cheek, Sophie still felt strangely flattered at the affectionate gesture from a woman whose personality and beauty were beginning to cast an enveloping spell.

Her spanking began to fade from her conscious memory.

Pride comes before a fall!

On the next Saturday, Elspeth watched her young helpmate like a hawk, without giving her the remotest hint that her bottom was in for it. She had been nursing the anticipation of renewing her acquaintance with that lovely firm, yielding flesh for seven whole days, and had been in an inner fever of anticipation since before breakfast.

However careful, assiduous and painstaking Sophie proved to be, her fate had already been decided.

In fact, Elspeth did not have to look too hard for an excuse. Sophie cheerfully acknowledged a shouted instruction to remember to polish the knocker on the front door, but was so wrapped up with the silver that it slipped her mind.

The mid-morning inspection of work-in-progress revealed the lapse, and Sophie's blushing apology was to no avail.

'Another spanking, I'm afraid, dear,' Elspeth announced with convincing but wholly false solemnity. 'Take your time over what you're doing and I'll deal with you after we've had coffee.'

It may well have seemed cruel to keep the woebegone girl waiting for the best part of an hour for her punishment, but it was all part of the experienced Elspeth's devious plan. She was fully aware that a period of keen anticipation would make the reality come as something of a relief.

She was, as usual, absolutely right. Poor Sophie carried on as ordered but with none of the zest she had shown before. Her mind was in a turmoil, although her fears were subtly different this time. Now that Elspeth had seen her bottom all bare, she was rather less concerned with the assault on her modesty and, as she had already acknowledged to herself that the spanking had not been quite as painful as she had feared, the assault on her flesh no longer held the unbearable fear of the unknown.

What was making her feel literally sick was the feeling of rejection. Just as she had put the shaming events of the previous weekend out of her mind and was beginning to feel at home, she was about to be made to suffer it all again. Far too naïve to appreciate the sensual aspects of spanking, and far too lacking in self-confidence to believe that Elspeth could possibly like her and still punish her in such a degrading way, poor Sophie was at a very low ebb.

As the hour approached she felt worse and worse. Her hands were wet, her mouth dry, her heart pounded away and her bottom felt strangely big and heavy. Only the memory of the way Elspeth had been so friendly and warm to her after the first spanking prevented her from facing the problem head on and confronting her with the obvious fact that she was useless, and so it would be better all round if she looked for alternative accommodation.

She was just working herself up into a state of utter dejection when the hall clock struck eleven and she stumbled into the kitchen to make the coffee. Her legs trembled and her hands began to shake uncontrollably, so that she only just managed to fill the two cups without mishap.

To her amazement Elspeth breezed in, thanked her warmly for the coffee, and started an animated conversation about some people who had just moved in to a nearby house. To her surprise, Sophie found herself relaxing a bit and could actually drink her coffee without that horrible feeling that she was on the verge of throwing up.

When both cups had been drained Sophie took them over to the sink and turned on the tap. She jumped when she felt a firm pat on her bottom, and the less than subtle reminder of her immediate fate set her nerves jangling all over again.

'Leave those till later, dear,' Elspeth said. 'I'm sure you can't wait for your spanking.' There was a sympathetic smile on her face as she spoke, and Sophie couldn't help responding with a shy one of her own. In spite of all her worries, the thought that she was impatiently waiting for something she would have done almost anything to avoid was ridiculous enough to contain a trace of humour.

She followed Elspeth meekly into the sitting room and stood shakily while the appropriate chair was placed in the middle of the room. She dried her hands on the seat of her leggings, and the touch sent the nerve-ends in her buttocks into quivering life.

Swallowing convulsively, she was guided between Elspeth's parted legs, her back to her.

She desperately tried to get her breathing under some sort of control as her leggings were tugged slowly down to her knees.

She screwed her eyes tight and held her breath as she waited for the feel of fingers on the waistband of her knickers, and the degrading sensation of them sliding down over her trembling buttocks.

'I much prefer these panties to those rather indecent ones you were wearing last time,' Elspeth remarked thoughtfully.

Sophie couldn't think of anything to say, so she just stood there.

'Right, Sophie dear, over you go.'

Her lungs emptied in a gusty sigh of relief at the realisation that it wasn't going to be on her bare bottom and she tottered round, clumsily putting herself across the parted thighs.

The pressure on her tummy seemed to make the hollow feeling even more pronounced, and then she found a little distraction as she tried to remember exactly how Elspeth had positioned her last time, shifting her weight around until she felt a sense of uncomfortable familiarity.

A warm 'Good girl' from above and behind made her feel a bit better.

Then fingers took hold of elastic and she felt considerably worse, although she managed to quash the immediate protest before it passed her dry lips.

Cool air on her prominent bottom.

Then a soft, warm hand. Patting. Making her cheeks quiver embarrassingly.

Then a pause and that horrid sound of stiff palm on bare flesh rang out as an explosion of hot, stinging pain made her gasp.

She clenched her teeth and concentrated on her bottom, determined to show Elspeth that she could take it.

As far as Elspeth was concerned, this second punishment was already proving to be even more satisfying than the first. Having already seen Sophie's bottom and reassured herself that it was as pretty and spankable as she'd hoped, she was able to concentrate on spanking it properly.

She started off fairly lightly, working methodically from cheek to cheek and from base to apex, leaving cloudy pink traces on the clear white skin as she went, and continuing in the same vein until the entire surface was glowing nicely.

Then she paused for a good look and a quick stroke, automatically assessing how the girl was getting on and pleased that the only obvious sign of discomfort was her heavy and rapid breathing. She then raised her hand and slashed it hard into the lovely chubby curve at the base of the left buttock, her little finger driving accurately into the clearly defined fold.

Sophie cried out at the escalation in the pain, and her bottom bucked in her anguish and surprise.

Elspeth watched the darker patch take shape and let fly again, her heart singing with sheer joy at both the feel and sight of her hand sinking deep into the naked flesh just above the red stain marking the site of her previous effort. The sound of the spank and of Sophie's gurgling wail were music in her ears, and the dramatic change in the shape of her bottom as she frantically clenched it added an extra dimension to her pleasure.

The third hard spank landed on the upper slopes and Elspeth treated herself to another lingering look at the duotone bottom, the left side a bright rich red and the right a delicate pink.

Three spanks later, both sides matched nicely and Sophie was crying softly, her sobs making her submissively proffered buttocks quiver delightfully.

Sophie probably felt that she'd had quite enough but,

unfortunately for her, Elspeth was only just getting into the swing of things and began a repeat of the opening dose, her hand beating a rapid and mercifully lighter tattoo on the wobbling cheeks, happily noting that her victim was obviously finding this approach much easier to bear, as the sobs were replaced by softer cries and wails.

After five minutes altogether, Elspeth rested her warm hand on cool thigh, leant back against the seat of the chair, and looked down appraisingly.

Sophie's bottom was a lovely even red all over and she was crying softly again, clenching and relaxing her burning bottom in blatant, albeit totally unconscious, mimicry of sexual excitement.

Elspeth smiled tenderly and began to stroke the hot flesh. 'You took that very well, my dear,' she said, her tones soothing Sophie's mind as effectively as her hand was her bottom.

'Thank you,' the young girl panted and visibly relaxed, pushing her bottom tentatively against Elspeth's palm. 'Ooh, that *is* nice,' she added, rather unnecessarily.

Elspeth was more than happy to spend the best part of the morning with her hands on Sophie's bare bottom, but was sensitive enough to notice when the girl's reaction changed from relief to a certain embarrassment at the intimacy of their relative positions.

With an affectionate slap, Elspeth helped her to her feet, kissed her and then offered to help with the front door.

As before, it took time for Sophie to come to terms with her punishment. But eventually she relaxed and, by the evening, was back to her bright and cheerful self.

If her second spanking could be described as consolidating her acceptance of corporal punishment at Elspeth's hands, the next day saw the definitive first step in her progress to real submission.

She did not get spanked at all – and, as she lay in bed before going to sleep, realised that she felt slightly disappointed. The day seemed, in retrospect, uneventful and rather unexciting.

# Chapter Two

Five weeks later, Elspeth woke up unusually early, feeling a glow of anticipation flow through her as she remembered that it was another Saturday, so Sophie's bottom was available for the entire day. She decided against waking the unsuspecting girl, preferring to spend the next hour or so in happy contemplation.

She slipped out of bed, turned on the kettle for the first and most welcome coffee of the day, stretched luxuriantly and strolled into the bathroom, enjoying the slight chill of the air on her naked skin.

By the time she had washed her face and cleaned her teeth, the water had boiled, so she filled the cafetiere, let it stand for a couple of moments, her nostrils flaring as the scented steam reached her nose, pressed the plunger firmly down, filled the cup and took that first blissful sip.

With her caffeine level nicely topped up, she put her cup down, stretched again and then began her usual routine of exercises, beginning with deep breathing, her lips curving up in a smile as the blood started to flow through her veins. Her breasts shifted as her chest expanded and contracted and her smile took on a dreamy quality.

It faded as the exercises got more demanding, but there was a look of quiet contentment on her face throughout. With a realistic view of her figure, stopping short of vanity, Elspeth was able to imagine the sight she was presenting as she twisted, turned and bent, her fair skin gleaming in the subdued light: her nipples, tummy-button, and triangle of dark hair drawing her phantom spectator's eyes to her front. And the long tight cleft of her round bottom equally attention grabbing when she turned her back.

She felt her breasts quiver and her buttocks shake when she jiggled up and down on her toes.

Small but addictive thrills coursed through her middle when she bent right down to stretch her hamstrings and the action tightened her bottom, opening the cleft, allowing a waft of cool air to caress her neat little anus.

Lying on her back she moved her feet apart and raised her legs, holding them six inches above the carpet, keeping them there until her stomach muscles began to protest, distracting herself from the pain by concentrating on the soft prickle of the carpet on the skin of her bottom.

After six repetitions she raised her hips, supported them with her hands, did three minutes steady bicycling, before hoisting her legs right over her head until her toes touched the floor, then spread them wide, breathing deeply as she again imagined the look on the face of the ghostly admirer standing over her raised bottom, staring avidly at her blatantly exposed bottom-hole and fanny.

She smiled again as she stood up and wound down with some more deep breathing.

Then, glowing all over, she climbed back into bed, settled down and calmly reviewed Sophie's progress.

It was unquestionably a case of so far so good. She was learning fast. Elspeth smiled again as she pictured the expression on Sophie's gentle face whenever its owner was sentenced to a spanking – and the way that expression had subtly changed over the past few weeks. The look of outrage and horror on the first occasion had been slowly replaced, first with wry resignation and, last Sunday, something not far from excitement. She had certainly put herself across the waiting lap with far less reluctance, and had definitely lifted her bottom to make baring it easier.

At the same time the young girl had begun to come out of her shell. She was more confident in expressing her opinions, seemed more at ease around the house, and was showing increasing interest in all the subjects which Elspeth held dear, from art to music. She was proving to be good company.

In short, Sophie was already disproving the theory that corporal punishment inevitably reduced the recipient's personality.

Suddenly restless, as though unable to wait any longer to take Sophie's education a stage further, Elspeth slipped out of bed and crossed over to the window. Flinging it open she took in lungfuls of air, wishing for a moment that she was back in the country, but then appreciating that the wind was coming from the west and so was relatively unpolluted. Fairly confident that none of the occupants of the houses on the other side of the mews would be up and about so early, she stayed there for several minutes, her naked breasts to the breeze and her nipples tightening visibly in the chill morning air.

Then, a little ashamed of her display, she walked back to her bed and clambered under the duvet.

She tossed and turned, restlessly impatient.

Another cup of coffee calmed her a little and her mind cleared sufficiently to plot the next stage in Sophie's downfall.

Now that the young girl had come to terms with the effectiveness of a sound spanking on her bare bottom for all mistakes and misdemeanours, she was ready to receive some basic instruction in the finer points of corporal punishment. She already seemed to trust her mentor, and so the time was ripe to teach her that pain and pleasure can be linked.

Subtle questioning over the past weeks had given Elspeth a far clearer idea of what made Sophie tick. Her one unhappy little affair at Oxford had obviously retarded her development, but she showed no signs of any permanent scarring. She freely admitted to finding one of the male partners in her firm quite attractive, and yet had never recoiled from any of Elspeth's physical approaches. She still blushed prettily whenever they kissed goodnight, and seemed to welcome the intimacy of the post spanking cuddles.

The promise of what the day should bring had an immediate effect on Elspeth. The urges were so sudden that she couldn't be bothered to fetch her vibrator to bring herself to her usual deliberate climax, but spread her legs and, with various images of Sophie's bare bottom filling her mind, used her fingers with unashamed expertise to achieve a very satisfying result.

To say that Elspeth's expectations were exceeded would be an understatement.

Sophie had also woken up earlier than usual and had felt a similar restlessness as she lay in bed waiting for the normal time to get up and start getting breakfast. Unlike Elspeth, she was too inhibited to find relief in the same, time-honoured way – in fact, she had not touched herself since the night after her first spanking, so by the time she was ready to start her chores, she was raring to go.

The customary mid-morning inspection went without a hitch and the two of them chattered happily away over their coffee, with Sophie far too wrapped up in her own contentment to notice that Elspeth was definitely on edge.

As the morning passed, the weather changed. An early summer series of thunderstorms moved steadily towards London and the air got heavy and sultry. Sophie reacted by working even harder and, when the last job was done, she sank gratefully into the nearest chair, breathing heavily as she wiped the perspiration from her forehead.

Elspeth glided in.

'Finished already, Sophie?' she asked, smiling warmly.

'Yes,' Sophie replied with justifiable pride.

'Well done, dear. I'll just take a quick look round – just in case.'

Sophie smiled back nervously at the implied threat in the last phrase, but waited calmly enough while her efforts were checked out, fairly confident that she had done well enough to avoid a spanking.

Then it suddenly occurred to her that the prospect of being

put across Elspeth's knee no longer frightened her. Her face reddened as the import of this surprising thought struck home. She may have accepted the strange fact that she seemed to need an occasional spanking to keep her up to the mark, but the knowledge that she no longer minded presenting her bottom to be bared and smacked came as something of a shock. Just as she was asking herself what sort of spell Elspeth had woven over her, the object of her growing affections returned, beaming amiably.

'Very well done, Sophie. An excellent morning's work.'

Basking in the approval, Sophie was beginning to return the smile when the bombshell landed.

'But I'm still going to spank you!'

Sophie gaped as her face reddened. 'But why?' she asked plaintively.

'Because I feel like it – and you've such a luscious bottom,' Elspeth replied in her most matter-of-fact tones.

Poor Sophie. Her mind was in a complete turmoil as the shocks came one after the other.

To be told that her bottom was desirable was naturally flattering.

The fact that another woman desired it was a mixed blessing, to say the least.

Although when that other woman was the beautiful Elspeth, whose approval meant so much, it did put a rather different complexion on the matter.

Lastly, openly to express the desire to cause her pain in that part of her anatomy, however luscious it may be, was simply beyond normal comprehension.

She instinctively played for time. 'Um... I am a bit hot and sticky, Elspeth. Would it be all right if I had a quick shower?'

'Yes of course, dear. How considerate of you. I'll see you in the sitting room in quarter of an hour.'

Sophie tottered upstairs, undressed, her unsteady legs took her to the shower room, she turned it on, tested the temperature, remembered her shower cap in the nick of time and moved under the powerful spray, gasping with relief as the water immediately washed away the accumulated sweat. A thorough application of scented shower gel completed the process and she stood there letting the needle-sharp jets stimulate and relax her, while she collected her thoughts.

At last, she came to the conclusion that Elspeth must be a lesbian, so the first thing was to try and come to terms with that unpalatable fact. She recalled a conversation in her college buttery, when one of her acquaintances produced a juicy bit of gossip about the captain of the women's lacrosse team and stated that she'd suspected her tendencies all along. Sophie had found her gloating rather distasteful and said that Sammy's sexual preferences were as irrelevant as her religion.

She meant it at the time, but now she was facing a situation that affected her far more directly, she was less sure of her convictions.

And yet...! Elspeth admitted to finding her bottom attractive. Nobody else ever had. After all her spankings after the first one, she had held her down on her lap and stroked it for several minutes. Sophie remembered vividly how much she had appreciated the touch. Not only had it soothed the stinging, but there had been some almost magical quality in Elspeth's hands, which had made her feel so good and had compensated almost completely for the pain and humiliation of the spanking.

She leaned forward, resting her hands against the tiled wall so that the spray landed directly on her arched bottom.

The power shower was forceful enough to make her skin tingle and reminded her forcefully that she was about to be spanked.

The thought began to excite her.

The realisation worried her.

Even more confused than ever, she turned off the shower, dried herself briskly, hurried back to her room, found a clean pair of knickers and a light summer dress, brushed her hair, applied lipstick and eye-liner, and finally arrived in the sitting room only five minutes late, her heart pounding and still very confused.

Not that Elspeth was angry at Sophie's tardiness. Obviously it had given her an excuse for including an element of punishment to the spanking, but then she felt certain that she'd already reached the stage when she didn't need any such excuse. She had used the time to savour the forthcoming attraction to the full, anticipating the sight and feel of Sophie's bare bottom and composing her mind so that she could generate the right atmosphere.

She was fully aware that this spanking could well be as influential as the first in terms of Sophie's training. She knew that to get someone to accept the complex premise that pain and pleasure can be inextricably entwined meant influencing the mind more than the flesh, and so the right atmosphere was vital.

As the girl stumbled haltingly into the room muttering an apology for being late, and looking absolutely gorgeous, she beamed at her, stood up, crossed the few yards between them and folded the trembling body in her arms.

She breathed in the heady scent of fear, excitement, and expensive soap.

Sophie's irregular breaths felt warm on her cheek and neck.

Her waist was firm and slender in her grasp.

She leaned back so she could look into that flushed and troubled little face.

She smiled with real affection.

'You look really sweet, pet,' she said softly, and the pleased and shy smile which greeted her compliment was both reassuring and thrilling. 'I love that dress.'

'Thank you,' Sophie whispered, and her eyes dropped away. She took a deep, shuddering breath. 'Are you going to spank me really hard?'

Elspeth's peal of laughter brought Sophie's eyes flickering

up to focus on her tormentor's face, searching for even a hint of mockery. Her relief when she saw only friendly warmth was obvious.

'Of course not,' Elspeth reassured her. 'But I will keep you across my knee for some time.' The qualification was clearly less welcome and Sophie's mouth puckered slightly, the corners turning down almost sulkily. Elspeth's right palm began to itch and she lowered it slowly onto the pronounced curve where bottom swelled out from small of back. Her fingers pressed into the firmly yielding flesh, and the buttocks tightened nervously.

'Oh!' Sophie said resignedly. She blinked, and Elspeth saw the glistening evidence of the first tears. Both her excitement and determination grew.

'But one of the advantages of taking my time is that I can stroke and rub your bottom and let it cool off a bit before carrying on.'

'That sounds nice,' Sophie replied, after a thoughtful pause.

Elspeth's left hand dropped down to join her right, and Sophie rested her head on her shoulder again, sighing mournfully.

They stood like that for several minutes, each preoccupied with her own thoughts and feelings.

Sophie was not sure what to think. She still found it hard to accept that Elspeth actually wanted to spank her, especially on her bare bottom. As far as she was concerned, the bottom wasn't exactly the most pleasant part of the human anatomy. Comfortable to sit on – well, hers was, anyway – but its other usual function meant that it was far better kept completely private. On the other hand, feeling Elspeth's hands kneading her cheeks was proving to be surprisingly nice. And she had said nice things about it. And if she wasn't going to smack it that hard, well maybe it wouldn't be too bad. Still more than a little embarrassing, though. Bent across her lap, bare from waist to knees. Horrid and vulnerable.

But it did feel nice, being cuddled like this. Without the

distraction of a sore bottom, she could appreciate the physical aspects more clearly. Elspeth's front was all soft and womanly. Not firm and muscular, like Gerry at Oxford. Not that he'd cuddled her much.

'Right, let's have you across my knee.' Elspeth's brisk voice shattered Sophie's reverie and her heart started to pound again. In her confusion she again had that strange feeling of being out of control, with the even stranger feeling of enjoying being controlled.

Elspeth took her hand and led her over to the big sofa, sat down in the middle, and suddenly Sophie found herself lying on her lap. She wriggled into position, with her groin resting on Elspeth's right thigh and the left one supporting her chest just below her breasts, and the realisation that having her head and feet resting on the sofa was significantly more comfortable and relaxing than her usual position.

She held her breath as she felt her skirt start its upward journey, but had to let it out again before it was even up to her bottom, as Elspeth was taking so long about it.

Quite deliberately.

Familiarity with Sophie's behind had not bred contempt, and Elspeth was not going to ruin a promising little session by rushing it. She inched the loose skirt up Sophie's nice round thighs, pausing now and then to feel her satiny skin and assess the increasingly yielding flesh as she travelled upwards.

When, at last, only a pair of pretty white knickers covered Sophie's bottom, Elspeth paused again. She looked for several minutes, her eyes focused on the enticing sight of the thin, shadowy line of Sophie's bottom-cleft, just discernible through the clinging nylon. The knickers had rucked up slightly and the further extremities of her gluteal folds were peeping out, sweet and innocent.

She trailed the tip of a forefinger along the exposed creases, enjoying the soft warmth.

The touch of naked skin galvanised her into activity and

she reached for the elastic waistband and pulled the girl's knickers down, with tantalising pauses every couple of inches.

She heard Sophie's breathing change as her bottom was bared, becoming shallow and irregular. With instinctive modesty she clenched her buttocks briefly. The cleft tightened until it was the thinnest of creases and little dimples flared up over the lower curves of her cheeks, subtly altering their smooth shapes. Then, with a sigh, she accepted the inevitable and relaxed.

Elspeth felt an insistent tingle between her legs as she looked down at arguably the nicest bottom she had ever had under her control, and the tingles increased when Sophie actually pushed it up, in tacit invitation.

Rather distractedly, Elspeth tidied the rumpled knickers as her unblinking gaze locked on to the inviting display. Only their laboured breathing disturbed the silence as the older woman looked, and the younger one found that she was almost enjoying being looked at.

'Did you really mean it when you said you like my bottom?' Sophie asked, unable to hide the tremor in her voice.

'Are you accusing me of lying?'

'*No*, honestly,' Sophie shrieked, her bottom quivering in sympathy with her sudden panic. 'It's just that nobody's ever said anything nice about it before.'

'You surprise me,' Elspeth responded. 'But I'll like it even more when it's nice and red.'

'Oh dear!' Sophie wailed, but belied her apparent unhappiness at the prospect by lifting her hips again.

Elspeth kept the girl waiting for a little longer while she rolled up her sleeves, then made her final preparations, which did not take long, consisting only of placing her left arm across Sophie's bare waist, taking a firm grip of her hipbone, resting her right palm on the base of the left buttock and giving it a squeeze.

'Ready?' she asked sweetly.

'Yes, Elspeth,' Sophie replied, rather tremulously.

'Then let the entertainment begin!'

Despite her seething excitement, Elspeth was experienced enough to keep herself under control. She spanked Sophie with calm deliberation, slapping the entire surface of her bottom with crisp spanks but allowing a significantly longer interval between them so that the sting was beginning to fade before the next one landed.

It was a sight to delight any connoisseur of the art. Two singularly attractive women, the younger one lying gracefully in the time-honoured position, her skirt neatly folded up on her back and her pristine knickers turned inside-out, with the gusset trapped between her thighs, like an arrow pointing up to the bare bottom four inches above.

A genuinely lovely bottom it was too. Sophie may have found it hard to credit that anyone should be attracted to it, but even a dedicated fashion freak would have had to admit that it had great charm, however much its plump curves would have disqualified its owner from a career as a model.

As Elspeth's hand sank into the relaxed mounds, they reacted beautifully. Sophie's bottom was fleshy enough to wobble under the assault, but the firmness of her flesh prevented that wobble from even the gentlest accusation of flabbiness. It was a springy ripple, which spread rapidly out from the point of impact, up to her hips to the north and down to her upper thighs in the south.

Her flawless skin was another plus point. Lingering traces of the previous summer's occasional sunbathe in her ultra-decent bikini had resulted a discernible difference in the colour of her buttocks compared with the exposed skin above and below; pure white versus creamy. Her bottom coloured quickly and prettily, although it took an expert spanker like Elspeth to strike with an ideal angle of her wrist and so avoid the blotchiness made inevitable if the fingertips are allowed to lash indiscriminately, which may be permissible when the sole objective is to punish. But as always, part of Elspeth's pleasure was to produce an even escalation through several shades of red.

If Sophie's bottom was unusually beautiful, the rest of her did not lag all that far behind. Her face may have been pretty rather than gorgeous and, at that particular moment, not perhaps at its best. She was flushed and her nice honey-coloured hair was in some disarray, getting less and less tidy as her spanking progressed and she tossed her head in reaction to the mounting pain – an admirable alternative to moving her middle and spoiling Elspeth's aim. Her eyes were wide open but unfocused as she concentrated fully on the varied sensations afflicting her naked bottom.

Her arms were folded under her breasts, propping up her torso.

There was a discernible tension in her body, especially in the way her bare feet dug into the sofa cushions but, even to an inexperienced observer, her compliance was obvious, mainly from the determined way she was keeping her rear end still and relaxed.

If the spankee presented a delightful sight, then so did the spanker. Elspeth's body language was understandably much more relaxed than Sophie's, and her movements were as graceful as ever. Not that these amounted to much more than the smooth sweeps of her right arm as it rose slowly, paused for a fraction, and then flashed down onto whichever specific part of Sophie's bottom most needed a dash more colour. The impact of each spank did send a little tremor through her breasts, more noticeable on the right than the left, making it obvious that she was not wearing a bra.

Her face would have held a spectator's attention more than any other part of her, especially as it was only inches above Sophie's bottom, so that the eye could flick from the main centre of attention to the secondary without having to re-focus.

Two small creases in her normally smooth forehead indicated the level of her concentration. Her eyes were fixed to the two buttocks just below but, given the beauty of

Sophie's bottom, neither that nor the unholy gleam in them were anything but understandable.

Her lovely mouth was curved in a smile, communicating both enjoyment and triumph.

Her straight back showed confidence and authority, but there was also a relaxed air about her which clearly showed that she was completely at ease.

Elspeth had turned Sophie's bottom a delightful shade of deep pink before the young girl began to breathe in that audibly disjointed way which suggested that she was beginning to feel a degree of discomfort. It was time to acknowledge that this was not a punishment, so Elspeth began to rub the warm cheeks, firmly enough to shift them around but without adding to the pain.

Her smile broadened when she heard a grateful sigh from her left and felt an increase of the weight on her legs as Sophie relaxed.

'Is that nice?' she asked softly.

'Very,' came the not unexpected reply.

After a few more soothing minutes, she tightened her grip on Sophie's hip with her left hand and raised the right. She paused, waiting to see how Sophie reacted to the obvious sign that hostilities were about to recommence. To her evident delight, she lowered her head and cocked her bottom up. Not much and certainly not blatantly, but enough to show that she was beginning to discover that there can be more to a smacked bottom than just pain.

Elspeth sighed happily and redirected her spanks, concentrating on the centre, driving the tips of her fingers into the soft division so that the ripples stimulated Sophie's anus and fanny, deliberately adding pleasure to the pain.

The effect was immediate. Sophie buried her head in her hands and spread her legs, offering her quivering bottom in a way that was, by her standards, indecent. Small, inarticulate cries underlined both her pleasure and her surprise in it.

Given all her skill and experience, it was hardly surprising

42

that Elspeth brought Sophie to the brink of orgasm quite quickly – nor, given her dominant personality, that she took her time in bringing her to fulfilment. Every time she saw and felt the signs she changed course and let the waves settle. Then she started all over again, mixing the direction and strength of her spanks, then stroking the scarlet flesh and rubbing both cheeks vigorously, running a fingertip along the folds between thigh and buttock, the cleft, the insides of the parted thighs. Then delivering another volley of stinging spanks, until poor Sophie was in a complete daze.

At last Elspeth judged the time was right and her left hand wriggled under the soft tummy, riffled through the neat bush, found the swollen clitoris and rubbed away, while her right hand administered a series of ringing spanks to the lower part of the bottom.

Sophie was so far gone that her screams were hoarse and relatively subdued, belying the basic fact that she had never felt anything quite as intense in her life.

And it didn't end there. When she eventually clambered shakily to her feet she was calmly told to strip off completely, go up to Elspeth's bathroom and fetch the special lotion, in a plain white jar marked, *For use on bottoms only*.

Too dazed even to wonder why Elspeth should have something that strange in her possession, she obeyed, and then went back across the familiar lap. The ensuing five minutes, as the cream was gently spread, were such bliss that she didn't even notice that Elspeth parted her buttocks several times, exposing her anus. The only thing occupying her mind was the incredible warm glow suffusing her entire middle.

By the end of the weekend she had made further progress.

Later that evening Elspeth took her into the guest bedroom. She stood her with her back to the full-length mirror, held her skirt up, pulled her knickers down, and made her turn her head so she could see her bottom, pointing out all its good features, going some way to convince her that bottoms are

43

appealing, and hers especially so.

She was made to spend the rest of the evening naked. It took her time to get used to it, but eventually she relaxed a bit and was beginning to find being the object of Elspeth's undisguised admiration rather morale boosting.

On Sunday they took a picnic into the park, managed to find a place to sit out of earshot of all the others with the same happy idea and, after a cold game pie, salad, early strawberries and cream, accompanied by a bottle of champagne, they both felt relaxed enough to discuss Sophie's feelings.

Not surprisingly, Elspeth took the initiative.

'How's that lovely bottom of yours?' she asked, out of the blue.

Sophie blushed and squirmed, her instinctive action pressing the part in question even harder into the grass below the rug.

'Fine,' she answered after a pause.

'Good. I'll have a look at it when we get back,' Elspeth said firmly, brooking no argument.

Sophie's face went even redder and she wriggled again. 'That would be nice,' she whispered, and Elspeth's keen eye noticed the conflict between uncertainty and desire on her face, and she laughed. 'You know something, Sophie my sweet? You should never take up poker. Every time you got a decent hand you would go bright red.'

Sophie grinned ruefully and agreed, describing a night at Oxford when she had been coerced into a friendly game and lost all her matchsticks in ten minutes.

'You quite enjoy my seeing your bare bottom now, don't you?' Elspeth asked suddenly.

'Yes, I suppose I do,' Sophie admitted.

'Good. I thoroughly enjoy looking at it. And the rest of you. I love your firm little boobs – and that lovely golden bush.' Elspeth continued remorselessly. 'Now don't tell me that you find my interest unappealing.'

Sophie's face turned scarlet as she gazed blindly into the distance. Her hands writhed on her lap, her fingers intertwining in her confusion at this unexpected prompting to come to terms with the feelings which had already caused her so much confusion.

'No, I suppose not,' she said eventually and, to her surprise the confession came as a considerable relief, and she suddenly felt inexplicably happy.

'Excellent.' Elspeth swivelled round until they were face to face, took Sophie's hands in hers, and looking her straight in the eye moved in for the kill. 'Now listen, Sophie. I am not a dyed-in-the-wool lesbian, but I find the female body more appealing aesthetically than the male. It's as simple as that. I find you especially attractive and I adore your bottom. I also like you. Very much. And I really appreciate having you in my house. But, if you're not comfortable with what I did to you yesterday – and what I've just said – then I really do think it would be best if you looked for somewhere else to live. It's not that I want you to go, but I don't want you staying unless you really feel happy with me.'

Elspeth could not have thought of a more persuasive argument, but it was not really needed. Now that Sophie had actually faced up to the extraordinary fact that being spanked could turn her on, as well as correcting her faults more effectively than anything else she had ever experienced, the revelation that Elspeth had designs on her came as much less of a shock. She couldn't remember ever having harboured similar feelings for another girl, and so her reactions to both the previous day's events and Elspeth's declaration of intent were still essentially beyond her understanding. On the other hand, now she had tasted the heady delights there was no way she was going to deny herself more of the same. Nevertheless, her lawyer's mind prompted her to take the opportunity to clarify things a little.

'You'll still spank me when I don't do my chores properly?' she asked, her voice remarkably steady.

'Yes, of course,' replied Elspeth, frowning as though surprised that there was any alternative. 'Why do you ask?'

'I'm not really sure. I suppose after yesterday, I thought you might just spank me when you feel like it. Not when I deserve it.'

Elspeth smiled. 'So you now agree with me that a smacked bottom is the best punishment for you?'

'Yes,' Sophie admitted, blushing again.

'And you're also happy to be spanked simply when I feel like getting my hands on your bare bottom?'

'Oh, yes.'

Elspeth continued remorselessly, happily seizing the opportunity to establish the ground rules for the future – the immediate future, anyway, because if all went to plan, details of Sophie's more distant future would have probably sent the girl screaming for sanctuary.

'Well that's fine. You'll get spanked both when you've been a bad girl and when we both feel like it. And I'll undoubtedly make you strip completely naked from time to time. I hope you won't make any silly objections to that? Even when you have to scrub the kitchen floor in the nude.'

To Elspeth's amazement that threat did not make Sophie blush. Instead, she looked her straight in the eye and acceded without a moment's hesitation.

'Excellent!' She was just about to carry on when a young couple strolled past and they both deemed it more sensible to wait until they were out of earshot. Two pairs of eyes followed the departing rears, both flickering from the male to the female and both then concentrating on the girl.

'I'm going to put you to the test right now, sweetheart,' Elspeth said, as soon as it was safe. 'We'll go back home and I'll put you straight across my knee, pull your skirt up and your knickers down. When I've had my fill of both looking at and feeling your bare bottom, I shall then spank you. Quite hard. Certainly harder than yesterday. And when you think you've had enough I am going to strip you, make you kneel with your head down and your bottom so high in the air that it's spread widely enough to expose your bottom-hole. Then I'll spank you again. Like that. It hurts more on a tight bottom, and the sure and certain knowledge that all your considerable charms are in full view will add significantly to the occasion. And will test your ability to behave properly under punishment, because if you huddle your bottom in so your anus is hidden, I'll simply start all over again.'

This time Sophie did blush. But not solely from embarrassment. Elspeth saw that the red stain reached her neck and disappeared into the top of her blouse. Her lips were parted and her breasts shifted enticingly.

As she gazed thoughtfully out over the busy park she presented a picture of both innocence and wantonness, and Elspeth felt the wetness begin to seep from between her tightly closed thighs.

At exactly the same moment, Sophie was aware of her own arousal. Oblivious to the risk of being seen, she reached out, took hold of her mentor's right hand and kissed the palm, her submissive gesture earning her one of Elspeth's most dazzling smiles. She felt an exhilarating glow flood through her, intensifying the natural spurt of trepidation at the threatened severity of her spanking.

Instead of recoiling from the usual and expected symptoms of fear – the sensation that a hand was squeezing her heart and constricting her throat; the dry mouth and wet hands; the hollowness in her tummy and the prickling in her bottom – she found that she was actually savouring them. She felt incredibly alive as the adrenaline surged through her veins.

It was going to hurt. Elspeth had made that absolutely clear. She began to anticipate the stinging pain, building up her determination to show that she could take it and not disgrace herself.

She acknowledged to herself that the promise of comforting words and gestures when it was all over would give her the required courage.

Hopefully Elspeth would make her come again.

Her thoughts encompassed other implications. If she was excited by the prospect of Elspeth's dark eyes focused on her nudity, how did she feel about the other side of the coin? Did the idea of seeing her new friend's bottom have any appeal? She felt a new and different sense of excitement as she pondered what had until that moment been the unthinkable, and rapidly came to the conclusion that the vision of a nude Elspeth could be an enticing one.

She remembered the couple who passed close by only five minutes before; how she had stared at both rear ends before concentrating on the girl, and how she had really noticed that distinctively beguiling feminine walk for the first time. The memory proved to be a decisive factor. The thought of naked, intimate contact with Elspeth added to the warm moistness.

She was in such an euphoric state that her natural caution deserted her and she made her first serious mistake.

'Will you let me see your bottom?' she asked softly.

Elspeth's smile vanished, replaced immediately by a stern and disapproving look. 'It's for me to decide when you can see it, Sophie. Not for you to ask.' The steely tone of her voice reminded Sophie forcibly of their relative positions, and the taste of fear filled her mouth.

'I'm sorry,' she whispered, looking down at the grass.

She was so obviously contrite that Elspeth's expression softened. 'If you're very good, I'll certainly consider it,' she replied, with some of her usual warmth.

Sophie's relief at the speed of her forgiveness was evident.

'I'll do my very best,' she promised avidly.

'I'm sure you will.'

They packed away the remnants of their picnic and walked briskly back to the house, Elspeth carrying only the rug and walking a proprietorial couple of paces ahead of the laden girl. Sophie stared at the seat of her skirt, fascinated by the subtle hints of fleshy mobility beneath and reminding herself that Elspeth hadn't actually ruled out the prospect of letting her see her in the nude.

Sophie was intelligent enough to realise that she had just taken a major step forward. She was still far too inexperienced to appreciate what lay ahead but, underneath her burgeoning excitement at the way her life had changed out of all recognition, she felt a new and welcome sense of security and fulfilment.

Elspeth, on the other hand, knew exactly what lay ahead for Sophie, and the prospect could only be described as delightful.

# Chapter Three

Sophie firmly shifted all the uncomfortable and distracting aggravations that were making life singularly unpleasant for everybody to the back of her mind, and devoted her full concentration to her work. It was Monday, and one of those especially trying summer days; hot, airless and muggy, and their offices may have had a certain old-fashioned charm but were horribly stuffy. Tempers were frayed and the atmosphere was tense and unpleasant.

The case she was working on didn't help. Their client was a thoroughly nasty piece of work, whose father was one of the firm's oldest clients and who therefore seemed to think that this gave him the right to demand both the impossible and the unethical. He had been breathalysed after skidding off the road – only by a complete fluke avoiding an elderly couple on the pavement – had been nearly three times over the limit, and was being charged with driving without care and attention in addition to being under the influence.

As far as Sophie was concerned, a year or two in what one of her more cynical colleagues called 'Her Majesty's Rest Homes for the terminally idle' would have done young Simon a power of good, but it was her job to try and help him get off as lightly as possible.

With grim satisfaction she confirmed that the police had carried out all the basic procedures by the book, that there were no appropriate mitigating circumstances, and that he would be hard pressed to claim that his career depended on being able to drive. As objectively as possible she dictated her summary, took it to the typist, sorted all the papers out, and then sat back with a weary sigh.

She saw that it was half past twelve, remembered that she had not taken a lunch break for over a week, and so decided to do just that.

Ten minutes later she was happily ensconced in an air-conditioned wine bar, an ice-cold spritzer in her hand and a Salade Nicoise on its way. She decided to take stock of her life.

On the one hand, she was growing increasingly disillusioned with her career. When she had first decided to read Law she had nurtured dreams of helping to combat injustice in general, and was beginning to realise that practising it was a different thing altogether. She was honest enough to admit that her present job was not right for her and that she would probably have been more content in a less high-powered firm, with more Legal Aid work. With equal honesty, she realised that she was not tough enough to make a success of taking on the big battalions on behalf of the proverbial little man – and/or woman. The sad fact was that the big battalions were by their very nature, powerful and well armed, and victory over them required more courage and determination than she had.

It did not help that she had failed to make any real friends at work. Nor had she felt able to discuss her growing unhappiness with Elspeth. She was not only feeling more and more isolated, but was facing the unhappy prospect of working with the one partner she disliked. Known generally – but behind his back, and at a safe distance – as Weasel, he was acknowledged by one and all as a brilliant solicitor. Sophie knew she would have the chance to learn a lot under his guidance but, as she sat picking at her food, she felt increasingly sure that she did not really want to end up resembling him in the least. Neither personally nor professionally. Earlier that morning she had heard him tearing a strip off one of her colleagues, a promising lad and one of the few who had been reasonably nice to her.

Not that Simon had done anything wrong. There had just been a conflict of priorities. He had been asked by another partner to drop everything for an hour and give him a hand. The Weasel had objected in principle to having his case sidelined, even though it had not mattered one bit. His face, red with embarrassment and resentment, had been as eloquent a sign of things to come as anything.

The other side of the coin was, of course, home and Elspeth. Sophie had left for work that morning even more reluctantly than usual after an exciting weekend and, as she pushed her empty plate aside and took the first sip from her second drink, she sat back and reminisced, her frown replaced by a happy little smile.

She had only been spanked twice but both had been, in very different ways, incredibly satisfying. The first had been on the Saturday morning, for failing to hoover behind a chest in the hall. Elspeth's attitude had been very much as usual – more sorrow than anger, brooking no excuse and making no effort to disguise her pleasure at finding a reason to administer the customary spanking to Sophie's bare bottom.

Not that she objected to Elspeth's enjoyment. Quite the opposite. Underlying the normal sense of nervous trepidation at the prospect of a painful punishment, there was an extra feeling of almost sexual excitement. Ever since that fateful picnic in the park, when Sophie had finally faced the fact that Elspeth fancied her, her punitive spankings had been much easier to bear. She was still afflicted by the old symptoms, ranging from a dry mouth, a butterfly-filled hollow in her tummy and a draining of her strength, especially in her legs, but she had soon found the sensations almost addictive.

They had been especially strong on that last Saturday. Elspeth had insisted that the hoovering had to be done thoroughly, and Sophie had simply forgotten. She therefore knew that her spanking would be unusually rigorous. She had been made to wait for over half an hour before presenting herself for punishment and, for once, had been glad of the delay.

She had sat quietly in the kitchen, keeping her breathing

regular and even, steadily building up her mental reserves to cope with the forthcoming pain. With her eyes closed, she had taken herself mentally through the preparations, which for punishments were brisk and efficient rather than sensual.

She imagined the feel of first her leggings and then her knickers being drawn down over her prominent bottom, the feeling of fresh air on naked skin making her buttocks feel immediately vulnerable, the inevitable pause of a minute or so while Elspeth studied her bare bottom. Sophie dreamily relived her usual feelings at that stage, from the comfortable intimacy of Elspeth's lovely thighs supporting her to the rather less comforting knowledge that very soon the pain would begin.

Since her first spanking she had learned a great deal about pain. Specifically, pain in her bottom. She was still as wimpish as ever over things like a stubbed toe or twisted ankle, but a smacked bottom had a markedly different quality as far as she was concerned, whether she was being punished or Elspeth was simply indulging her bizarre tastes. It helped that the punishments were always for an actual misdemeanour, so that her mind was attuned to contrition rather than resentment.

The spanks were always hard enough to make her bottom wobble like a jelly and each one stung, but only enough to make her blink. It was the cumulative effect which made the difference between punishment and play. Slowly and steadily, with the regular, rhythmic sound of Elspeth's hand on her flesh ringing in her ears, Sophie would lie as still as she could for as long as she could, grimly hanging on to the thought that she was getting exactly what she deserved. No more, but certainly no less.

The pain, the submissiveness, the intimacy of their relative positions and the odd sense of security she found whenever she was being held securely down across Elspeth's knee, all combined to make her determined to do better and, after it was over, genuinely grateful for the trouble taken to correct her faults.

And afterwards there was the nice glow of the aftermath and the knowledge that the slate had been wiped clean and all was forgiven and forgotten.

Until the next time.

That last Saturday's session had gone according to the established custom, until the end.

Sophie had been very close to tears after an especially testing punishment, convinced that her poor bottom was hotter and more painful than ever. When Elspeth's hand had stopped beating her she slumped over her lap, gasping with tears in her eyes. As usual she panted out her apologies and thanks for the punishment, and had been more than a little dismayed at Elspeth's reaction.

'I'm afraid it's not over yet, darling,' she had said firmly.

'Oh!' Sophie responded, her voice high-pitched and tremulous.

'Get up and go and stand in the corner,' Elspeth ordered. 'And hold your shirt well up so I can see your bottom.'

She had stood there, gratefully feeling the burning ebb slowly away, quite frightened at the thought of further punishment, but with her fear tempered by a combination of curiosity and adrenaline.

Elspeth had left the room, returning quickly and resuming her seat.

'Come here, Sophie.'

She had seen the wooden hairbrush as she hobbled across the room, and the extra surge of fear left a metallic taste in her mouth.

Elspeth carefully positioned her, draping her across her parted thighs with the left one lowered so that Sophie's torso sloped downwards, elevating her bottom. She then increased its prominence even more by making the trembling girl draw her knees up and move them apart.

Sophie had felt hideously exposed and in no doubt that her fanny was fully visible. Elspeth stroked and squeezed her rounded cheeks and then pulled them wide apart, causing a brief flash of pain in her anus, before letting go and retrieving her implement.

'I'm going to give six of the best, Sophie dear,' she had announced grimly. 'Right here, on the base of your bottom. It'll make sitting rather uncomfortable for the rest of the day, but that's just too bad. Understand?'

'Yes, Elspeth,' she had quavered, relieved that it was only going to be six but still dreading the unknown bite of the seemingly innocent implement. 'Thank you, Elspeth.'

'Good girl. I'll tell you what, you can choose. Either I give you three on your left buttock and then three on the right, or I can go from buttock to buttock. Which would you prefer?'

'Oh... from buttock to buttock, please.'

'Fine. Now brace yourself.'

Sophie had felt the cool smooth wood tap the lowest part of her left cheek and had held a deep breath behind gritted teeth. She felt the slight movement as Elspeth raised her right arm to her shoulder and then a loud *Thwack*! had reached her ears, just as considerable pain flooded through her soft flesh. It had taken most of her determination to stop herself from screaming aloud, and the rest of it to keep her bottom in position.

Then the adrenaline had come to her rescue, helping her to stiffen the sinews and take the remaining five without letting herself down. In fact, as the pain had mounted she discovered new reserves. By the end she found herself almost revelling in the fight between the escalation in severity and her ability to conquer her natural instincts to protect her suffering buttocks.

Sophie looked at her watch and happily noted that she still had at least fifteen minutes before she had to get back to the office. With a slight start, she realised that the intensity of reverie had dampened her knickers and, with a rueful shrug decided to recall Sunday's contrasting session.

Elspeth had ordered her to spend the entire day in the nude and had warned her that she would help herself to handfuls of flesh whenever the mood took her. As her bottom had not fully recovered from the hairbrush it had only been spanked once, in the late afternoon, but that spanking had been rather memorable.

Sophie had been standing by the mantelpiece in the sitting room, happily studying the painting of the naked girl, when Elspeth had come in.

'Don't move, darling,' she said immediately – and slightly huskily.

Sophie obeyed, holding her breath as the excitement surged and her bottom tingled. It had been the obvious target of Elspeth's attention, and therefore it was a reasonable assumption that something was going to happen to it.

She soon discovered that she had adopted that lovely relaxed, feminine stance, with one leg forward and slightly bent, the other one straight. One buttock plumped and firm, the other softly sloping. Elspeth described the contrasting shapes in some detail and her hands had added emphasis. Then she made her stand quite still to be spanked, and both had enjoyed the difference in the pliability of her cheeks, with Sophie furthering her education by analysing the difference in feel between spanks on a compact buttock and on a softly relaxed one. Slightly to her surprise, they had been noticeably less painful on relaxed flesh and she made a mental note that it was in her interests not to tense her bottom on future occasions.

She had ended up with a hot, red, and deliciously sore bottom, so turned on that she had gratefully seized on an excuse to slip up to her room and bring herself to a terrific climax.

With a start Sophie realised she was on the verge of being late, so paid and trotted back to the office, trying to quash the feeling of slight nausea by reminding herself that in about four hours she would be back home. With Elspeth.

The Weasel greeted her at reception. 'Where the fuck have you been?'

Sophie blushed furiously, then felt icily calm. 'At lunch.'

'What about the Dyson case?'

'Being typed up.'

'Oh. Well don't sneak off again, I might need you.'

Without another word, Sophie marched to her office, wrote out her resignation and took it straight to the senior partner, who tried to persuade her that it was all a storm in a teacup. But Sophie sensed his heart wasn't in it and stuck to her guns. The net result was that she was told to hand over all outstanding work to Tony, clear her desk and leave. A cheque for three months' salary in lieu of notice would be sent to her home address.

Half thrilled at the possibilities of a new life, half frightened that she had done something very stupid, Sophie quickly put an end to her short and unhappy professional career.

In the meantime, Elspeth had decided that it was far too hot to arrange a liaison with one of her lovers, and had spent the entire morning relaxing.

When Sophie had been slaving away in her hot office, she had been lying languorously on the sofa, naked, listening to Mozart's *Don Giovani* and reaching the conclusion that Sophie was now ripe and ready to be plucked. As the peasant girl, Zerlina, began to sing the lovely and highly appropriate aria, 'Batti, batti' (beat me, beat me), she recalled the sight of Sophie's beautiful and beautifully presented bare bottom, shuddering under the hairbrush. Her fingers delved into her wet fanny and played her instrument in time with soaring voice and orchestra until her hoarse cries drowned the music.

And so, when an increasingly apprehensive Sophie arrived unexpectedly, Elspeth was already in a receptive mood. When she heard the sound of Sophie's key in the front door she was in her bedroom having just enjoyed a long shower, and so, had time to throw on a pair of knickers and a cool summer dress. She appeared at the bottom of the stairs looking her usual unflustered self.

She took one look at Sophie's troubled face and knew that something fairly dramatic had happened.

'Well?' she asked simply.

She listened impassively as the girl stammered out a halting explanation for her unexpected arrival and, when the flow eventually dried up, had a struggle to keep any signs of the inner surge of exultation from either her voice or expression.

'I see,' she said. 'So, completely out of the blue, you take it upon yourself to change – and radically change – my life as well as yours.'

As the full implications of her actions struck home, the blood drained from Sophie's face and she began to tremble all over.

'Please, Elspeth, don't throw me out. I'll look for another job. Waitressing. Anything. I'll not get under your feet. I promise.'

Elspeth stared steadily at the desolate little figure, rather moved by her desperate attempt to act with dignity.

'Very commendable,' she replied acidly, and felt a pang of conscience as Sophie's face crumbled pathetically, followed by a surge of real affection as she took a deep breath, straightened her shoulders and forced herself to look into her mentor's eyes. 'Let's discuss it properly,' she continued, after a meaningful pause. 'In the sitting room. Make a pot of tea, first. Earl Grey.'

She swayed gracefully into the sitting room and waited with bated breath for the sound of breaking china, knowing that Sophie was hardly in a fit state to work with her customary care.

There were no such disasters, and ten minutes later she drained her second cup, brusquely ordered Sophie to finish her first, took a deep breath, and began the speech which was to seal Sophie's fate irrevocably.

'I'll start by reminding you of some pertinent facts, Sophie. I am extremely fond of you. I find you physically very attractive, especially your bottom. I believe in firm discipline, especially for young women, which I know had helped you to improve a great deal, both in terms of your housework and as a companion.

'It isn't that I hate the thought of having you around all day, I promise. The thing is, I have my own life to lead during the week and, if I wasn't completely free to come and go as I please, I would very soon get irritable. I know you said you would find other employment, and I am sure you would succeed sooner or later and we would get back to where we were. On the other hand, you're a bright, competent girl and I don't like the thought of you slaving away in some job that is beneath you.

'There is also the basic fact that you didn't see fit to bring me into your confidence before resigning. In other words, I am not sure that I can trust you... now, come on Sophie, don't cry. Here you are, blow your nose and pull yourself together. That's better. Now, where was I?

'Oh yes. Basically, I think we have two choices. The first is that you find somewhere else to live, and the second is that you stay, but very much on my terms.

'These are that in effect you become, for the want of a better expression, my slave. You will do exactly as I say. Your body in general and your bottom in particular, will be mine. If I want to beat you, then you will submit without any fuss. If I have guests, I may well lock you in your room for the whole time they are here. You will perform the most intimate services for me and you'll do them willingly. Is that quite clear?'

'Yes, Elspeth.'

Elspeth heaved a sigh of both triumph and relief when she saw the dawning of hope in Sophie's haggard face, leaned forward and kissed her hard on the lips. 'I want you to think it over properly, my sweet. I'll do the tea things while you stay here and do just that.'

While she appreciated the gesture, Sophie did not need more than a second to make up her mind. In a nutshell, the addictive, thrilling fear when Elspeth sentenced her to a spanking was so far removed from the sick feeling in the pit of her stomach when the Weasel so much as looked disapprovingly in her general direction that there was no doubt in her mind.

She sat waiting for her mistress, a warm sense of calm spreading through her as any uncertainties faded away.

Elspeth came back. 'Well?'

Sophie drew a deep breath. 'I would love to be your slave,' she whispered.

'Good girl. Now come here and we'll seal our contract with a kiss.'

With her usual brisk efficiency, Elspeth started as she intended to carry on. Sophie was ordered to crouch down. 'Take my shoes off, kiss my feet, and then suck my toes.'

Sophie flung herself down, her shaking hands fumbled the shoes clear, and she bent to Elspeth's elegant and well manicured feet, before a sudden flash of inspiration earned her a number of brownie points. She knelt up and caught Elspeth's eye.

'Would you like me to bare my bottom, so you can look down on it?' she asked nervously.

'That would be nice, darling,' came the very welcome reply and, with her heart singing happily, she hoicked her skirt up, her knickers down, and bent to her humble task, with the added pleasure of feeling relatively cool air on the naked skin of her parted buttocks and, especially welcome, on her hot fanny.

After that she was caned. By the time Elspeth sentenced her to the most severe punishment she had faced, Sophie had already begun to recover her equilibrium and so was able to react more normally to the prospect.

First, there was fear. The cane was, in her very limited knowledge, almost the ultimate threat. She had read the various articles covering its use in schools and the European Court's judgements prohibiting it. It's reputation sent shivers down her spine.

Second, there was gratitude. She knew she had committed her worst ever crime as far as Elspeth was concerned, and to be punished properly was absolutely right. Another reason for thanking her was that after she had sucked her toes – which had proved to be far nicer than she would have thought possible – Elspeth leaned forward, stroked her jutting bottom, and immediately suggested that she would appreciate a shower.

So, she was standing blissfully under the hissing spray, revelling in the sensation of accumulated tension disappearing down the drain. She hated being hot and sticky at the best of times, and if she had been forced to proffer a bottom which was anything other than pristine, she would have felt far too ashamed to have gained the full benefit from her punishment.

As she washed her buttocks, she stopped with a start. Elspeth hadn't actually said that her bottom was to be the target. Wasn't the cane used on the hands? She felt uneasy at the thought, standing stock still, with her lathered hand clutching her right cheek.

Her uneasiness developed into near panic at the prospect of presenting anything but her bottom. She tried to envisage what it would be like to hold out a hand to be beaten, and was convinced it would be far less satisfactory. For both of them. Elspeth definitely liked her bottom and Sophie found it hard to imagine that she would choose a less interesting and exciting target.

Relieved, she carried on washing herself and, as she did so, her recovering mind tried to analyse the importance of her bottom to her. She was still inexperienced enough to feel self-conscious when her knickers slithered down over her buttocks and she knew that Elspeth was looking at it. She couldn't quite understand how bottoms could be truly beautiful, in spite of the nude statuettes and the painting over the fireplace, but if Elspeth said that hers was attractive, then that was good enough for her. So, when she presented it all bare for a spanking, there were two sources of pleasure. The first was that Elspeth presumably enjoyed the view, and the second was that being smacked on her bare bottom was inherently humiliating, which was exactly the way she wanted it.

She smiled to herself when she worked out that the fun spankings also contained an element of embarrassment, which also added to the intensity of the experience.

Then, having convinced herself that she was going to be beaten on her bottom – and in all probability with her knickers pulled down – she tried to imagine the degree of pain.

The hairbrush had come as a rude shock at first, but she soon found that she was able to cope with the escalation in pain, and had then risen to the challenge.

The cane would obviously challenge her far more, and she fought her growing nervousness with a determination to be as brave as she could be.

She was caned on her bare bottom.

It proved to be far more painful and testing than she had imagined.

She did rise to the occasion.

When it was at last over, Elspeth's respect for her new slave had grown considerably. Everything was happening more quickly and satisfactorily than she had dared hope. Sophie's hasty resignation had genuinely angered her at first, but the dear girl's attitude since breaking the news was more than making up for it.

She had kissed her feet with an almost ideal combination of submissiveness and enthusiasm. The way she had offered to kneel there with her bottom naked had been a nice gesture, and had provided a delicious view.

As Elspeth had fetched the cane from its hiding place she heard the sound of the shower, and the thought of that curvy body, all pink and shining, made her look forward to the next hour or so even more keenly.

She was thrilled at the prospect of putting Sophie through her first really serious test. She had already proved herself to be Elspeth's best ever conquest, even including Helen, her immediate predecessor. Elspeth stood for a moment, the cane swinging loosely in her hand, her head cocked slightly to one side as she compared the two, debating whether there was any point in getting in touch with Helen and spending a day or so with both together.

Perhaps, she thought, but not for some time. She briefly conjured up a vision of Helen's bottom – bigger and softer than Sophie's, and less shapely. Lovely tight division though. And she did miss the girl's extraordinary ability to withstand pain. Twenty-four hard strokes with the crop had barely moved her.

Elspeth's face cleared as she came to the conclusion that Sophie's responsiveness to pain was just as satisfying and, most important of all, she was far more intelligent and entertaining company, and even the most submissive slave can't be bending over all the time.

On that cheerful note she began to plan how best to introduce Sophie to the cane. By the time the object of her desires appeared, looking utterly adorable in a simple loose skirt, a white blouse, bare legs, and with her hair tied back in a suitably youthful pony-tail, all memories of Helen vanished.

She decided that she had two main objectives for the caning. Obviously the first and main one was to punish her. More severely than she was used to. That would be best achieved with six or a dozen proper strokes, all on her bare bottom and with the girl made to bend over in a position which made her bottom nicely prominent but without stretching the skin too much. Ideally, she would be aware that both her fanny and anus were visible, although Sophie was quite intelligent enough to work out that they could only be seen by someone directly behind her, whereas Elspeth would be standing to her side. That problem was easily solved by moving behind the girl after every stroke, ostensibly to check the effect but also to have a good look at every detail of her suffering bottom. Apart from the fact that Sophie still found having her bottom-hole examined embarrassing, it was one of the prettiest Elspeth had ever seen, and definitely worth looking at.

The other point of the exercise was to introduce her to new levels of pain, without running the risk of undoing all the good work of the past months. Elspeth was sure she could achieve both ends, but knew she would have to proceed with an element of caution.

She began by working on the girl's mind, treating her gently, because she understood that the day's events had left her pretty shell-shocked. She reminded her of her affection and then of the punishment awaiting her.

'I am not going to give you a fixed number of strokes, darling, but to beat you in rather the same way I spank you. In other words, I'll keep going until I feel that you've been adequately punished. Any questions?'

'Er… just the one. You will be beating me on my bottom, won't you? Not on my hands?'

Elspeth smiled. 'Of course it'll be on your bottom, you silly goose. I don't want you to end up unable to do your chores. Oh, and bare, naturally.'

Sophie blushed and Elspeth saw the movement of her throat as she swallowed nervously. 'Elspeth?' she whispered.

'Yes dear?'

'I'd just like to say thank you. For beating my bare bottom and not throwing me out. I really will try and be good.'

'A proper slave?' Elspeth asked lightly.

'Yes,' Sophie replied, after a deep breath.

'I really am pleased. Now, let's get your beating over with. Then I can make a start with your enslavement.'

Her tone may have been light, but the implications were hardly lost on Sophie and, after an initial surge of doubt, she began to feel an expectant glow about her future.

But first she had to be beaten.

Nothing else mattered for the next half an hour or so, as Elspeth calmly and expertly orchestrated an experience she would never forget.

She moved smoothly through the preparations, starting by applying vaseline to the corners of her mouth, before producing a hard rubber ball gag.

'Open wide,' she said to the anxious girl, adding that she did not want her to feel inhibited about crying out with pain, but neither did she want the neighbours to be frightened. With Sophie's first restraining device carefully inserted and with the straps firmly tied round her head, Elspeth made her stand for a moment with her hands on her head, while she walked slowly around her, savouring the view.

A very pretty girl, her blonde hair shining with health, looking delightfully traditional in her old-fashioned, flared summer dress, her plump little breasts heaving as she fought for breath, yet to work out how to breath properly.

Her eyes wide open with fear and gazing into the distance.

The gag giving her an open-mouthed look of sheer terror.

Trembling gently from head to foot.

Elspeth also noticed her head was held high and that she was refusing to let herself be defeated by the problems posed by the gag. She was already beginning to master the knack of slackening her mouth so she could breathe around the ball; yielding to the restraint, not battling helplessly against it. Excited by her looks and impressed with her attitude, Elspeth got down to the preparations for the beating.

She had decided to bend Sophie over the back of a suitable chair, knowing from long experience that it was just about the right height. So she guided the trembling girl into place and pressed down on her shoulders to make her bend over.

A little whimper escaped when Elspeth tied Sophie's hands

to the front legs, and another when she did the same to her feet, before completing the task of rendering her victim almost completely helpless by running more rope from each knee to the front legs of the chair, forcing them even further apart and bending them inwards.

She could then address the task of baring the girl's beautifully presented bottom. The skirt rose easily and was soon folded neatly on her back, but her parted thighs made it impossible to pull her knickers down to her knees, and Elspeth was quite content to leave them tightly stretched about half way.

She could not resist helping herself to a lingering look at Sophie's helplessly naked bottom, nor to a thorough feel, running her hands over each buttock in turn, enjoying the satiny skin and the way her fingers sank into the flesh, in spite of her bent position.

Then she picked up the cane, placed it carefully across the lowest part of Sophie's trembling bottom, made a slight adjustment to her stance, and then settled down to beating those beautifully curved and widely separated globes with all the expertise at her disposal.

Her approach may have been considered unconventional but, given that she wanted to do more than simply punish Sophie, was undeniably effective. She spent the first couple of minutes flicking away at the girl's helpless bottom, using her wrist more than her arm and with only the slightest pause between smacks. It was more of a spanking than a caning, but even so, her new slave's buttocks quivered every time the cane landed and before long the individual lines left in its wake had all joined up, so that her whole bottom gleamed like a pink beacon in the subdued light.

Then it was time to introduce the punishment element. Elspeth was certain that Sophie would have found the overture more pleasant than painful, and a quick check confirmed the point. She was quite still, not fighting her bonds and breathing easily. She debated whether she should be kind and break the news that a proper stroke was on its way. The day before she certainly would have done, but Sophie was a slave now, and therefore less entitled to consideration. Apart from that, the shock of the unexpected would be good for her training.

With a tight smile she wiped her hand on the seat of her skirt, took a firm grip of the smooth yellow cane, took careful aim at the roundest part, and let fly. The flexible rod hummed through the air, sank into soft flesh and rebounded. Elspeth brought it up to her lips and kissed it absently as her glittering eyes feasted on Sophie's reaction.

She had obviously been lulled into a sense of false security by the introduction, and the searing bite of a full-blooded stroke had come as a total shock. The gag effectively reduced her scream of pain to a choked gurgle, but the way her head flew up, the creaking of the chair as she strained against the smooth nylon ropes, her wildly staring eyes and reddening face, were all equally eloquent.

Elspeth moved round to crouch behind her, watching the tramline weal rise proud of the surrounding flesh and quickly darken. Satisfied that it was parallel to the floor and was evenly etched across both churning buttocks, she resumed her stance and began to flick the cane against Sophie's much less relaxed bottom, reddening the skin slowly and steadily and watching carefully as Sophie began to relax, until her buttocks were quivering prettily. Then she drew the cane right back and delivered the second proper stroke.

All in all, the beating lasted a full thirty minutes and, by then, Sophie's bottom had been reduced to two helplessly quivering mounds, both stained a lovely rich dark red and with five purple weals to add variety. Elspeth looked at her handiwork with excusable pride, especially pleased with the way she had used the tip of the cane in a concentrated assault on the left buttock, ensuring it was as well and thoroughly reddened as the right one.

The owner of the dramatically punished bottom was clearly at the end of her tether. She was slumped over the chair, with the only visible movement from Elspeth's viewpoint an occasional muscular spasm, which made her thighs and buttocks shudder deliciously. Her breathing was short and fast, whistling through the confines of the gag. Her eyes were closed, her face bright red from the combination of pain and effort and marked with the drying tracks of her tears.

Elspeth resisted the temptation to begin her planned soothing session and took a firm grip of her cane. 'Just one more stinger, darling, then it'll all be over.'

A muffled sound from her left managed to communicate Sophie's intense relief at the news, and Elspeth felt a surge of pleasure and pride as she saw the girl make a visible effort to present her bottom, pressing down with her legs to lift it up.

She had always maintained that the final stroke should be even more memorable than all that had preceded it, and long ago had worked out how best to achieve that admirable aim. She rose up on the tips of her toes, angled the cane so that it rested diagonally across Sophie's quivering bottom, and let fly. With superb accuracy and with devastating effect the cane lashed in, crossing all five previous stingers and reviving the fading sting in each.

For the sixth time Sophie screamed and the chair creaked alarmingly before the last of her strength ebbed away and she slumped over the chair, weeping helplessly.

With a glow of triumph Elspeth untied her, helped her up, took out the gag, and held the sobbing girl close until she had recovered enough to stand upright without collapsing on the floor.

After that it was a simple matter to guide her over to the sofa, stretch her out across her lap and apply the special ointment, lovingly prepared by one of her close friends, whose interest in herbal remedies allowed her to gain almost as much satisfaction from restoring beaten bottoms as she did from marking them in the first place.

Then it was a light supper and an early night for Sophie, who slept like a log in spite of her aching buttocks, because every instinct reassured her that she had made the right choice and that from then on, her life would have the security she had subconsciously longed for.

Over the following three weeks Sophie had no cause to change her mind. Her new status made little difference to the basic friendship that had already grown between her and Elspeth. If she now had to call her mistress, it did not stop her making her views known on those relatively few subjects on which she was better informed, albeit considerably more diffidently than before.

They still shared the pleasures of music and art and Elspeth took the same amount of trouble to explain and enlighten as she had done previously.

She spent much of the time in the nude but had lost most of her modesty before her enslavement.

She was spanked more often and often much harder but learned to appreciate the pain, rather than simply accept it.

The main change was that Elspeth now expected those threatened intimate services on a regular and frequent basis.

Sophie had been introduced fairly gently, starting the day after her first beating, when Elspeth had decided that they should have a special dinner to celebrate the new arrangement. A caterer had supplied lobster salad and tirimasu, Elspeth's cellar had produced a bottle of vintage champagne, posh frocks and jewellery had been put on and, as the dinner progressed, Sophie had gradually forgotten both her aching bottom and her less than happy immediate past. Elspeth had been on glittering form and their uninhibited laughter rang through the candlelit room.

Afterwards, with the washing-up left for the following morning, they had taken coffee and port into the sitting room, comfortably nestling together on the sofa in companionable silence. Sophie had enjoyed little exposure to the finer things in life and the delicious food and wine, the strange formality on which Elspeth had insisted, had all made her feel rather out of her depth at first. Then she had relaxed and was just thinking how to broach the delicate subject of showing her gratitude, when Elspeth forestalled her.

'Strip naked, darling,' she ordered.

Blinking in pleased surprise, Sophie scrambled to her feet and obeyed, soon standing stark naked, except for her silver bracelet and black choker. She looked so gorgeous, standing there at attention, pale and rounded, her head held high but with her usual anxious expression on her pretty face, that Elspeth stared for even longer than usual. Then, with her juices beginning to flow copiously, she issued her instructions.

Sophie happily knelt, slipped off Elspeth's expensive shoes, and bent her mouth to feet and toes, feeling a glow of satisfaction at the sighs of pleasure.

The glow intensified when she was calmly informed that she had earned the right to see Elspeth's bare bottom. She watched with bated breath as those lovely slender hands inched black skirt up shapely legs and round thighs until her unblinking eyes focused on the seat of a pair of diaphanous black knickers. She did not notice Elspeth holding the skirt under her elbows, but just her freed hands moving down to her waist, tucking her thumbs under the elastic and, wide-eyed, she followed the slow unveiling.

Her breath gusted out as the rumpled knickers slithered down to Elspeth's ankles and, keenly aware that she was very privileged to be allowed to look, stared open-mouthed, still innocent enough to feel slightly embarrassed at the close view of another woman's naked bottom, but sufficiently advanced to appreciate its beauty.

Then she was ordered to kiss it. Every inch.

Her head began to swim as she breathed in the complex perfume, consisting mainly of feminine skin and expensive soap. Her lips brushed the top of Elspeth's left cheek, and she gasped at the feel of warm satin against them.

Even the gentlest pressure of her mouth made it sink into the softness of Elspeth's flesh.

She ran her pursed mouth down the cleft, where it was even smoother and warmer. Bending her head back, she managed to follow the tight division until it disappeared between the thighs.

Then Elspeth broke the charged silence. 'I'm going to bend forward a little, and you are going to part my buttocks and kiss my anus.'

Sophie was too far gone even to contemplate hesitation, and slowly reached up, placed a hand on each cheek, pressed in with her thumbs and eased the cleft open, holding her breath and swallowing nervously.

She was relieved to find that being so close to another woman's bottom-hole wasn't unpleasant, and so she could concentrate on enjoying the total subservience of the gesture.

Her gorge rose a little when she was ordered to lick it, but she obeyed and was able to control herself. Then the volume and frequency of Elspeth's sighs of pleasure increased, which helped.

Then Elspeth told her to stop for a moment and knelt on the sofa, thrusting her bottom right out, exposing everything.

'Lick my cunt, Slave Sophie, and if you please me I'll let you share my bed tonight.'

She moved forward immediately, too surprised at first to take in the unexpected crudeness, just desperate to earn the right to sleep in her mistress's arms.

The heady, musky scent which reached her nose, proving that she had done well up to that point, thrilled her and, boldly resting her hands on the tautened buttocks framing her target, she applied her mouth with an instinctive expertise.

# Chapter Four

Using the time-honoured stick and carrot approach, Elspeth brought Sophie on steadily but surely, careful to enhance her submissiveness without subduing her attractive personality. To the uninitiated, Elspeth was often guilty of confusing stick and carrot and they would have been amazed to witness Sophie being rewarded for efficiently completing a hard morning's work by being put across Elspeth's knee for a sound spanking. Had they noted the dreamy look on Sophie's face as her bare bottom was slowly and expertly reddened, perhaps a glimmer of understanding would have made them re-examine their prejudices.

If they had been able to talk to Sophie, then she would have explained that, as far as she was concerned, it was all perfectly simple.

When she was naughty, Elspeth ticked her off, sentenced her to whatever punishment suited the offence and her mood, and administered it. In the three weeks that had passed since she had resigned, Sophie had felt Elspeth's hand on numerous occasions, the hairbrush twice more, and had been introduced to strap and paddle. She was moving beyond just accepting a sore bottom in return for slackness and inefficiency in her work, and beginning to show signs of grasping the real implications of submission to pain.

She and Elspeth had developed something of a punishment ritual, best illustrated by describing more fully her first meeting with the paddle.

She watched Elspeth make a leisurely inspection of her work and, because another sultry day had drained her energy, she was pretty sure that her bottom was going to suffer. All the familiar symptoms – the beating heart, dry mouth, tingling buttocks and wet palms – began to make her feel at the same time both strong and weak. On the one hand, the challenge of submission stiffened her resolve. On the other, knowing that she was about to submit made her feel helpless and compliant. She knew she was fast becoming addicted to punishment, but that no longer worried her greatly.

Closing her eyes, she started to anticipate the inescapable ordeal, savouring the prospect, tasting the fear and looking forward to the climax, when the burning pain was at its peak and she could relax in the knowledge that there was no more – and wait for the afterglow.

Her failings were discovered and described and she was duly told that she was going to be spanked. On her bare bottom. That was always part of the ritual, because she had never been punished in any other way. But she now enjoyed hearing that phrase as much as Elspeth enjoyed using it.

Then there was the unspecified threat of extra severity, and the symptoms intensified as she remembered the burning sting of the hairbrush.

Elspeth made her walk ahead of her into the sitting room and then move the spanking chair into the usual place.

The next few minutes saw nothing out of the ordinary. She put herself across the parted thighs, lifted her hips until her bottom was bared, settled back, gritted her teeth and meekly submitted to a perfectly normal spanking. Hard, fast, and very effective.

She took it with her normal resilience, although in something of a mental turmoil because she couldn't put the extra element out of her mind.

When her spanking was over she was not allowed to rub her bottom, but had to strip naked and then stand in the corner with her hands on her head while Elspeth fetched the implement.

This turned out to be an authentic wooden American paddle and Elspeth, noting that Sophie looked at it with interest as well as fear, promised to tell her more about it later. She did say that it had been a feature of sorority initiations in colleges in the good old days and said that Sophie should adopt the classic posture, namely with feet about half a metre apart and elbows on knees.

Nervously, Sophie complied.

And waited.

Nothing happened, so she let out her breath and risked a quick look over her shoulder, seeing that Elspeth was studying her intently.

'What do you think of the position?' she asked unexpectedly.

Sophie thought for a moment or two. 'My bottom feels pretty tight and vulnerable,' she admitted. 'But I'm generally quite stable and not uncomfortable. Is my bottom-hole exposed?' she added daringly.

'No. Your fanny is – but that's all.'

With both parties satisfied with the pose, six firm strokes were administered, two on each cheek, and then the last couple across the division, adding considerably to the level of pain as the impact forced Sophie's buttocks further apart and so stung the soft skin of her cleft, and even hurt her anus. Not severely, but enough to make her eyes water. She was made to stay bending while Elspeth had a good look at the damage, then was asked what she'd thought of the paddle.

'The first impression is of a really hot sting,' she said. 'Then the pain seems to go quite deep into my flesh. Not as sharp as the cane – and maybe not as hot as the hairbrush. But the effects last for a long time before fading. My bottom is still burning like anything. Especially in the middle.'

Pleased at her analysis, Elspeth let her rub her bottom for a moment before submitting to the next part of the ritual – standing in the corner, hands on head and her naked bottom on display for leisurely contemplation.

After five minutes came the newly established finale.

'Right, come here, Sophie.'

'Yes, mistress.'

'Kneel. Show your gratitude for the punishment.'

'Yes, mistress. May I kiss the hand that beat my naked buttocks?'

Elspeth imperiously extended her arm and her hand was kissed all over.

'May I kiss the thighs which supported me?'

Elspeth whisked up her skirts and stood as Sophie's soft lips moved slowly up her right thigh, brushed against the bulge in the front of her knickers, and then down to her left knee.

'May I kiss the bottom which was crushed under my weight when you had me across your knee?'

'You may, slave,' Elspeth replied, then turned and lowered her knickers.

When both buttocks, her cleft and anus had been reverentially kissed, it was back to work.

Soon after that episode Sophie was introduced to her new uniform, about which she had mixed feelings. It was highly appropriate for her new role in life, consisting of a very short skirt, stockings and suspenders, a white blouse, and a minuscule lace apron. She was too naïve to realise that it was essentially a fetishist's dream of a French maid's outfit, but intelligent enough to see it was a parody of what a real servant would have worn.

It also resulted indirectly in another very significant step in her training.

The measuring session had been the catalyst. The first problem had been with the attractive woman who had supervised the operation. Elspeth had referred to her as her dressmaker, but the obvious rapport between them suggested a far more intimate relationship, and Sophie had been hard pressed to disguise the pangs of jealousy that made her feel unpleasantly vulnerable.

She had felt a lot worse when ordered to strip naked and

stand in the middle of the sitting room while she was studied, poked, prodded, her private parts discussed in embarrassing detail, before she was measured with intrusive thoroughness.

Worst of all was that Elspeth and the stranger treated her as though she was a dumb animal with no feelings whatsoever. The only way she could handle the situation was to tense her muscles to stop them trembling, gaze at the far wall, and try to think of more pleasant and distracting subjects.

Her ploy was not wholly successful, especially when her breasts and buttocks were the subjects of her tormentors' undivided attention.

But things *did* get worse!

Apart from the occasional appreciative murmur, neither Elspeth nor the so-called dressmaker had commented on her charms, and Sophie was just beginning to relax a little when the strange woman suddenly broke the silence.

'Elspeth, dear, you told me she's got a very pretty little anus. I'd love to see it.'

The remark itself was enough to take poor Sophie's breath away, but the obvious implications – that Elspeth had actually discussed the most intimate and private part of her body with someone else – brought tears welling up in her eyes. It was not only incredibly embarrassing, but also shattered the protective shell she had begun to build around her as soon as she had devoted herself fully to Elspeth. For the first time in weeks, she wanted to protest at her treatment and was almost prepared to take the consequences and face the insecurities of the outside world again. As her thoughts whirled through her brain she stood trembling uncontrollably, her shoulders heaving as she tried to stifle the sobs which threatened to overwhelm her completely.

Elspeth could hardly fail to spot Sophie's distress, and appreciated immediately that both were facing a minor crisis. For once her intuition failed her and she couldn't understand what had upset the girl, but realised that she had to act both decisively and quickly.

It was time to apply the stick, metaphorically if not literally. The carrot could be offered later – if Sophie took the stick in her usual co-operative way.

'You don't seem to be paying attention, Slave Sophie,' she said icily. 'Mistress Daphne has said quite clearly that she wants to have a look at your bottom-hole, and so I expect you to bend forward, reach behind you, and part your buttocks so she can see it. Now!'

The two women crouched and watched as the sobbing girl did as she was told, her trembling hands reaching tentatively for the cheeks of her bottom and drawing them haltingly apart until the pale, pinky-brown circle came into view.

The two heads moved close together for a better view. Two pairs of gleaming eyes focused intently on Sophie's indecently presented rear. Two foreheads creased in disapproval.

'Bend over more and move your hands further apart,' snapped Elspeth. 'We can't see the actual hole,' she added, rather unnecessarily.

A whispered 'Oh no!' from the other end was accompanied by a reluctant revelation of the desired part of Sophie's anatomy, and Elspeth let out a silent sigh of relief.

The proffered anus was studied with expert appreciation.

'You're right, Elspeth, it really is *very* pretty. Such a neat little surrounding bit, and the opening is beautifully round.'

Elspeth smiled in agreement, and then trailed the tip of a well manicured fingernail all around the patch of slightly darker skin, before following one of the tiny wrinkles onto the opening itself.

Sophie gave a little moan.

Daphne and Elspeth ignored her and continued with their examination, with the former following her hostess's example by gently fingering the object of their undivided attention.

Sophie was too miserable to take much notice of what was happening to her. She was vaguely aware of an rather pleasant tingle in the middle of her bottom, but was basically still too preoccupied by being forced to expose herself to a stranger in such a degrading way.

She instinctively did her best to be suitably compliant, but her inner resentment came very close to the surface when she felt something pressing against the tight ring of her virgin anus, wriggling determinedly around as though trying to force its way up her bottom. It took a fair amount of resolve to stop herself jerking upright, but she was unable to suppress an anguished groan as the finger finally penetrated her.

She crouched there miserably, her anus prickling unpleasantly as the intruding digit worked its way implacably into her cringing rectum, tears pouring down her face and no longer able to contain her sobs of humiliation.

Then, to her inexpressible relief, she felt the finger slide out. The flow of tears dried up and a series of convulsive swallows successfully combated the nausea that had threatened to disgrace her completely.

'She really hasn't behaved very well, has she Elspeth?' announced a gloating Daphne.

'No,' her mistress replied evenly.

Sophie desperately tried to collect her scattered wits as the acid taste of panic filled her mouth.

'I shall punish her. Quite severely. Starting off with a sound spanking.'

Sophie felt a surge of relief as Elspeth's sentence penetrated her overloaded brain. Being spanked was familiar ground, even though being punished in front of a stranger was something she would have found pretty frightening had she been faced with the prospect only an hour or so beforehand. As it was, it was infinitely preferable to having her anus examined and invaded.

Her legs were so shaky that she stumbled over Elspeth's lap with none of her usual grace, and had to spend longer than normal settling into the well-established position; arms and feet on the floor, legs straight and slightly apart, Elspeth's left thigh supporting her torso just below her breasts, and with her groin pressed into the firmly yielding support of her mistress's right thigh. Her back was arched downwards and Elspeth's left hand pressed firmly but comfortingly on the small of her back. As she lay there, trembling all over, she vaguely heard Daphne and Elspeth discussing the pose of her bottom, but did not listen to what they were saying.

She was so pre-occupied with her own muddled thoughts that she hardly noticed the first ringing spank, other than feeling another surge of relief now that she was being subjected to something she knew how to handle.

In a few moments her sense of panic had all but disappeared, and she found her head had cleared to the extent that she was able to review the events of the last half an hour fairly constructively.

As she began to appreciate how badly she had taken the inspection, she felt really ashamed of herself. Elspeth had wanted her to display her bottom-hole and let Daphne have a long look at it, and so that was what she should have done. Immediately. Without hesitation. Glad to be the focus of their attention.

Then, wincing as the stinging pain spread through her buttocks, she started to grasp the true nature of her slavery. Her likes and dislikes were totally irrelevant. If she felt awkward about being put on display, poked, prodded and examined, then it was too bad.

She loved Elspeth and so pleasing her was paramount.

And as long as she felt that Elspeth at least liked her in return, then she would do anything required of her.

And like it.

Losing her place in her mistress's affections was the worst fate imaginable.

Infinitely worse than having to open up her own bottom so a complete stranger could see what was usually decently hidden.

Even having a finger pushed into her rectum was acceptable.

Now she was being punished.

As she deserved to be punished.

On her bare bottom.

In front of that stranger.

Hard.

Painfully.

Aware that she had made a significant step forward, Sophie composed herself to accept her spanking creditably. She had not fully appreciated how hard Elspeth was spanking her, and the realisation that her bottom was already pretty sore made her gasp. She gritted her teeth, dug her toes and hands into the carpet to keep herself steady, and concentrated on her bottom, reminding herself that it was less painful on soft relaxed buttocks than on tense, nervous ones.

As she did so, the first seeds of understanding some of the more advanced complexities of CP were planted in her mind. With that insight often brought on by stress, she began to sense that Elspeth was not simply spanking her harder, but also in a different way. Until then, she had known that the fun spankings caused her less pain than the punishment ones, but had never given the matter a great deal of thought, simply attributing the difference to a combination of atmosphere and frequent rubs.

She could not only feel that the spanks were more severe, she could hear a difference. They sounded sharper and crisper, with a clearer ringing tone.

The basic approach was as usual; moving from cheek to cheek and from base to apex then down again.

Sophie wracked her brain to try and identify the difference and, just as a rather breathless and sore-palmed Elspeth decided that it was time to finish her off, she thought she had got it. During the fun spankings, Elspeth had always spent some of the time concentrating on the cleft, using little more than her fingertips so that the main parts of her buttocks were left untouched. Sophie had always welcomed these intervals and had recently admitted to herself that being smacked there and like that actively turned her on, sending tingles into both her anus and fanny. Unlike the pure punishment she was currently undergoing, which contained no mercy whatsoever.

Pleased with her powers of deduction, she decided it was time she let her mistress know that she was genuinely suffering. Her bottom had been bobbing and weaving gently for several minutes, but she had restricted her vocal contribution to hisses and gasps. She began to wail and cry out in distress, and as soon as she had done so realised there was no need to pretend. Her bottom was stinging ferociously, and suddenly overcome with the pain, she burst into tears.

Elspeth immediately stopped and sat back, nursing her right hand in her left and gazing down at the crimson bottom with a satisfied smile. She turned to Daphne, who had been leaning forward, her gleaming eyes glued to Sophie's bouncing bottom from the first spank to the last.

'She took that pretty well, don't you think?'

Daphne smiled and then licked her lips slowly. 'She certainly did, Elspeth. It's a long time since I saw such a red bottom. Quite delicious. May I take a closer look?'

'Feel free.'

For the next couple of hours, Sophie was subjected to an ordeal which tested her physical and mental stamina to the limit. She was made to stand in the corner with her red bottom on display.

Then Daphne spanked her until the tears flowed again.

After another session in the corner, she was instructed to act as maid to both her tormentors, and undress them completely.

She was made to grip her ankles and was then caned. Six strokes from each naked woman, and she was ordered to turn her head and look at her punisher. In spite of the pain, she found pleasure in their gleaming white curves and the movement of their breasts as they swung the golden wand against her meekly offered bottom, with Daphne's big, rather

81

pendulous bosom providing a dramatic contrast to Elspeth's firmness.

They made her kiss them. All over. Breasts, inner thighs, buttocks, clefts, bottom-holes and fannies.

She was just able to appreciate the differences in their scents, in the feel of their skin, the consistency of their flesh and in the taste of their intimacies.

Her sense of achievement when both women climaxed under her ministrations made the pain and embarrassment she had suffered earlier all worthwhile.

And when she stood, trembling with exhaustion, and watched them enjoy a graceful *soixante-neuf*, she was able to quash the surge of jealousy by comforting herself with the thought that although Mistress Daphne was a very attractive woman, with lovely auburn hair and soft breasts, she couldn't hold a candle to Elspeth.

It took the best part of a week for Daphne to finish making her uniforms and, by the end, Sophie sensed with huge relief that she had been completely forgiven for her childish tantrum when ordered to show off her anus. At first, Elspeth had been disturbingly distant with her, but Sophie had accepted that she deserved a period of relative isolation and grimly set about the task of getting back into Elspeth's good books.

The first sign of approval was when she was ordered to help her mistress in the bath. The specific request was to wash her back, and the hint of reconciliation made it all even more pleasurable. She gently worked the scented lather all over, enjoying the satiny feel of her skin, the firm pads of muscle on either side of her spine, her long and graceful neck and the swell of her hips away from her narrow waist. Best of all were the sighs of pleasure that accompanied her efforts.

Taking a deep breath, she softly asked Elspeth's permission to attend to her bottom, and her relief when her offer was eventually accepted was intense. As was the pleasure when her hands smoothed carefully over those softly yielding mounds.

At that stage, her pleasure was not overtly sexual. Sensual, certainly, as she had lost the shyness she had at first experienced at the sight and feel of Elspeth's nakedness, and was even able to see and kiss the tight little pale brown anus buried in the depths of the cleft without any hesitation.

What she did feel was very privileged. Seeing the intimacy between Elspeth and Daphne had hurt at first, but her severe punishment had effectively cured her of childish jealousy. And as she worked the lather into the middle of her mistress's bare bottom, a glow of satisfaction at the knowledge that she was probably one of the very few who had performed the service made her feel special.

An even more welcome sign that she had been forgiven was when Elspeth announced that they had earned a day in the country.

On the following Saturday, with all the housework done the day before, they set off early and drove south to West Sussex. Sophie had at first felt a little unsure of herself once they were outside the secure and familiar walls of their house, and had watched the passing streets in wary silence. But before very long Elspeth's happy and relaxed mood put her completely at ease, and by the time they were on the Guildford by-pass both were chatting away like the good friends they essentially were.

They stopped briefly in Petworth, wandered around the narrow streets, admired some beautiful Georgian town houses near the Square. Elspeth saw a pretty little porcelain figurine of a naked dancer in the window of one of the many antique shops, marched in, asked if she could look at it, and made Sophie go red with embarrassment when she declared that the bottom was nowhere near sensual enough for her tastes. Elspeth's wicked little smile as they left the shop brought on a fit of giggles in both, and Sophie suddenly blossomed in the new atmosphere between them.

She had never been to that part of the world before and was very taken with the long sweep of the South Downs.

She loved Chichester.

Elspeth pointed out that most of the old wall around the city was still standing, and then led her through the lovely Georgian back streets. They looked round the Cathedral and Sophie listened spellbound to Elspeth's expert and enthusiastic judgement of the Piper tapestry behind the altar. She found it hard to reconcile its almost garish modernity to the ancient grey surroundings at first but, after a few moments contemplation, began to grasp its significance. She felt much more comfortable with the Sutherland painting in an adjacent chapel.

They had a decent lunch and, with energy levels suitably restored, Elspeth announced that they had time for one more treat before heading back to London.

It turned out to be Goodwood racecourse, or more specifically, a hill above it. After a short but quite steep climb up from the car park they came to a ditch, with an even steeper slope above it. Elspeth pointed out that it was, in fact, the site of a prehistoric fortress, which had also probably been used by the Romans. There was a path at the top of the steep bit – the 'Vallum' or wall, reinforcing the 'Fossum' or ditch, as explained to a fascinated slave – and they walked slowly around the perimeter of the fortification.

Sophie loved it. The view to the north was enough to make her exclaim with delight. Rolling hills, copses, fields, and with the spectacular racecourse in the foreground, the main grandstand an amazingly delicate structure, with white eastern-style domes shining in the sunshine.

To the south, the view took her breath away. To their right the Isle of Wight loomed out of the sea. Following the coastline eastwards, the complex inlets of Chichester harbour held her eye and then, almost directly below, Chichester itself, the Cathedral spire dominating the city. Sophie breathed in the fresh air and did a slow twirl so she could take in the whole panorama.

Elspeth's voice broke into her reverie. 'Bend down and touch your toes!' she ordered.

Only a barely audible gasp betrayed Sophie's shock as she immediately did as she was told, feeling her light skirt tighten across her buttocks.

Her brain seethed for a few moments. Her first and most natural concern was that somebody would see them. She frantically searched her memory to try and recall if there had been anyone near, but she had been so entranced with the view and the heady freshness of the air that she had been oblivious to everything else.

In a logical progression, she hoped for the first time in ages that Elspeth would spank her over her knickers and spare her the extra embarrassment of total strangers seeing her bare bottom. Daphne had been bad enough!

But she was not altogether surprised when she felt her skirt being tugged upwards and then her knickers sliding down to her ankles. The wind felt deliciously cool on her flesh, especially so when it gusted and she could actually feel it on her fanny. Without thinking, she dipped even further and its breath right in the centre of her bottom made her exposure almost pleasurable.

Then she heard a hollow *Thwack* and hot pain flooded her left buttock, the impact jolting her forward. She blinked and tried to identify the implement. It was certainly something new and, just as the second blow on her right cheek sent the breath whistling from her lungs, she worked out that it could only be Elspeth's shoe. They had left their handbags securely in the car and her dress was too figure hugging to provide concealment for anything bigger than a handkerchief. A brief glance behind confirmed that her conclusion had been spot on and, with a glow of pride, she took an even firmer grip of her ankles, bent her knees for extra stability and thrust her bottom out, subtly but clearly indicating to her mistress that she was quite happy to be beaten, even with the high risk of attracting an audience.

Sophie did not have long to reflect, as Elspeth was no more enthusiastic about drawing possibly antagonistic attention to her sexual preferences, so administered a round dozen in quick time, leaving the girl totally breathless and on the brink of crying out in distress by the end. Even so, as she gritted her teeth under the alarmingly painful barrage, she did manage to appreciate the subtleties of the lesson she was being taught, namely, never take anything for granted. As the last two strokes landed right across the base of her cleft, the leather sole driving her buttocks apart, hitting her anus and fanny, sending flashes of hot pain right through her body and making her see stars, she suddenly felt an even greater adrenaline surge than usual.

The complete lack of warning, the urgent preparation and the dangerously exposed circumstances, all combined to give the beating an especially exciting quality, a quality which added a lot to the joy of submitting to Elspeth and which drew her even closer to her beautiful mistress.

It therefore seemed utterly logical to kneel at her feet and slip the shoe back on to her elegant little foot.

It did not even occur to her to adjust her clothing before she did so, because the thought that Elspeth would have a different view of her bare red bottom as she knelt made the fear of discovery fade into insignificance.

And the pleasure she saw in Elspeth's face when she straightened up and made herself decent was all the reward she expected. So when she felt soft lips on hers, then a tongue forcing them apart and swirling around her open mouth, she felt giddy, standing stock still for a second, until Elspeth's hands reached round, gripped her throbbing bottom and pressed her close.

She had never been kissed with such incredible sensuality. Or, she pondered later, it could have been that she had never been kissed when her senses were generally so receptive. Whatever the reason, the touch of Elspeth's lips and tongue, her scent, the soft firmness of the front of her body pressed tightly against her, her pulsating bottom, all combined to turn her on in a way she had never experienced in her life.

It got better. After they had separated to draw breath, Elspeth cuddled her briefly, then stood back, reached down, clenched her fist with her thumb extended, and ran the nail purposefully up and down the slit of her fanny.

Sophie shuddered violently as the sweet and sour thrill flashed through her middle. Her legs threatened to buckle and a laughing Elspeth moved quickly forward to support her. She felt her knickers cling damply and the realisation that she'd almost had a climax after that one touch made her blink.

They stood in each other's arms for several moments.

Sophie tried to come to terms with the strength of her sexual feelings towards Elspeth.

Elspeth simply looked forward to consolidating her advance.

On the drive back, Elspeth decided to tell her slave exactly what was required of her when they got back home.

She was to strip naked the moment they crossed the threshold, escort her mistress upstairs, undress and bath her. Then take a shower.

'After that, we'll go into my bedroom and you will kiss and lick me all over. Starting with my boobs. Then tummy button, feet and toes, inner thighs, buttocks, bottom-hole, and finally my cunt. Properly. Understand?'

'Yes, mistress,' whispered Sophie.

Her ignorance of the various ways of pleasing another woman slightly irritated Elspeth at first, but then she discovered that it was almost as satisfying to instruct her as they went along.

'...Try and force your tongue right up into my bottom, sweetheart. Aaahh! That's better.'

'...Now hold the lips of my cunt apart and suck my clitty into your mouth...Yessss... Now nibble it... *gently*... that's it... *wonderful*!!'

And so on. After Elspeth had come three times, a much wiser Sophie was laid gently on her back, her thighs eased apart, and an experienced hand began to stroke her matted, dark-gold curls, gradually opening the glistening entrance until her protruding little clitoris stood proud, so it could be flicked and rubbed until she came.

When Elspeth allowed Sophie to share her bed for the night, the young girl made a mental note to remember the date and log it in her memory as the happiest and most exciting day of her life.

Now that she knew Sophie was completely devoted to her, Elspeth intensified her training. Every morning began with a naked, freshly showered slave bringing in a cup of coffee and the morning paper. She would sip and read, while Sophie stood quietly beside the bed, her back to her mistress so that her bottom could be fondled as and when required.

Then her bath was run, she was washed thoroughly and with increasing expertise and, while Sophie prepared breakfast, she would dress with her usual care. Her slave was again made to serve her naked and to stand by her side while she ate. As soon as everything was washed up and put away, the main business of the day could begin. After a thorough inspection of her body, Sophie slipped back to her bedroom and put on her uniform, returning within ten minutes for a final check before starting the housework.

Elspeth knew she could now trust Sophie to carry out the designated tasks efficiently and without supervision, though she looked so adorable in her skimpy outfit that she found the temptation to keep an eye on her all but irresistible.

The black skirt only just covered her bottom when she was standing upright, and so whenever she bent down there was always the arresting view of her white knickers stretched across the plump mounds of her bottom. Daphne had originally suggested especially high-cut ones, leaving her bottom as good as bare, but Elspeth had decided they would make the preparations for her regular punishments that much less exciting, and so had insisted on more normal ones, which covered her buttocks – except for the gluteal folds.

The result was a delicious twinkle whenever Sophie was walking away from her, and if Elspeth felt like spanking her, then it was a simple matter to lead her into the sitting room, where the spanking chair was kept more or less permanently in position, and putting the willing girl across her knee. Then the fuller length panties came into their own, as she was of the firm opinion that baring an errant bottom which was almost naked before one started wasn't half as exciting as exposing one which was decently covered to start with.

One development inspired by their day in Sussex was a fitness programme for Sophie. Elspeth had noticed that she'd arrived at the top of the hill above Goodwood racecourse rather out of breath and so, dead on midday, Sophie had to report to the sitting room, take all her clothes off and do thirty minutes of exercises. Not surprisingly, Elspeth enjoyed these sessions rather more than Sophie, who clearly found having her naked charms bouncing and wobbling under her mistress's eagle eye a little disconcerting, and the stretching and bending exercises embarrassing.

After a month or so, she readily admitted that the improvement was marked.

The half-hour inevitably ended up with a moderate punishment, with Elspeth rather enjoying the change between baring an already positioned bottom and watching a bare one present itself as commanded.

Then it was back into the uniform for lunch, with either more chores to be done or an afternoon relaxing, with Sophie near to hand so that Elspeth could see and fondle any part of her delightful body which took her fancy.

The Sussex outing seemed to have had a far greater effect than simply a break in their routine. Ever since that enjoyable day, Sophie had moved from acceptance to enjoyment of her status. She still blushed prettily whenever she was told that she was in for a spanking, and her expressive face made it perfectly clear that the prospect of a sore bottom still made her nerves twitch. The change in her feelings was shown more in the way she got into position and, having done so, the way she added a small but noticeable thrust to her buttocks, cocking them up or pushing them out in readiness. She was also far more resilient. It took many more spanks or strokes before she started to react to the pain, and her cheeks were often quite red before her hips began to churn and her sighs and gasps changed to those addictive little cries of distress.

All in all, Elspeth was delighted with her progress.

It was time to take her a stage or two further.

Elspeth gave the matter a great deal of careful thought and eventually came to a conclusion. She worked out that, as Sophie's abiding fear was that she could be thrown out at any moment, it would be a good psychological move to play on that fear. Not only would her relief when she was welcomed back into the security of the house make her even more compliant but, by facing her fear, she would probably learn how to conquer it.

And so Elspeth made Sophie go out on local errands dressed in her uniform. On the first occasion her face went pale rather than its usual pink, and she tottered nervously out of the front door.

Several times Elspeth followed her at a discreet distance, and was pleased to see that the girl's stride soon reverted to normal and, eventually, she began to walk with conscious pride in her striking appearance.

The next stage was to remind Sophie that Elspeth controlled her body as much as her mind. The process had been started right at the beginning, of course, when the shy and modest young girl had been forced to face the fact that all punishments were administered to her bare bottom, and the workouts had taken things several steps further. Elspeth smiled as she conjured up memories of that nice body, all white curves, glistening faintly as Sophie began to sweat, firm breasts bouncing as she moved, her round bottom quivering, bending, opening, closing, bouncing.

She decided it was time that Sophie lost her pubic hair. She had a very pretty little fanny anyway, and the loss of those golden curls would enhance rather than detract from it, but the key point was that she would find the idea both peculiar and demeaning. Elspeth picked up the phone, made an appointment with Simone, another member of her intimate little circle of likeminded friends, rang for a taxi, ordered Sophie to dress in her uniform and, an hour later, they were in Simone's salon, anonymously sited in a little alley in Soho.

With the door locked and the blinds drawn, Elspeth turned to her apprehensive slave and brusquely told her to strip naked.

With memories of the humiliation she had felt when Daphne had measured her for the uniform flooding back alarmingly, Sophie took off all her clothes and automatically stood bolt upright with her hands on her head and her feet apart, trying her hardest to compose her thoughts and telling herself firmly that one of Elspeth's motives in making her show herself off was pride in her slave's appearance.

With that to comfort her, she found the inevitably detailed inspection of her charms far easier to bear, and actually bent over to open her bottom so that her anus could be scrutinised without a second's hesitation.

She was so pleased with herself that she didn't wonder why both Elspeth and Simone spent so long peering at her bush, tweaking the tight curls and pulling them aside to assess the tightness of her slit. To her surprise and embarrassment she began to find it rather sexy, and had to concentrate quite hard on safer matters, like the inside of Chichester Cathedral, before she could feel confident that her fanny was not betraying its arousal to the eyes and noses hovering so close to it.

She felt a stab of loneliness when Elspeth departed. 'I'll

leave her in your capable hands, Simone,' she announced breezily. 'I'll be back to collect her in – four hours?'

'That will be perfect, darling.'

Sophie damped down the surge of unworthy jealousy at the endearment and concentrated on the person in whose charge she had been placed.

Simone was prettier than Daphne but lacked the latter's cheerful earthiness. Almost as dark as Elspeth and best described as petite, with few curves to disturb the smooth sweep of her white coat, either fore or aft.

Her hair was cut in a neat bob and gleamed healthily in the bright light of the salon. Sophie began to relax, only hoping that she was not going to have her hair cut too short, as she liked the way it flowed over her shoulders.

The plastic of the chair seat felt cold to her naked bottom as she sat in front of the mirror. The sight of her bare breasts bobbing gently as she settled into a comfortable position made her blush, and the squeak caused by bare skin on plastic as she shuffled her bottom made her go bright red.

Simone was clearly an expert and highly trained hairdresser, and Sophie relaxed as she set to work, finding the feel of her hair falling onto her naked skin amazingly pleasant. Her fanny began to tingle again and she squirmed on the fulcrum of her flattened buttocks to excite herself even more.

'Sit still!' Simone snapped.

'Sorry, mistress.'

But the sensations persisted and she couldn't resist another wriggle or two.

'I warned you, Slave Sophie. Stand up, turn around and bend right over.'

'Yes, mistress.' Sophie gulped and leapt up to obey, blushing again at the horrid sound of her warm and slightly sticky buttocks tearing themselves free of the plastic.

She thrust her bottom out and waited for her punishment, her heart hammering, her thoughts whirling.

The first flare of resentment died as quickly as it had come, and was replaced by a sense of curiosity as she wondered whether a spanking from Mistress Simone would feel any different to one from Elspeth.

Three minutes later she straightened up, panting hard and just able to grasp that, as far as her bottom was concerned, a dozen from the back of a larger, heavier hairbrush hurt her just as much as anything Elspeth had dished out, but that the lack of any emotional ties between spanker and spankee made the pain much sharper somehow.

Suitably chastened, she sat as still as a mouse until her new, much shorter but quite flattering hairstyle was done. Relieved that she hadn't been cropped, she admired her reflection and felt pleased that it had been nowhere near as bad as she had feared.

But things *did* get worse!

She was taken through to an inner room, and gasped when she saw the apparatus waiting for her. Suddenly everything fell into place, from the anonymous front of the salon to the attentions they had paid to her bush. The clinical couch with the two stirrups at the end facing her could have only one purpose, and Sophie's fanny tingled with alarm as Simone took her by the elbow and led her firmly to it.

In a daze, Sophie lay down and lifted each leg in turn to allow Simone to strap them in place, almost as wide apart as she could stretch them.

'Move your bottom down, please. I can't see your anus.'

She obeyed and felt horribly exposed.

'Excellent,' Simone said, peering into her raised and splayed crotch. 'Very pretty.'

The compliment made her feel a bit better, and she lay quietly as Simone sat down on a low stool and got to work. At first, when she realised she was not being shaved, she felt rather relieved. The thought of a sharp razor scraping away at such a delicate part of her anatomy had genuinely frightened her, but then the implications of what was happening struck home and her eyes filled with tears. She knew from the regular little pricks and tugs that Simone was using electrolysis, and therefore the depilation would be permanent.

For the first time, she had to come to terms with the fact that there was no going back. She was a slave for the foreseeable future, and it took several minutes before a sense of relief and contentment with her lot enabled her to relax and begin to enjoy the attentions to her most sensitive parts. Especially when she peered down between her legs and watched Simone's elfin face, frowning in concentration as she wielded the neat bit of apparatus, carefully trapping a hair at a time, pausing and then drawing it out.

When Elspeth returned, Sophie was starting to feel quite sore and distracting herself by trying to estimate how many individual hairs her fairly sparse bush had contained. Her Mistress smiled warmly at her and then joined her friend at the scene of the action.

'Oh, that *is* better,' she exclaimed enthusiastically, and Sophie felt first relief and then a sense of curiosity. The two women discussed the operation in detail, with Simone explaining that she had cleared all the hair from her lower lips, that there had only been a few tiny ones around her bottom-hole and that they were all gone, and that she'd made a start on the main triangle.

'As you can see, darling, it's quite a bit thinner.'

Sophie craned her neck but couldn't really see any difference.

Then Simone kindly produced a mirror and she gasped at the sight of the base of her fanny, noticeably red, quite inflamed and as bald as a coot.

She was then untied, helped to her feet and allowed to get dressed, and she and an excited Elspeth caught a taxi back home, where the first thing to do was to strip naked and sprawl on her bed for a lingering application of cream to the afflicted area.

Three weeks later, with two further sessions having completed her pubic transformation, Sophie was standing in the middle of the sitting room, nervously building up her mental resources to enable her to cope with what Elspeth had promised would be her most severe beating to date.

She had done nothing wrong, but had advanced so much that her innocence of any crime did not matter one bit. All that did matter was that she should put on as good a spectacle as she could, because both Daphne and Simone were present as witnesses. Her bare bottom had already been subjected to a hard spanking from each of them and was throbbing warmly as she stood waiting meekly for them to finish their coffee.

She was naked, the ball gag filled her mouth, her hands were tied behind her back and, worst of all, Elspeth had made her bend over so she could lubricate her rectum and then thrust the handle of her largest hairbrush right up her bottom.

Her sphincter was aching from the intrusion and she knew she looked pretty ridiculous with the main part of the brush protruding obscenely from between her clenched cheeks. Then the clatter of cups being replaced in their saucers made her catch her breath. The action was about to start.

Daphne and Simone crouched at her feet and strapped on a couple of leather anklets. Sophie risked a quick downward glance, saw the heavy rings on each side and tried not to think about their purpose, sensing that she would find out soon enough.

She did. Her hands were untied, similar straps buckled to her wrists, she was made to bend over and the wristlets and anklets were then clipped together.

Daphne's comment that she looked really sweet with the brush poking out of her bottom made her feel a bit better.

Then she felt it sliding out and bit into the hard rubber of the gag, bending her knees to keep her bottom thrust out with proper submissiveness.

The three women took it in turns to beat her, calmly and deliberately, slowly transforming her rounded buttocks into twin mounds of blazing agony.

She was soon glad that her groans and cries of pain were stifled by the devilishly effective rubber ball.

They gave a much needed rest while they moved around her crouched, sweating body, toying with whatever part took their fancy, from her seething buttocks to her dangling breasts. Daphne asked permission to stick a finger up her bottom. Elspeth granted it, and then she and Simone did the same.

The pain, the public exposure, the feeling of helplessness, the obvious excitement shown by the three mistresses, all combined to give her a deep inner glow of contentment. She felt she was at last sensing the real meaning of her new role in life. To please. Elspeth first and foremost, but the presence of the others now enhanced the experience and no longer made her squirm.

They helped her to her knees and she needed no further instruction to press her breasts to the carpet and stick her bottom out as far as she could.

They spanked her again, concentrating on her yawning cleft and pouting anus.

The different and even more personal nature of the pain made her eyes water.

They slippered her.

She was lifted to her feet and her hands tied behind her back again.

They slapped her breasts and thighs, both back and front. She writhed and groaned at the unaccustomed pain.

Her gag was removed and all three of her tormentors kissed her aching mouth.

The tears flowed freely.

Her legs trembled.

She felt dizzy.

The mistresses sensed she was nearly at the end of her tether, replaced the gag and bent her over the back of an armchair for her caning, first of all finding some silk scarves to tie her wrists and ankles to the feet of the chair.

The slender length of rattan whirred and hummed as it sped through the air before slicing into her scarlet bottom. Each stroke made her limp cheeks ripple and the array of characteristic raised weals steadily covered her bottom from apex to base.

Sophie grunted at each new narrow strip of fire, but was so weakened by the combination of pain and martyr-like ecstasy that she was incapable of much else in the way of reaction.

By the time the last stroke had landed perfectly in the twin folds at the tops of her thighs, she was little more than half-conscious, and only began to come to when a cold wet cloth was gently placed on her bottom.

Finally, Elspeth suggested she should be allowed to go up to her bedroom and recover.

Sophie looked her straight in the eye. 'Thank you, mistress,' she replied, her voice remarkably steady, 'but before I go, may I have your permission to kiss your bottoms.'

To Sophie's credit, despite her pain and exhaustion, she was able not only to appreciate the differences in the three bottoms, but also to get a thrill from the sight, feel and scent of each.

# Chapter Five

For once, Sophie was up early enough to take her time before going up to Elspeth's bedroom, and so was able to linger in front of the recently installed full-length mirror in her own room.

She rather liked what she saw. Vanity had never been one of her failings and therefore she did not have the benefit of a clear picture of what her figure had been like before Elspeth started the keep fit routine, but her mistress's detailed analysis of the improvements had at least shown her what to look for.

Her waist was definitely trimmer. Her clothes were looser, to the extent that she would soon have to buy a new belt for the jeans she was occasionally allowed to wear when she was not on duty.

Her breasts? They had been pretty firm beforehand and there didn't seem to be much change there.

Legs? Sleeker. No doubt about it.

She swivelled round and peered over her shoulder at the part which Elspeth freely admitted was her favourite. She ran her hands over the smooth curves, noting that the marks of her last caning had disappeared completely. She patted each cheek in turn and frowned slightly at the way they wobbled freely, still finding it a little strange that Elspeth approved of her fleshiness, even to the extent of restricting her to the minimum of buttock tightening exercises, on the basis that she didn't want it to get 'all firm and masculine'. Shaking her hips vigorously from side to side set the twin mounds into even more pronounced motion, and Sophie suddenly saw the attraction of a bottom which wobbled under stress.

She smiled at the revelation and then tested her new-found

flexibility by bending over and resting her palms on the floor without bending her knees. She looked back into the mirror and gasped at the sight. Her bare fanny seemed to jut out beneath her rounded buttocks, plump, the slit tight and with no sign of protruding inner lips. Unlike Mistress Simone, whose convoluted architecture had come as something of a shock at first.

Sophie stood up, and with her back still facing the mirror, mentally compared her reflection with memories of the only other bare female bottoms she had been able to study at any length.

Elspeth's first, of course. And foremost. A lot smaller than hers, although beautifully feminine. When her neck began to ache, she had the brilliant idea of fetching the small mirror on her dressing table and using it to look at her rear view in greater comfort.

Now able to compare at leisure, she studied her reflection carefully and as objectively as possible. The most striking difference to her relatively untutored eye was that her folds where buttocks joined thighs were a lot wider and deeper than Elspeth's. And curved upwards noticeably. She was rather less happy with the slight jodhpur look at the very tops of her thighs, but did admit that it added to the overall curviness of her middle.

Her skin was creamier than Elspeth's, but then Sophie comforted herself with the thought that she had never seen such an alabaster-like – and flawless – complexion on anybody, so dismissed the critical comparison at once.

Otherwise, she could with all modesty, understand that her mistress liked her bottom. It was certainly shapelier than Daphne's and much more prominent than Simone's tiny little behind.

Elspeth's cleft was tighter, though.

She shifted her weight slowly from one foot to the other, marvelling at the way each cheek changed shape and smiled reminiscently at the memory of Elspeth making her stand like that in front of the mantelpiece and describing the difference in feel as she spanked her.

A quick glance at the clock reassured her that she still had ten minutes in hand, and so she decided to delve more deeply.

When Elspeth had first shown an interest in her anus, Sophie had found it basically incomprehensible and inwardly recoiled when she had first been ordered to lick her mistress's. At the time she had been in a totally submissive frame of mind and had obeyed without hesitation, only feeling serious qualms.

Since then she had done it more times than she could count and, while she no longer felt queasy when she parted Elspeth's buttocks, it was only fairly recently that she had stopped closing her eyes as she bent her mouth to the task. Now she had seen that unmentionable part of the body so often, she had begun to find it less unattractive and almost interesting. It helped that Elspeth's highly developed sense of self-discipline extended to her personal cleanliness.

She remembered that embarrassing episode when Daphne had measured her for the uniforms. Bending over and reaching behind to pull the cheeks of her bottom apart. The feeling of total disbelief that Elspeth had actually discussed her bottom-hole with one of her friends.

She felt she had to try and see why they found it pretty and so knelt and, after a fair amount of awkward shuffling, managed to get a view of her splayed bottom. She stared with growing fascination and a sense of relief. Her anus was even smaller and pinker than Elspeth's and certainly much more attractive than either Daphne's or Simone's. Reaching back, she trailed a finger over the pinky-brown surround and then onto the pouting opening, and the thrill of it took her breath away. Her hand brushed against her fanny and she felt an urgent need to bring herself off, but knew that time was running out. She took a last, lingering look and promised herself that the next time she had to lick Elspeth's bottom, she would approach the task in a very different frame of mind. No longer would it be simply the most debasing service she could offer, and therefore a perfect indication of her slavery. It would, from then on, be a pleasure as well.

She scrambled to her feet, replaced the small mirror, brushed her short hair, and trotted off, her bottom jiggling and her heart singing. Somehow she had a strong feeling that, if she had begun to feel her education was just about complete, she had been wrong. She was, in fact, only just starting to understand it all.

Elspeth's first order of the day not only confirmed that her education was only just moving up from kindergarten level, but also came as a shock.

'Don't go, Sophie,' she said calmly. 'I haven't been to the loo yet and I'd like you to wipe my bottom afterwards.'

'Yes, mistress,' Sophie said, her gorge rising.

It turned out to be less of an ordeal than she had feared. Elspeth sat and ordered her slave to stand immediately in front of her, facing away, her bottom in reach. The powerful extractor fan proved remarkably effective and, when the dreaded moment came, Elspeth simply raised her bottom clear of the seat and bent forward, so that Sophie could perform that most subservient role able to see what she was doing, but not in unpleasant detail.

Afterwards she found herself washing her mistress's bottom with all of her usual care, and soon came to terms with the prospect of having to carry out her new task on a regular basis. In fact, as she soaped the soft buttocks, she suddenly felt elated at the intimacy of the service. Then, when Elspeth crouched down and presented her open bottom so that her anus was fully accessible, Sophie felt turned on. She could actually feel her fanny getting damp.

Not surprisingly, she addressed herself to her mistress's most sensitive parts with special enthusiasm and, equally unsurprisingly, the experienced Elspeth noticed the difference immediately, crouched even lower and closed her eyes blissfully as her slave carefully soaped and rinsed every little nook and cranny.

The next part of the morning was rather less satisfactory. Sophie's new-found feelings were enough to spoil her usual deft poise when serving breakfast and she spilt some milk, then coffee, into Elspeth's saucer, and finally forgot the marmalade. Crimson with embarrassment at her clumsiness, she stood rigidly at attention, the skin on her naked bottom crawling with apprehension as she waited for the inevitable punishment.

With slightly mixed emotions, Sophie learned that she was going to have to wait to be dealt with, as Daphne was coming for coffee and would obviously like to watch. On the one hand, waiting to be punished was always something of a trial. On the other, the thought of having two pairs of eyes on her suffering bottom was actually quite stimulating.

As she scuttled around the house making sure that all was ship-shape for their guest – still naked, as Elspeth wanted her uniform in pristine condition – Sophie began to get nicely churned up in anticipation of her beating. Not that Elspeth had specified the details of her punishment, but she was pretty certain that a mere spanking would not be considered anything like severe enough, bearing in mind her many failings.

Had she known that her punishment would involve rather more than simply a very red and sore bottom, perhaps she would have been less excited. On the other hand, it turned out to be another advance in her education and, with her growing ability to get both satisfaction and pleasure from being tested mentally and physically, she found herself even more devoted to her mistress than ever.

It started innocently enough. As soon as she had handed out the coffee and was about to make a discreet withdrawal to the kitchen, she was told to wait and stand with her back to the sofa, upon which the two older women sat in confident expectation of an entertaining morning. They agreed to start things off by making Sophie stand there with her skirt up and

102

knickers down to her knees, proving that Daphne was absolutely right in thinking that contemplating a pretty bare bottom made Elspeth's excellent coffee taste even better.

Sophie was then sentenced. Firstly to a sound spanking. She fetched the chair and waited while some vital piece of gossip was savoured to the full, her heart pounding away and her tummy full of butterflies, but at the same time, aware that her arousal had not been diminished in the least.

'Pull your knickers back up, Sophie,' Elspeth said as she stood up, stretched luxuriantly and flexed her right hand threateningly.

Sophie did so and the thought of Elspeth's lovely hands easing them down over her upthrust bottom made the tingle between her legs even more pronounced.

Over she went. Up came her skirt. Down slipped her knickers, stretched tightly across her buttocks so that the flesh bulged out in the wake of the elastic waistband.

Her cheeks were poked and prodded.

Daphne made some flattering comments about her bottom.

Sophie felt a slipperiness on the insides of her thighs.

The spanking began, Elspeth's rigid palm dancing rapidly all over the full surface of her quivering bottom, warming the skin up steadily.

Sophie lay quiet and still, savouring the warm pain, the movement of her flesh, the feel of Elspeth's thighs under her tummy, the crisp sound of the spanks.

Daphne's flushed face loomed in front of her, tense with excitement, despite her smile. Suddenly she leaned forward and kissed the slave's dry lips, working her tongue into the panting mouth.

Sophie could not believe the surge of lust as the two contrasting sensations of expert kiss and equally skilled spanking joined up, seemingly right in the core of her womb.

Daphne retreated to get a closer view of her bottom, and Sophie could concentrate on keeping it under control, huddling it briefly in acknowledgement of the effectiveness of each spank and then raising it to invite the next.

Soon, breathing heavily but otherwise showing no signs of discomfort, she was ordered to stand up and strip naked, while her tormentors huddled in conference, obviously planning the next move.

In almost perfect unison, the two of them steadily reduced Sophie to a quivering wreck.

They took it in turns to smack her breasts.

She had to bend over the back of the armchair and they spanked her together, one hand per buttock in a fusillade of punishing blows which were too fast to let her move in time to them. All she could do was press her front as hard as she could into the padded top of the chair and keep her gluteal muscles relaxed, so that her bottom wobbled as a punished slave's rump should.

Her thighs were slapped. Hard and fast. Back, front and both sides.

Daphne then said she just *had* to climax. She couldn't wait a second longer. Glad of the break, Sophie helped her undress and then buried her face between the older woman's big soft buttocks, her stiffened tongue flickering over smooth skin until it felt the corrugated surround of her anus, and then she could zero in on the hard sphincter.

She felt it writhe as she licked as hard as she could and then she felt it relax. The tip of her tongue was tightly enclosed and she realised it was actually up the squirming bottom-hole. But then a groaning Daphne rolled over onto her back, pulled her knees back to her chest and ordered Sophie to go straight for her clitoris. Breathing deeply, enjoying the female muskiness, Sophie sucked in the flesh surrounding the stiff button and wiggled the stiff tip of her tongue against it, holding grimly onto the taut, surging buttocks as their owner shrieked her way to a clearly satisfying climax.

Then Elspeth decided that some of the same was just what the doctor ordered, and Sophie could not hide her smile as she bent towards an even smoother, considerably firmer, much neater and infinitely more desirable bottom. When Elspeth's anus relaxed, allowing her tongue to penetrate, Sophie felt no horror at what would have made her feel quite ill not long before. Only gratitude for the chance to show her love.

Then she was paddled, having to adopt the traditional elbows on parted knees position, and the jolting thump of America's worthy contribution to the art of CP had her groaning with pain and fighting to stay on her feet.

Her dark red bottom was inspected and admired.

'Beautiful,' announced Daphne.

'I think we deserve some champagne,' said Elspeth.

Again, desperately pleased to be given a break, Sophie stood up to go to the kitchen and was brusquely told to bend over for another half dozen for moving without permission.

She was in tears by the end, mainly from shame at her own carelessness, but her incredibly sore bottom certainly contributed to her distress.

Elspeth opened the bottle, filled a couple of glasses, and she and Daphne walked slowly round the trembling girl, sipping contentedly and stroking, prodding and commenting.

Sophie stood, trying to control her shaking legs and arms and, as the minutes passed and the pain faded to that throbbing glow to which she was becoming rapidly addicted, her mind cleared. The sexual excitement began to grow again and she was able to concentrate on each sore area and to savour the sensations – from the still intense heat in her bottom to the inflamed warmth in her thighs and breasts. At the same time, being so blatantly on display simply added to the thrill.

The final stage of her punishment was the most educational of all. Daphne insisted on the martinet, which was a new one for Sophie and, encouragingly, she looked forward to feeling it with as much curiosity as fear.

Before she felt the new implement, Daphne suggested something about rings. Sophie had been too preoccupied with her thoughts to pay much attention and only pricked up her ears when Elspeth replied that she had been saving them for another occasion but, on second thoughts, it was not a bad idea.

It was, in fact, her introduction to nipple clamps, and the novelty of this fairly refined form of torment added an extra dimension to the final stage of her beating, especially as Daphne was not satisfied with clamping only her nipples.

After her neat little protrusions had been admired and then pinched into unnatural prominence, Sophie watched with appalled fascination as the intricate and beautifully made clamps were applied and then tightened until sharp stabs of pain made her hiss.

She was then told that the martinet was best on a really tight bottom. Her sore breasts prevented her from paying full attention to start with, but as a gloating Mistress Daphne waved the threatening weapon before her face, the two points of sharp pain in her front seemed to fade away a little as the skin of her bottom crawled in anticipation.

'I love the martinet,' Daphne told her with relish. 'As you can see, it consists of a dozen whippy thongs, flexible enough to wrap round a nice curvy bottom like yours, but stiff enough to sting like mad. Especially the tips, as you'd expect.'

Sophie gazed at the gently swaying strips of shiny black leather and shuddered gently at the thought of them biting into the stretched skin of her tender bottom. The chains hanging down her front from the clamps jingled. Then, once again, she felt a keen curiosity about the actual quality of the pain she was about to experience, and her nipples puckered with excitement.

To her relief she saw Daphne hand the whip to Elspeth. Although she had learned that the older woman was just as competent a punisher as her own mistress, there was far more satisfaction in submitting to the woman she now truly loved than to a relative stranger. And knowing that Daphne's gleaming eyes would be glued to her naked bottom as it suffered under the lash made it all even better.

She was made to kneel on the footstool, with her knees wide apart and her breasts pressed painfully into the upholstery.

Her buttocks loomed up in the air, the deep cleft between them completely open, and she shuddered as she realised that her anus was fully exposed and horribly vulnerable.

She kept her breathing steady, building up her reserves of courage.

And things *did* get worse!

She felt fingers delving into her fanny and gasped with shock as the lips were pulled apart.

Her clitoris was rubbed and she could feel it swell out of its protective hood.

She was desperately trying to make sense of it when a sharp pain flooded through her and even her new-found sense of discipline was tested to the limit. She began to pant frantically in shock and real fear of damage to the most sensitive and tender part of her body. And when Elspeth's lovely face swam into her vision, it was very hard not to cry out in protest, to say that a smacked or beaten bottom was one thing but torturing the essence of her femininity was going too far.

Elspeth's reassuring smile calmed her. 'Don't panic, Sophie,' she whispered, 'it's only another clamp, like the ones on your nipples. It won't harm you.'

Sophie let out a huge sigh of relief and then saw the glitter of excitement in her mistress's eyes, and found it contagious. The pain in her fanny subsided as the thrill of submission and pain took over.

Hands delved between her thighs again. She heard the tinkle of the chains and then a series of tugs re-lit the sparks in nipples and clitoris.

She whimpered softly.

Elspeth's face reappeared. 'We've joined all three clamps

together. You'll be fine as long as you keep in position while I'm whipping your bottom, but if you try and straighten up, then it will hurt.' Sophie saw her face loom closer, those lovely lips pursed. They felt so soft and warm against her dry mouth and the affection that obviously inspired the kiss brought a nervous smile to her face.

Then her whipping started.

The martinet proved to be marginally less horrendous than expected, although testing enough considering it was lashing into a bottom which had already been soundly spanked and paddled.

Sophie's growing curiosity about the differences in Elspeth's seemingly endless range of implements made it quite easy for her to crouch there, taking the first half dozen or so without either moving or crying out. Daphne had been quite right about the tips of the thongs. They did sting. A lot. Not that the thongs themselves lacked bite. Each stroke left a swathe of hot pain across her bottom, wider on her right buttock than the left, but the pattern of small spots on the flank had a very special quality.

Even the steadily increasing pain in her rear was not enough to drown the throbbing tingle affecting her nipples and clitoris when the linking chains tugged at all three as her body jerked every time the martinet lashed her, in spite of all her efforts to keep absolutely still.

Slowly but surely, she began to submit totally; to her obscene pose, with her bottom-hole and fanny on full display: to the pain: to the knowledge that Daphne was drinking in her nakedness and suffering.

All that mattered was to give her beloved Elspeth the means to gain full satisfaction from administering the beating. To present her bottom properly. To make as little fuss as possible. Preferably none at all. To please her by impressing her friend.

To be a good little slave.

The pain spread through her body and flashes of light exploded in her brain at every lash of the devilish whip.

She sensed that Elspeth was subtly changing her aim and, after a few moment's concentration on her gaping bottom, she realised that her mistress was being her usual considerate self and moving fractionally backwards, so that the tips were no longer hitting her flank but moving steadily inwards.

Towards her open cleft!

She shuddered with renewed fear, and the clamps tightened and the flare of pain from her nipples and fanny made her whimper.

A pause. Bliss. She could blink back the tears and do some deep breathing.

Her bottom burned and ached and throbbed.

Daphne and Elspeth crouched behind her and she heard them discussing the state of her flesh.

One of them was stroking her taut curves. The touch reawakened the pain before it began to soothe.

Then she heard the sound of the whip on its way down.

The tips bit into her left buttock and she cried out in relief at the change.

Again the threat of the clamps helped her to stay in position and, as Elspeth took her slowly into new realms of suffering, she found that the new levels of concentration required to keep her bottom well presented kept her mind reasonably clear, allowing her to learn more about pain, how to absorb it and, above all, to learn a bit more about herself.

Perhaps in the nick of time Elspeth brought the whipping to a halt. Sophie was sobbing helplessly and was clearly beginning to lose control of her muscles, so that the danger of the clamps being pulled off her delicate tissues was suddenly alarming.

Sophie saw the blurred image of the whip on the stool in front of her, but was in such an emotional state she didn't appreciate that her ordeal was over for several minutes. As she collected her scattered wits she heard voices from close behind, and then gentle touches on her bottom and fanny confirmed that Elspeth and Daphne were inspecting the damage.

'She really is lovely, Elspeth,' Daphne breathed.

Sophie felt a bit better and her tears began to dry up.

Fingers probed around her swollen clitoris and her relief when the tiny silver jaws were removed made her cry out.

The nipple clamps stayed in place, though, and after a twinge of dismay Sophie was quite glad of their presence, for the small pain in her breasts seemed to help her overcome the massive pain in her bottom.

Then she felt the fingers on the opening to her fanny.

'She's sopping wet!' Daphne cried, at the very moment that Sophie heard the faint squelching sound as she was easily penetrated. She felt ashamed and very self-conscious at first, but then realised that to have found such a sound whipping actually arousing was as good a testimonial to her talents as a slave as anyone could wish, and she was suddenly rather proud of herself.

'I'll just go and fetch Miranda's special cream,' Elspeth announced. Sophie had the presence of mind to whip her head round for a glimpse of her bare bottom swaying and twinkling as she left the room, and the sight was a welcome distraction, especially as the pain in her clitoris began to fade as healing blood flowed back into it.

Four hands smoothed gently over her sore bottom and, before long, the pain ebbed away and that delicious glow spread through her.

She heard the lid being screwed back on to the jar and waited for the order to get up. It did not come. Instead, the two naked women moved around in front of her, lay down on the carpet and proceeded to make love before her eyes until they came.

Sophie felt no jealousy as she watched the two lovely writhing bodies, except for an occasional pang when Daphne applied her mouth to Elspeth's bottom and fanny, and they only lasted for a moment or two. Otherwise she was happy to watch them, to enjoy the views of Daphne's big brown-tipped breasts, her broad buttocks and thighs, her conspicuous anus and glistening fanny.

And, of course, to enjoy Elspeth's body even more.

Three weeks later, Elspeth took advantage of a very wet Sunday to begin the next stage of Sophie's education, which was progressing very satisfactorily.

She was now a far more skilful lover and knew exactly how to use hands, fingers, lips and tongue to best effect.

Her ability to accept pain had improved less dramatically but, as she had shown a natural talent in that direction from the beginning, that was not really surprising.

The increase in her self-confidence was clear. She now actively enjoyed being naked and walked about the house with a free swing of her rounded hips which was a delight to see. She bent for punishment in exactly the correct manner – quickly, submissively and with quiet pride in her attractiveness – and performed her intimate duties humbly and efficiently, and was generally a greater asset than ever.

The time had come to broaden her horizons, Elspeth decided, as Sophie gently wiped her bottom.

In her bath and over a silent breakfast, she thought long and hard, beginning with the few areas where her slave failed to reach the highest standards. The first to come to mind was her inability to control her anus. She did not like having it penetrated and although she had learned not to make a silly fuss as she presented her bottom, it had always been something of a struggle to get even a finger up into her tight rectum. She looked up from the paper and gazed affectionately at her favourite possession. Dear little Sophie. Her shorter hairstyle suited both her face and status, the former by showing off her features much more effectively – especially those lovely big blue eyes – and the latter by being stylistically negative.

Her make-up was far more expertly applied nowadays, she realised. Martine had obviously given her some lessons.

Unobtrusive and subtle.

Her choice of clothes was another area where she had improved. Those leggings had gone, although Elspeth had rather enjoyed the early spankings, looking down on her nervous target, tightly encased in black nylon, the shape of her bottom quite clearly defined. Pulling them down had been quite entertaining, as well. The little black skirt was much better though.

Sundays were non-uniform days and Sophie was allowed to be more of a submissive lover and companion than an out-and-out slave. And on that particular Sunday she was wearing a light summer dress, tight enough at the top to show off her lovely firm breasts and with a flared, knee-length skirt to hide her even lovelier bottom completely. She looked clean, fresh, and in a slightly old-fashioned way, youthfully delicious.

Elspeth sighed, stretched, licked a stray bit of marmalade from a finger, and saw Sophie look up and blush a little as she licked with deliberate sensuality.

'Let's clear away and then have a nice relaxed morning, darling,' she said. 'I had hoped we could have another day in the country. Tunbridge Wells is always worth a visit, but even its charms are not worth getting soaked for. And the forecast is rain for the rest of the day.'

Half an hour later, she was sitting comfortably in the middle of the big sofa in the sitting room, with a slightly nervous Sophie lowering herself across her lap. During the washing-up she had broken the news that for 'bottom-hole training' she thought it best to get stuck straight in to her programme, rather than break the girl in gently, so had led her firmly – and unresistingly – to her fate.

She bared Sophie's bottom, enjoyed a close and lingering look at the fading marks left by the martinet, and then rested a hand on each cheek, the tips of her fingers pressing gently into the sides of the cleft. She paused, savouring the moment. Sophie's bottom was always a joy to behold and to hold, and she enjoyed both the sight and feel for a minute before parting her buttocks. She could feel the tension in her hands as her slave instinctively protected herself, and again when she extended her forefinger and started to tickle her anus.

The girl gradually relaxed as the pleasure of her mistress's touch conquered her awkwardness, and she was soon sighing audibly and raising her hips to make access easier.

Elspeth smiled, brought her right hand up to her mouth, licked her finger thoroughly, opened Sophie's bottom up again and pressed the slippery digit against the tight, pink ring.

Again, it shrank at her touch.

She smiled.

'Sophie,' she said grimly, 'I am going to stick my finger up your bottom and you are going to learn to take it. Then to like it. Now stop being silly and relax.'

Suitably chastened, Sophie did as she was told and Elspeth soon had her finger wriggling past the sphincter and into the tight warm tunnel beyond.

She then moved to stage two, reaching for the tube of lubricant in her pocket, applying it liberally to her finger and slipping it back into her slave's rectum, much more easily.

Ten minutes later, Sophie was on knees and elbows on the floor and Elspeth had her smallest vibrator deep in her bottom, moving it in and out with one hand while the other toyed with her sopping fanny. Her climax was, by her restrained standards, loud and prolonged.

Afterwards, Sophie willingly accepted that bottom-hole training was both instructional and enjoyable, and cheerfully agreed to an intensive course.

The next step was to bring her slave out in the open. Sophie had learned that if her mistress wanted her to perform in front of her friends, then she should do so and at least appear to enjoy it. But her basic shyness had clearly made it hard for her, and even with the relatively familiar Daphne, she tended to lose her new-found poise.

Once again, Elspeth knew that both carrot and stick would

be more effective in the longer term than the stick alone. She asked Daphne to come over and measure Sophie for a pair of leather trousers, pleased to see that the girl stripped and positioned herself far more willingly than she had the first time, but also that her face was pink with embarrassment throughout.

Two days later the trousers were ready and an entertaining fitting was under way. Sophie showed all the natural excitement of a girl being treated to an exotic new outfit, stripped both quickly and seductively, and quite enjoyed it when Daphne took a lot of care to fit the accompanying G-string exactly. Elspeth found it hard to tear her eyes away from Daphne's elegant fingers busying themselves in the deep tight cleft of Sophie's bottom, but raised them to see her face as Daphne explained that having her buttocks bare under the trousers would allow her to feel the leather against her skin, and make them even sexier to wear.

With a tight fitting white blouse, high-heeled boots and a black velvet choker around her throat, Sophie was transformed and paraded in front of her admiring audience with new assurance but no sign of unbecoming cockiness.

Daphne came up with the excellent plan of sending Sophie out for a walk, to show herself off.

Elspeth had an equally good idea. They should follow her at a discreet distance to see how she got on.

After a rather nervous start she soon settled into a stately stroll, her chubby round buttocks beautifully outlined in the softly clinging leather and, as she blossomed under the several admiring glances directed towards her, they noticed how she began to exaggerate the natural sway of her hips.

Hardly surprisingly, as soon as all three were safely back home Sophie was made first to strip, then to help the two women undress and then to parade around the sitting room, naked except for her choker and boots, her bare bottom proving to be even more seductive in motion than her leather clad one had been.

Daphne was slightly shocked when Elspeth actually kissed her slave's buttocks, unable to resist the heady scent of combined leather and clean, highly aroused girl.

Elspeth was tempted to give Daphne a sound spanking there and then, but held back on the grounds that it would not be good for discipline. So she sent Sophie up to her room before putting her giggling friend across her bare lap and reddening her broad cheeks to the satisfaction of both parties.

By coincidence rather than design, Elspeth killed one little seed of doubt which had been lurking deep in Sophie's subconscious mind, namely that she was something of a freak because she occasionally got sexual pleasure from a sore bottom.

Elspeth bought spanking books and magazines from time to time, and it had simply never occurred to her that it would be a good idea to let Sophie see them. She tended to read them, note any interesting points for future reference, and then throw them away. But for some reason she had left a couple in the sitting room.

Sure enough, Sophie found them as soon as she started her chores one morning. When Elspeth peeped into the room to check up on her, she was on the sofa, her eyes wide in amazement, reading issue number three of one of Elspeth's favourite magazines that concentrated on girls punishing girls.

'And what do you think you're doing?' she snapped.

Sophie leapt to her feet, sending the magazine flying, went pale, then bright red and stammered out her apologies.

Elspeth spanked her for slacking, forgave her, and five minutes later they were sitting side by side looking at the cause of Sophie's downfall, and Elspeth was enthusing over what she considered to be one of the best spanking illustrations she had ever seen.

The photo story consisted of a girl coming home, finding her girlfriend on the phone to a sex line and playing with herself. She decides to spank her and does so, starting on the seat of her skirt, then on the knickers, on to her bare bottom, and ending up using a plastic ruler.

Several things had inspired Elspeth to hang on to that particular issue. The spanker was appropriately stern, the spankee meek, pretty, and with a lovely bottom, the camera angles imaginative and in several shots, the punished girl was looking directly into the camera, giving an unusually vivid impression that the reader was actually a spectator.

Best of all was one half page, full colour shot, taken as the girl was having her knickers pulled down. Her face was out of shot but the photographer had managed to catch the tension of the moment very well indeed. Her bare buttocks were clenched tightly enough to dimple them, the dominant girl was holding her victim's arm in the small of her back with one hand while the other dealt with her knickers, pulling them hard enough to stretch them between her hand and the gusset, still trapped between the girl's thighs.

After a few minutes Elspeth broke the spell, told Sophie to get on with her work, and promised that they would have a proper look at both magazines later. With the varied, exciting and reassuring images of other girls being spanked and beaten in her mind, Sophie worked with extra enthusiasm.

The next stage in Sophie's development came when Elspeth quietly told her she had decided to send her away for a whole weekend. While she took the disturbing news reasonably calmly – certainly compared with earlier days – her failure to agree instantly and willingly gave Elspeth a perfect excuse for an extended punishment session.

And, at last, to introduce Sophie to the cellar, a treat she had been saving until she was fully confident in her slave's ability to cope with the much more intimidating atmosphere there. As she sat next to her on the sofa, holding a nervously trembling and distinctly moist little hand, she explained the reasons for wanting to lend her out.

'The thing is, Sophie, that I belong to a circle of people – mainly female, but not exclusively – who enjoy domination and punishment above everything else. You've met Simone and Daphne, but there are quite a few others, all of whom are longing to get their hands on you. None of us are sadists. We would not get any pleasure from tying up a totally innocent girl and thrashing her, however beautiful, and even if she had the most beatable bottom in the world. We like our partners to be willing.

'You've done wonderfully, Sophie, you really have. I liked you from the beginning. And fancied you! Now I really do love you and I want you to go to Mistress Devina with that very much in mind. You'll be back in no time and I'll be happy to have you back. And to hear all about it. All right, darling?'

'Yes, mistress,' Sophie whispered.

'Good. Now I'm going to punish you. Not that you've done much to deserve it. I'm in the mood, that's all. I want to see you naked. To smack your bottom and watch it wobble and redden.

'I'm going to smack your tits and watch them wobble and redden, too. And your thighs.

'You will be paddled, caned and whipped. But only on your bottom.

'Both nipples and your clitty will be clamped.

'Last, but by no means least, I'll have you on your back with your legs pulled back over your head and tied down so you're trussed up like a chicken, and then I will whip your bottom-hole and your cunt. I won't damage you there – I love them both far too much to do that – but it will hurt, that I do promise.

'Now get across my knee. I'll spank you here and now.'

Half an hour later, A stark naked and pink-bottomed Sophie stumbled down the stairs and followed her mistress nervously into the cellar. Her first sight of the bench, the gleaming chains hanging from walls and ceiling, the manacles, the bench, the odd-shaped vaulting horse – which immediately brought back unpleasant memories of school gymnastics – and, most of all, the array of wooden and leather implements hanging on the far wall, sent a shudder through her tense body.

But then, as Elspeth strapped on her wristlets and anklets, gagged and clamped her, she began to face up to the mental and physical challenges.

And Elspeth had just told her that she loved her.

She felt the adrenaline begin to flow as she laid her sweating torso on the cool leather of the horse, and felt her bottom tighten as her feet were parted and chained to the legs.

Her buttocks quivered as Elspeth patted them with the big American paddle.

Sophie closed her eyes and readied herself to show her mistress that she loved her too.

# Chapter Six

Sophie set out for her weekend away with distinctly mixed feelings. For all Elspeth's reassurances, it was still a lonely excursion into that wide world outside the haven of the house, reminiscent of the way she had felt in the last few weeks of her short legal career.

Reminding herself that Elspeth loved her and that she had both risen to and benefited from every challenge she had been made to face so far, she hefted her suitcase and walked down towards Marylebone Road, swivelling her head in search for a taxi and forcing her mind to concentrate on the delicious feel of her bare bottom cheeks sliding against her leather trousers.

An hour later she paid the cab driver, studiously ignored his blatant study of her breasts, took a deep breath and walked purposefully up the stone steps to the front door of a desirable riverside house, noting that everything was in immaculate condition and pondering the fact that members of Elspeth's mysterious Circle seemed to be comfortably well off, to say the least.

The door was opened by a very pretty, vivacious, dark-haired girl wearing an identical version of her uniform, currently neatly folded in her case. Hiding her surprise at the presence of what presumably was another slave, she simply gave her name.

The girl ostentatiously looked at her watch and scowled. 'Better come in,' she said ungraciously, and held the door wide open.

Puzzled by her reception, Sophie walked into the hall, glanced quickly round, came to the immediate conclusion that Devina and Elspeth shared the same discreetly excellent taste, and then followed the maid or slave up the stairs, fascinated by the excellent view of her plump bottom encased in a pair of white knickers, which again, matched her own uniform ones.

The immediate recognition of Daphne's contribution somehow made her feel much more at home, and she began to relax enough to try and work out why the girl had checked the time and seemed annoyed by the evidence of her punctuality. She had just worked out the probable solution – that, if she had been late, she would undoubtedly have been punished – when she was being ushered into a beautiful drawing room, with large windows giving a lovely view of the Thames.

'Do come in, Sophie. I have been longing to meet you.'

Slightly taken aback by the warmth of the greeting, Sophie turned, saw Mistress Devina sitting on a sofa, stark naked and with her legs elegantly crossed.

She blushed and instinctively curtsied, straightened up, lowered her gaze to the floor and composed herself while her temporary mistress studied her.

Even her brief glimpse of Devina had been enough for her to form a clear impression of a tall slender woman, probably in her late thirties, with lovely blonde hair, quite big breasts with pale nipples. She obviously kept herself in excellent shape, as there were no signs of a spare tyre around her waist and her thighs looked lovely and firm. Her ribs were nicely covered though. Certainly not afflicted with model-like scrawniness, although slim enough to appeal to those who liked the lean look.

A lovely warm smile.

Perfect teeth.

Enormous blue eyes.

A gentle, calm face.

Hardly fitting the image of a dominating mistress.

A cultured voice, with no exaggerated accent.

Sophie felt her breathing quicken at the thought of being at her mercy.

'Could you turn around, my dear?'

The command broke her train of thought, and Sophie slowly turned so Devina could study her back.

Three beautiful black and white prints of naked girls on the wall were now facing her. All showing their bottoms. Reassuringly plump bottoms.

Like the maid's, so there was the comforting thought that bigger curves were not regarded as unattractive.

'Carol.'

'Yes, mistress?'

'I would like to see Sophie's bare bottom. Act as her maid and take her trousers down for me, if you please.'

'Yes, mistress.'

Sophie blinked in surprise. What amounted to a sudden and unexpected rise in status was almost too much to absorb at once and she stood there quietly, desperately wondering if it would be a sound move to make some effort to help. Just as she decided that, as usual, it would be best to do as she was told, Slave Carol's frowning face swam into view and her hands were at her waist, undoing the button. As the harsh rasp of the zip's descent accompanied the inevitable slackening of the tightness around her middle, Sophie held her breath.

It occurred to her that she really had made progress. She blushed when she remembered her embarrassment when Mistress Daphne had measured her for the uniform.

As Carol tugged the trousers down over the pronounced swell of her hips, Sophie began to feel increasingly aroused, revelling in the novel sensation of actually getting turned on at the thought of two complete strangers looking at her bare buttocks. Not that her temporary maid did anything to make things easier for herself. With instinctive understanding, Sophie realised she would probably have made just as big a meal of what was essentially a fairly simple act had the positions been reversed, taking every possible opportunity to grope and squeeze.

Especially when it came to the delicate task of tugging the back of her G-string from its nesting place between the cheeks of her bottom, although Sophie admitted she was probably too inhibited to have indulged herself to quite the same degree.

Eventually all was laid bare and Sophie stood there, blushing prettily and hoping Mistress Devina was enjoying the view. She could hear Carol's heavy breathing from somewhere near her left shoulder, but could not get any indication as to her feelings on the quality of the exposed intimacies she was obviously studying closely.

With her bottom tingling, her fanny pulsing and her heart beating wildly, Sophie admitted to herself that only a few weeks ago she would have been longing for the order to get dressed again. Instead of which, she was actively dreading it.

To her relief, Mistress Devina asked Carol to guide her closer to the sofa and Sophie, somewhat hampered by her trousers, shuffled back the few paces, her excitement even greater at the thought of those amazing blue eyes peering at her from almost point blank range.

'Very pretty,' Mistress Devina breathed after several minutes. 'Don't you agree, Carol?'

'Not bad, I suppose,' replied the girl with studied disinterest, prodding the nearer buttock. 'Would you like to see her anus, mistress?' she added suddenly.

'Why not? Mistress Elspeth told me it is exceptionally lovely.'

'Come on you, bend over,' Carol snapped. Sophie reached for her toes in one smooth movement, momentarily distracted by the apparent familiarity in Carol's relationship with her mistress. Perhaps she wasn't a proper slave, Sophie wondered as two rather rough hands dragged her buttocks apart.

Vaguely hoping that her fanny hadn't betrayed her excitement by oozing too profusely, Sophie began to revel in her enforced exposure.

'Very pretty indeed.'

Devina's obviously genuine appreciation made Sophie feel even better, and she bent her knees slightly, increasing the pressure on her cheeks and sending a stab of slight pain from her obscenely stretched bottom-hole into her tummy.

Then, to her surprise, she was told to pull her knickers and trousers back up. She had already started to prepare herself for at least total nudity and probably a beating, but obeyed without fuss.

She was then turned round and Carol was ordered to uncover her breasts.

Once again, she showed no inhibitions about fondling them and tweaking her nipples.

Then her trousers and G-string were taken down again and her fanny examined.

Not surprisingly, Carol had a quick feel.

'She's quite wet, mistress,' she announced unemotionally.

Sophie held her breath, uncertain whether the news would be welcome or otherwise.

'Oh good,' came the reply.

The sense of anti-climax when she was ordered to cover herself up again was sharp enough to leave Sophie open mouthed, but she comforted herself with the thought that the chances of the morning deteriorating into a discussion on knitting and recipes over a cup of coffee were remote, and so calmly waited on events.

She was not disappointed. As soon as she had done up the top button of her blouse, Mistress Devina stretched languidly and smoothed her palms over her breasts, squeezing her nipples between thumb and forefinger with a blissful look on her face. The contrast between her cultured and polite way of talking and the blatant sexuality of her actions made Sophie blink, and she began to realise that there was more to her than met the eye. Her aroused curiosity stimulated her underlying excitement, and all thoughts of the safe haven of Elspeth's house faded away.

Devina stood up and stretched again. Sophie found she

was looking at the neat triangle of light gold hair at the base of her stomach, then at the slit below, clearly visible through the sparse curls, and the similarity between the bush in front of her and Elspeth's clearly suggested that Simone kept both in trim.

As she stared surreptitiously at Devina's thighs and enviably flat stomach, she also wondered if Carol had been totally depilated like her.

Then realised she would love to know.

The sweet and sour pulses from her fanny grew stronger at the thought of inspecting her fellow slave, especially if she found the inspection embarrassing. Sophie had not taken to Carol.

Devina's cultured voice broke into her reverie.

'You know, my dears, after all this excitement, I rather feel like administering a nice spanking. Yes, that would be just the ticket. I hope you don't mind, Sophie?'

'Not at all, mistress,' Sophie replied immediately, her steady voice disguising the surge of excitement.

But then Devina thought that a glass of champagne was called for and sat down again while Carol got it for her. Sophie stood quietly and nursed the anticipation.

She was looking forward to being spanked. For all the intensity of her emotions when Elspeth thrashed her, she still got a kick from the intimacy of being put across a dominant lap. The pain may have been considerably less, but was still sharp enough to get the adrenaline flowing and to make her bottom glow nicely when it was all over.

The strange and very different atmosphere in Mistress Devina's establishment was already getting to her, and making it especially exciting.

To lie on naked thighs.

A different hand and, presumably, a different technique, which would help maintain her curiosity and interest.

The challenge of showing Carol that she knew how to take punishment.

She began to try and visualise how Mistress Devina would go about it but then, sensibly, shied away from a mental process which she sensed could only lead to disappointment if things failed to turn out as she had imagined.

All too soon, a refreshed Devina announced that she was ready and asked Carol to go into the study and make sure the chaise longue was in its proper place.

The girl did so, shooting a gloating look in Sophie's direction as she passed.

Sophie felt her heart pound and wiped her moist palms on her legs, savouring the expectation of embarrassment and pain. Except, as she acknowledged to herself, the days when she was seriously embarrassed at being bare-bottomed were gone.

When Devina stood up and pointedly massaged the palm of her right hand, Sophie really began to feel fluttery, and so was a bit disconcerted when her temporary mistress announced that so much sitting had made her buttocks all numb and a massage would be most welcome.

At first Sophie was a little annoyed at the diversion, but then the thought of seeing a new bottom at close quarters aroused her growing interest in that part of the female anatomy, and she approached her task very willingly.

Mistress Devina's behind turned out to be broad, rather flat, and short-clefted. Very different from Elspeth's and Daphne's. More like Simone's, but bigger all round.

It was amazingly soft and Sophie was forced to concede reluctantly that her skin was just as enticing as Elspeth's.

After several deep sighs of contentment, Devina thanked her nicely and told her to follow her to the place of execution. A nervous, excited, aroused Sophie obeyed, and was even more distracted by the fluid movements of the bare bottom oscillating deliciously right in front of her.

They entered the study, with a beautifully upholstered chaise longue right in the middle and a smirking Carol standing beside it.

Sophie began her usual deep breathing exercises as her bottom began to tingle.

Then Mistress Devina told Carol she was going to be spanked for failing to treat their guest with proper respect.

Both slaves gaped at an impassive Devina. In the second or so which followed the announcement, Sophie felt a flash of disappointment at the realisation that all her mental preparations had been in vain, and then a surge of a completely different feeling of excitement. To her surprise, Carol's reaction was to protest at the unfairness of it all. By nature and training, Sophie had always managed to accept her fate more or less silently, and to hear a slave actually arguing with her mistress was incredible. Not that the red-faced girl was actually guilty of disrespect in anything she said. She was pleading rather than refusing to submit.

Sophie saw a sparkle in Mistress Devina's eyes, which made her suspect that she was missing some essential point and from that moment on, she listened carefully, sensing that she was about to learn some of the more subtle aspects of domination and submission.

Relaxing, she listened to the increasingly noisy by-play between the two protagonists with keen interest.

'Oh, please don't be awkward, Carol dear,' Devina begged. 'I do so want to smack your fat little bare bottom and you're making things very difficult for me.'

'My *bare* bottom?' Carol wailed plaintively. 'I don't want Sophie to see my bottom. It's not fair!'

'Oh dear. You *are* being a pest. Of course it's fair. You've seen Sophie's bottom.'

'That's true, mistress,' Carol replied grudgingly. Then she brightened. 'I know, I'll take my knickers down for her so she can see it and then I won't have to have it smacked in front of her.'

Sophie was amazed at the childishness of the exchange, but rather than dismiss it, she listened and watched even more closely.

Devina stamped her foot, which made her soft bottom quiver and her breasts shake. 'Please, Carol, let me smack your bottom?' she pleaded, her eyes shining even more noticeably.

'Oh, all right,' Carol said, and a little smile transformed her face from sulky child to mischievous young woman.

Sophie breathed out as she understood that it was a little game, enjoyed by both and, as Devina moved over to the chaise longue and sat down with the same gracefulness which marked all Elspeth's movements, her regrets at not being spanked gave way to a keen sense of anticipation at witnessing a spanking for the first time.

By the time a very red-bottomed Carol had been helped to her feet and kissed better, Sophie understood far more about CP than she had only fifteen minutes earlier. Her developing interest in bottoms ensured that she enjoyed seeing Carol's far more than she would have done previously, and the fact that she hadn't really taken to the girl meant she got a great deal of pleasure from seeing it wobble and redden under the steady rain of spanks.

She noticed right from the beginning that there were marked differences in Devina's methods to those she was used to at Elspeth's hands. For a start, she spanked much more slowly and deliberately, with a good five second interval between slaps. She would pat her chosen spot, raise her hand, pause, and then lash it down. As soon as her palm had rebounded from Carol's elastic flesh, she would rest it on the nearer thigh and watch the brightening patch with evident satisfaction. Then she would select the next part of the generous target at her disposal, pat it, and spank it.

Her spanks were also considerably harder than Elspeth's and each one made Carol's buttocks bounce and wobble dramatically.

It was also obvious that Carol did not share Sophie's view that punishment should be born stoically. Each time her mistress's hand landed she howled uninhibitedly, tossed her bottom around, clenched it as tightly as she could, and often added some comment for good measure, usually on the lines that her mistress was rotten and cruel to hurt her poor little bottie so much.

Apart from enjoying the physical aspects, from the movements of Devina's naked breasts as she swung her arm, to the fairly pronounced distortions which affected Carol's bottom, Sophie found other sources of pleasure.

Devina had told her that she could wander round and view things from different perspectives, and she took full advantage of the welcome freedom, soon realising that there was a strange beauty in punishment. The flowing curve of Carol's body; the graceful sweep of Devina's arm; Carol's multi-coloured bottom peeping naughtily out between her rumpled knickers and raised skirt; the rippling waves as the flattened flesh sprang back into shape; the gentle bounce and quivers of Devina's lovely breasts.

Then she began to analyse the strange relationship between the two of them, so markedly different to the more straightforward one she shared with Elspeth. She had grasped the fact that the exchange before the spanking was a bit of a game, but found it hard to understand the reason for it.

Until she concentrated on Devina's face for a while, and the soft expression of pure happiness as she gazed down on her slave's naked bottom brought a glimmer of comprehension. From her attitude right from the start, Sophie guessed that she was essentially a calm and gentle woman, and the role of the steely-eyed and grim dominatrix would not have come naturally.

On the other hand, Carol's childishness and sulky protests spurred her into acting more forcefully, while still maintaining the mild mannered and gentle persona which was apparently her favoured attitude.

Sophie also began to appreciate that Carol's behaviour as she was spanked also helped the atmosphere. She may have reacted far more noisily and physically than Sophie would have considered appropriate, and certainly gave the impression that her bottom was awfully sore, but always had it cocked up ready for the next spank.

Pleased with her deductions, Sophie moved around freely. She stood directly in front of Devina, her eyes flicking from her smiling, slightly flushed face, to the shuddering bottom immediately below it, to Carol's expressive features, and then to Mistress Devina's mobile breasts.

She went to Carol's head and smiled into her gleaming eyes, and somehow communicated her understanding to her fellow slave, because she was treated to a conspiratorial wink. Raising her eyes, she enjoyed a very different view of the girl's bottom, looming dramatically above the folds of the skirt and the small of her back, the curves into her cleft especially obvious.

All too soon, it was all over and Carol burst into a noisy flood of tears and clambered to her feet, hopping round the room clutching her bottom and wailing that she had never felt so sore in her life.

When she had calmed down a bit, Devina asked her tentatively if she would like to sit on her knee for a cuddle.

'Yes please, mistress,' she replied eagerly, and held her skirt right up to her waist as she perched, finally proving to Sophie that her fanny was also completely hairless.

Carol sighed deeply as she rested her head on Devina' shoulder, and again when her mistress reached down and began to stroke her tightened bottom.

Sophie watched avidly as the hand eased towards the open cleft and began to delve gently between parted thighs and buttocks, obviously roaming freely around the two openings made accessible by their owner's position.

The contrast between the vaguely maternal position and the blatantly sexual actions of the hand took Sophie's breath away, and her own juices ran freely as she saw Carol move inexorably to a surprisingly restrained climax.

Her overwhelming desire to be spanked, to feel the differences for herself, to experience a new lap and another hand made her screw up her courage.

'Mistress Devina?' she said, as soon as Carol had recovered.

'Yes, Sophie,' Devina replied, smiling vaguely at her.

'It was just as much my fault as Carol's and so I think it's only fair that I should get spanked as well.'

'Oh no!' Devina exclaimed with convincing horror. 'You're a guest.'

A great deal wiser, if only an hour or so older, Sophie caught on immediately and begged to have her bare bottom soundly smacked.

Mistress Devina caved in, but on the condition that she had another glass of champagne first, so poor Sophie had to hang around in a fever of anticipation while the refreshing nectar was enjoyed to the full and at considerable length.

Even then, she had to be patient. 'Which do you think you will find more embarrassing, Sophie my dear?' Devina asked seriously as soon as they returned to the study. 'To take your own trousers down or to have Carol do it for you?'

Forcing herself to give the matter proper consideration, Sophie thought that to have one's bottom bared would be worse.

At last, after a gloating Carol had taken her trousers and knickers down, she was able to lay herself across Devina's slender but surprisingly comfortable thighs and set herself up for a serious assessment of the different spanking techniques between the two mistresses.

She ended up feeling that a spanking from Elspeth was definitely a more fulfilling experience, but that Devina's methods were certainly not to be dismissed lightly. Her bottom was deliciously painful and her punisher's nudity had certainly added another dimension.

On the Sunday evening Sophie walked wearily into Elspeth's house, her buttocks throbbing and glowing but inwardly satisfied that she'd done nothing to discredit her mistress's training.

Over supper Elspeth listened with amused intensity while Sophie gave a blow by blow description of her weekend, asking questions firstly to clarify certain physical details and later about Sophie's reactions. Typically, several of the questions made Sophie think quite hard and, when she grasped the reason for the interrogation, realise that she had missed the point at the time.

For example, when she listed all the implements used, Elspeth laughed.

'Dear Devina hasn't changed. She still insists on using normal household things rather than anything made specifically for punishment. I prefer implements that are the results of hours of thought and effort, all with the express intention of causing the right degree of pain and redness to a naughty girl's bottom. Except for the hairbrush, perhaps. That has such delicious undertones of strict but loving nannies.'

The happy look on Elspeth's face made Sophie wonder for a second whether her bottom was fit enough to offer it for a demonstration, but a quick squirm made her decide that discretion was more sensible. Then she kicked herself for failing to spot that it had felt the differing effects of a slipper, two hairbrushes, a wooden spoon, a ruler and a leather belt, all of which as Elspeth had noted, had other uses.

As she reminisced under persistent questioning, she was brave enough to mention Carol's lack of inhibition under punishment, and to ask Elspeth if she preferred her to try to keep still and quiet or to buck and howl. Elspeth was fairly non-committal, and Sophie resolved to react a little more in future and see what happened, happy with the prospect of something else to add interest to her punishments.

She also admitted that the biggest turn on for her had been when she was made to lie on her back, with Carol straddling her head and holding her legs right back so that Devina could smack the inner curves of her buttocks, her anus and fanny with a baby's hairbrush, ending up by applying the soft bristles to the reddened skin. The pain had been markedly different and the worms' eye view of Carol's bare bottom had been spectacular to say the least.

Elspeth laughed. 'Of course, I've never queened you, have I?'

Sophie looked blank, and a couple of minutes later was enjoying a similar view of her mistress's bottom. As Elspeth slowly lowered herself, Sophie was entranced by the way the buttocks changed shape and the tight cleft opened up, and so was more than ready to apply her tongue when her face was enveloped in soft, sweetly scented bottom flesh.

As a reward for a glowing report from Devina, Elspeth decided to take Sophie away for a couple of days and that the Wye Valley would make a pleasant change. She booked a double room in a quiet country pub outside Ross-on-Wye, broke the glad news to Sophie, and they eventually set off, delayed first of all because Sophie forgot her toothbrush and secondly because Elspeth had to give a sound paddling for her carelessness.

They were both therefore in an excellent mood and still had enough time in hand to stop off in Oxford on the way, so that Sophie could show Elspeth her college and other haunts from her innocent past.

As they drove round the edges of the Forest of Dean, getting close and beginning to feel an almost childish excitement at the prospect of three days in that lovely part of the world, Elspeth really noticed a change in Sophie. Her weekend with Devina had clearly given her food for thought, and her innate diffidence was already less marked. Going back to Oxford had obviously given her confidence another boost. Elspeth had watched her carefully, seeing how the memories of her three years there had flooded back as they wandered around. Her descriptions of places and occasions had got steadily more detailed and cheerful, as though remembering that to have got into Oxford in the first place had been quite an achievement, and her eventual degree an even greater one.

Elspeth was aware of the danger that her slave could suddenly reach the conclusion that her present status was arguably a denial of all she had gained, and decide to rejoin the outside world. She knew Sophie well enough to be sure that if she did decide to put slavery behind her, she would only do so after a great deal of thought and very reluctantly. As she drove, Elspeth tried to imagine how she would feel if that did happen, and hardly surprised herself with the conclusion that it would be a very sad day indeed.

Sophie was special. Very special, and her intelligence was a key factor.

She tried to reconcile the two contrasting sides to the young girl's character, summarised perfectly by her confidence on the tour of Oxford on one hand and, on the other, by an hour or so on a recent evening, when she had wanted to concentrate on a television documentary, had sensed that Sophie was not wildly interested and so made her go on all fours by her feet. Her naked back made a convenient stool and her bare bottom was within easy reach of her right foot, providing a pleasant area to explore during the breaks in the programme.

She had behaved exactly as a well trained slave should, kneeling absolutely silent and motionless, except for an occasional sigh of pleasure when Elspeth prodded away in the soft warmth of her bottom cleft with her big toe.

Just before she had to devote all her concentration on following the complex directions to the remote pub, she vowed never to take Sophie for granted and to make sure that she gave her enough opportunities to be herself, rather than train her so intensively that her personality was totally subdued.

Their holiday provided an excellent opportunity to do just that. Elspeth treated her as a friend first and foremost, and was pleased by the way she began to relax.

There was a trace of awkwardness when they went to bed, with Sophie not quite sure where to look as Elspeth undressed.

But she dealt with that by asking Sophie to give her a massage, with the specific request to spend some time on her bottom, which, she claimed, was still a bit numb after all those hours behind the wheel. The intimacy clearly pleased Sophie, whose touch had a new sensuality as she worked.

They made love rather than fucked.

They did a lot of walking and, again, Elspeth worked on generating an atmosphere in which there was something approaching equality between them.

They explored Ross-on-Wye, Gloucester and Hereford.

The owner of the pub told them about the Sculpture walk in the Forest of Dean, so they tried it and agreed it was the high point of the break. The idea behind it was simple and very ingenious; a well marked seven mile walk through varied parts of the forest, seeing a number of very different and interesting sculptures on the way round, ranging from a twenty feet high wooden chair on an open hilltop to a large stained glass 'window' suspended between two trees in a narrow gap in the woods, carefully positioned to catch the flickering sunlight.

They talked. Elspeth gently prodded away until Sophie was able to discuss her feelings about their relationship with less inhibition than before, and by the time they were on their way back home was actively questioning her mistress about punishment implements, increasingly keen to discover the differences in technique and application.

As she settled down to sleep on their first night home, Elspeth felt quietly confident that Sophie was ready for greater things.

She sent her out to spend whole days with other members of the Circle, and the girl's general behaviour was invariably complimented, so that Elspeth's reputation as a trainer reached new heights.

So did Sophie's as a slave. The combination of her intelligence, interest in all aspects of submission, her lush bottom, skin which reacted prettily and quickly to punishment, her tiny anus and neat fanny, firm breasts and pretty face made her an exciting diversion.

Her education proceeded apace.

Mistress Beatrice, a fervent traditionalist whose punishment room boasted a genuine whipping bench, introduced her to the fierce kiss of a properly assembled birch, and Sophie came away with a ferociously sore bottom, which was still burning some time after she had got back home.

Mistress Mae Wong taught her that the Chinese have an even longer tradition of refined punishment. She tied her to a dining room table, face down and at full length, and with her slave, a tall blonde Swedish girl who provided a startling contrast to her bird-like mistress, spent half an hour rhythmically applying thick bamboo rods to her bare buttocks. Neither punisher put any real weight or force behind the blows and, for the first part of the session, Sophie found it intensely arousing. But gradually the repetition made it extraordinarily and deeply painful. She could hardly walk when they eventually let her up, and it was only when Mistress Wong made her lick her bottom-hole that Sophie was able to pull herself together, the pleasure in seeing her neat little bottom all bare providing the necessary incentive.

Mistress Bettina loved the role of leather-clad dominatrix and, in between slaves when Sophie called, had to greet her at the front door personally. Her costume of thigh length boots, a short corset which narrowed her waist dramatically and left her breasts, buttocks and fanny completely exposed, reduced Sophie instantly to a quivering wreck.

Sophie found that submitting to the frightening figure was extremely easy, meekly submitting to being trussed up like a chicken and hung from the basement ceiling by her cuffed wrists and ankles to have her widely splayed bottom whipped with devastating skill.

After every visit Elspeth questioned Sophie closely, and expanded her own activities to include anything which seemed to have appealed to her slave. For example, she obviously found bondage especially challenging, and so visits to the cellar became more frequent.

In complete contrast, Beatrice had put her across her knee for a very prolonged spanking before applying the birch, and Sophie had admitted she still found that being spanked turned her on more than anything else, even if it no longer produced the same sort of adrenaline surge as more severe sessions.

On the few occasions when Sophie seriously annoyed Elspeth, she was neither spanked nor beaten, but sent to bed immediately after supper.

That was the worst punishment of all.

Then Elspeth reckoned that Sophie was nearly ready for the two final tests in her training and began to prepare her for the first, broaching the subject of male domination while a naked slave was lying across her knee. She had coated her right forefinger with lubricant, parted Sophie's buttocks, and was gently preparing her anus for the vibrator her slave was holding and studying uneasily. Extremely life-like and bigger than anything she was used to, the tension in her little sphincter suggested that Sophie doubted her ability to take it with the ease she had shown in recent weeks.

It proved to be less of a problem than she feared, and Elspeth was soon able to ease the tip rhythmically in and out, enjoying the sight of it disappearing into the depths of her cleft.

'Do you ever look at a man – passing in the street, for example – and fantasise about making love with him?' she asked innocently.

Sophie denied harbouring such thoughts, but not totally convincingly, and Elspeth breathed a sigh of relief.

As soon as she had slackened her slave's bottom-hole, she had her on knees and elbows on the floor, ready to be penetrated properly and, after a lingering look at the delicious view, she set to work. Sophie hissed with pain as the large knob stretched her anus, but before long, was groaning with pleasure and moving her hips in perfect time with the slow thrusts of the intruder.

Elspeth switched it on and Sophie's groans got louder.

Then, in a low voice, she told her that at the centre of the Circle, so to speak, was the master, who had heard such good reports of Sophie that he was favouring them with a personal visit in two days' time.

Sophie's groaning and moving stopped. 'And you want him to put his cock up my bottom?' she asked flatly.

Elspeth's eyes widened with surprise at the speed with which the girl had assessed the situation.

'Yes, darling,' she replied simply.

'Will he let you stay with me while he's doing it?' Sophie's voice was small and tight with fear, and Elspeth felt moved by her courage, and then again surprised that she had so quickly grasped the essential fact that the master would take full charge of the proceedings.

'I expect so,' was all she dared say in the way of reassurance.

'Would you mind carrying on, mistress? Make sure my bottom really can take it.'

'Good girl,' Elspeth said with real warmth, and increased both the depth and the speed of the thrusts.

At the appointed hour a nervous Sophie opened the front door, half expecting some monstrous ogre, and was so relieved to see a perfectly normal man smiling at her that she welcomed him with little of her usual calm poise. He was about six feet tall, probably in his early forties, and cast in the same mould as Elspeth, in that he was a picture of understated elegance. His dark grey suit could only have been Saville Row, his tie a plain maroon silk, his shoes both well worn and immaculate, his voice low and cultured, and his smile calm and friendly.

Her instant judgement was that he was handsome, very attractive, and with an air of quiet assurance which was more threatening than any amount of posing and bluster.

Sophie's nerves jangled and her 'Please come in, master' emerged as a humiliatingly childish squeak.

Not daring to say anything else she led him to the sitting room, and was able to steady herself while he and Elspeth greeted each other like the warm friends they clearly were.

By the time she had opened the champagne, poured out two glasses, handed them round and offered the tray of canapés, she was nearly back to normal and the master's approval of her uniform made her feel even better.

Then, out of the blue, he ordered Elspeth to give her a sound spanking.

The extra and unaccustomed element of knowing that a pair of male eyes were watching made her even more determined to show what she could take and, although Elspeth set to with a will, she easily managed to keep silent from beginning to end.

His spontaneous comment 'what a lovely bottom' when her knickers slithered down her trembling thighs did her morale no harm at all.

Nor did his insistence that, after she had been spanked, she removed her knickers completely and tucked the back of her skirt into her apron strings so that her red bottom was in full view.

She managed to put the fact that he was going to bugger her before the afternoon was out to the back of her mind, and concentrated on doing her level best to be a credit to a patently nervous Elspeth.

Before she served lunch, he told her to take all her clothes off – except for her stockings and suspender belt.

Every time she walked out of the dining room the conversation stopped, and knowing that both pairs of eyes were following the movements of her bare bottom made her even more self-conscious.

After lunch, she had to put her uniform back on to serve the coffee.

Then the master put her across his knee, peeled down her knickers and helped himself to a leisurely feel of her buttocks. She waited breathlessly for him to pull them apart and inspect

138

her anus. He didn't, and she was faintly disappointed.

But he did spank her.

Much harder than Elspeth and it hurt considerably.

She had the wit to thank him when she eventually clambered to her feet, and saw Elspeth's relieved look out of the corner of her eye.

'It was my pleasure,' he replied dryly, but his smile suggested he meant it.

Sophie began to feel more confident.

When she had finished the washing-up, she reported back to the sitting room, her anus beginning to tingle expectantly.

'You really have got a lovely bottom, Slave Sophie,' he said suddenly.

'Thank you, master,' she acknowledged, her face burning with pleasure.

'So I have decided to cane it. Twelve of the very best. On the bare, of course.'

The blood drained from her face. 'Thank you, master.'

The master and Elspeth had a brief discussion on the relative merits of total nudity versus a bared bottom, agreed that the latter was better, and Elspeth produced her best rattan cane.

The master swished it through the air, nodded approvingly, handed it back, and started to take his jacket off. Sophie watched with growing apprehension as his tight shirt made it quite clear that his broad-shouldered litheness was natural rather than an illusion caused by expert tailoring.

The master rolled up his sleeves and his muscular forearms made her shudder.

She swallowed hard and began her mental preparations, anticipating the pain rather than trying to put it out of her mind.

Deep, slow breaths.

Suddenly he was standing right in front of her, his eyes close and penetrating, as though he was trying to search the inner recesses of her mind. His hand cupped her cheek and she sensed sympathy behind the power and authority. She began to look forward to being beaten by him.

'As I said, Sophie, it will be twelve of the best. On your bare bottom. I want you to call out the number of each stroke soon after I've delivered it. Understand?'

'Yes, master,' she whispered, unable to tear her eyes away from his. They were grey. With a hint of green? He smiled and her heart lurched as she realised she was attracted to him. As a man. She had forgotten what it felt like. Her pent up breath shuddered out.

'Be brave, Sophie. Now turn round, lift up your skirt and bend over. Right over, touching your toes.'

'Yes, master.'

She caught a quick glimpse of Elspeth's pale, strained face as she turned, and her nerves jangled again.

She lifted her skirt, rolled it around her waist, took a really deep breath, and slowly reached down to her toes. Her knickers were stretched tightly over her protruding bottom.

She waited for him to take them down and wished he'd told her to do it herself. It would have been that much more submissive; willingly baring her own bottom for punishment.

More slave-like.

He asked Elspeth to do it. The next best thing.

She fumbled as she pulled them halfway down her thighs. Then she undid both back suspenders and tucked them into the belt. Her bottom was completely bare.

It felt big, prominent, soft. Terribly vulnerable.

The cane tapped her, high up, just below her tailbone.

She closed her eyes, took another deep breath.

She sensed his movements as he began his swing.

The cane hummed loudly as it cleaved through the air on its way to her soft, intimate flesh.

She heard the sharp crack of the impact.

She felt the rippling of her bottom flesh.

Red, yellow and orange lights exploded in her brain.

Her held-in breath whooshed out of her lungs in a strange, choking gurgle.

It was the most painful single blow she had ever experienced, and it was all she could do to stay in position.

Her mind cleared as the initial searing heat of the thin line of agony etched right across her bottom ebbed away. Just a little but enough.

'One, master,' she cried.

She fought back her rising panic at the thought of another eleven like the first, and then reminded herself that she was being challenged, not punished.

She just had to rise to the challenge. For her own pride. And because she loved Elspeth.

The cane tapped her again. Just below the raised, throbbing weal left by the first stroke.

She realised he had given her the time she needed to compose herself and inwardly thanked him as she braced herself, dragging air deep into her lungs.

'Six. Thank you, master.

Halfway. That last one had forced a loud cry from her but her hands had hardly moved from her toes. Her confidence began to grow.

The pain was horrendous. The top half of her behind was a wealed mass of burning, stinging agony. The backs of her thighs ached. Her back hurt. She had bitten her lip at some stage.

But the sense of achievement eased the pain.

She hoped Elspeth was more relaxed.

And that she was proud of her slave.

That she was enjoying the view of her bottom.

Her bare bottom.

Nice phrase.

'Aaaarghhh! Seven. Thank you, master.'

He hadn't told her to thank him. It just seemed the right thing to do.

'Nnnngggg! Eight. Thank you, master.'

It didn't seem quite so painful in the middle of her bottom.

Fleshier? Or because it was near her anus and therefore sending some stimulating messages into her vitals.

'Ooohhh! *Nine*. Thank you, master.'

God, that one hurt. Feeling a bit faint.

Breathing, Sophie, concentrate on the breathing.

Beginning to get a bit sweaty.

'Aaaahhh. Ten. Thank you, master.'

Not quite as bad, that one.

Two more. She could do it.

'*Oh God*! Eleven. Thank you, master.'

The last one will land in the folds.

Agonising.

Deep breaths. Deep breaths. Last one.

'Ahhhh… nnggg. Oh God, oh God, oh God. Twelve. Thank you, master.'


Pain, relief, exultation, gratitude, all combined to drain the last vestiges of strength from Sophie's legs and she toppled onto her face, moaning incoherently for several minutes before the red mists faded and she struggled to her feet. Tears of pain and relief poured down her very red face as she tried to stammer out an apology for her lack of self-control.

She was told to lie face down and her bottom was examined, admired, and then soothed with the magic cream. Her tears dried up, she apologised again and claimed that she was fine, proving it by getting up unaided and standing quite steadily.

A drink of water helped and she was fit enough to take all her clothes off and stand in the corner, where she gratefully allowed her mind to drift over recent events. She told herself she had not done badly, but there was room for improvement.

As she analysed her reactions, she came to the conclusion that she had finally grasped what was arguably the key element in her chosen way of life. It occurred to her that if at any stage she had decided that enough was enough and refused to take any more, neither the master nor Elspeth would have forced her into continuing.

It would have been the end of her progress and possibly the end of her relationship with her mistress.

Therefore true submission had to come from within. It could not be forced on one from the outside.

That crucial piece of self-discovery allowed her to submit to being buggered with far more than the good grace which was all that Elspeth expected of her.

She knelt on the footstool and thrust her wealed bottom out as blatantly as she could, thrilling to the master's exclamations of delight at the prettiness of her bottom-hole and fanny.

When Elspeth wriggled her lubricated forefinger in her tingling rectum, the contrast between the delicious sensations in the middle of her bottom and the burning pain still affecting her buttocks had her gasping with pleasure.

The very different pain as he penetrated her, stretching her anus and filling her back passage almost to bursting point made her see stars.

She remembered Elspeth's advice and rhythmically tightened and relaxed her tight sphincter against the velvety hardness of his cock, and his groans were music in her ears.

He began to thrust in and out and she moved in concert, crying out when his hard stomach rammed against her sore buttocks, but not retreating an inch.

She felt his increased urgency and her own arousal threatened to take over and disrupt her rhythm, but then he came, so all she could think of doing was to keep her bottom pressed as tightly as she could against him, sensing that the deeper his penetration, the greater his pleasure.

She felt the hot spurts and cried out in sympathy with him.

Then Elspeth's beautiful face swam into her vision and her lovely soft lips were on hers, her tongue forcing her mouth open.

She felt his prick go soft in her bottom and her anus clamped around it, as though reluctant to let it go.

The master thanked her warmly before dismissing her, and

she staggered up to her room, collapsed on her bed – face down – and went out like a light.

# Chapter Seven

Sophie peered out of the taxi window as they approached Mistress Simone's salon in Soho, and heaved a sigh of relief when she noticed that the driving rain which had forced Elspeth to abandon plans for a few days in the Peak District was definitely slackening. She had been praying for a break in the weather, hoping she would be able to follow her usual practice and, having paid the cab off at the far end of Soho, walk the rest of the way. She still got a kick out of being seen in her leather trousers, especially now they had softened with use and clung to her bottom even more sensuously. And especially when the twelve weals left by Elspeth's cane were still raised and tender, so that the slithering of her mobile buttocks against the seat constantly reminded her of the thirty minutes in the cellar earlier that morning, lying prone on the whipping bench, her legs together.

'Your bottom really does look sweet in this position, Sophie. It swells beautifully up from the small of your back and then down to your thighs. And your gluteal folds mark the limits of the target delightfully.'

She squirmed reminiscently and the friction sent little sparks of pain inwards, upwards and downwards.

'Are you a working girl, love?' the driver asked as he came to a halt.

'No, I do it for pleasure,' she laughed, handing him the fare, and then she scampered through the drizzle to her secluded destination, still smiling at the memory of his lame attempt at a seductive leer.

Simone was waiting for her, looking calmly severe. Sophie curtsied and kissed her extended hand, straightened, slipped

145

off her coat and stood at attention, waiting for orders and quietly looking forward to the next couple of hours while her temporary mistress walked around her, speculatively feeling her breasts, thighs, tummy and buttocks through her clothing.

'Touch your toes.'

She swooped down, resisting the temptation to show off her vastly improved fitness and rest the palms of her hands flat on the floor and, while her taut cheeks were poked, prodded and squeezed, she remembered her last visit. The metallic taste of the fear which had thrilled her more than the eventual pain filled her mouth and her nipples and fanny tingled as the memories flooded back.

Naked, on the examination bench, her legs tied back over her head while her obscenely displayed femininity was closely examined to see if any hairs had had the temerity to survive the original depilation.

Her relief when Mistress Simone had announced that her cunt was quite clear.

Mistress Simone's undisguised pleasure at finding two on her anus.

The sharp prick of the needle and the duller burning sensation of the electric charge.

Her relief when that was all the electrolysis required and then the earnest, whispered discussion between Elspeth and Simone.

And things *did* get worse.

Flat on her back, with Elspeth holding her hands tightly, telling her to close her eyes.

Icy cold liquid on her left nipple.

Metallic rattling, which made her long to try and see what they were going to do to her.

Her nipple being squeezed into painful prominence.

A sharp, stinging pain. Penetrating.

Forcing herself to take it calmly, to concentrate wholly on

the quality of the pain and not worry about the cause.

Something hard being forced through her nipple. A tugging sensation being added to the sting.

Then the same for the other nipple.

Less testing, as she knew what to expect.

Then her legs were drawn up again, splayed wide. Fingers squeezing her clit. Pain and pleasure. That rattle again.

Similar pain, but sharper and more invasive.

A strange pressure and a similar tugging.

Then they had led her to a mirror and shown her the gleaming little rings, one through each puckered nipple and a third poking out of the top of her fanny. After the first shock at the evidence of her mutilation, she looked with growing fascination.

She had healed quickly and was now so used to them that she could hardly remember what it had been like before. Especially in bed at night, nearly always with vivid memories of a variety of sensual experiences to recall, relive and inspire her to bring herself to her usual discreet climax, twiddling the steel rings for added affect.

Mistress Simone finished groping her bottom and Sophie began to tingle expectantly as she waited to be ordered to strip for a more detailed examination before the next, and apparently last, electrolysis session on her legs.

Simone stood in front of her and Sophie looked steadily and affectionately at the subtle beauty of her elfin face, with its lovely big brown eyes and full, sensual lips.

'Before we proceed, Slave Sophie, I would like you to help me.'

'I'd be delighted, mistress.'

'I have a new slave and it would be good for her to act as my assistant with you. To show her the high standards I eventually expect of her.' Sophie realised that Simone was tense, as her French accent was far more obvious than usual.

'With pleasure, mistress,' Sophie replied with genuine warmth.

Penny turned out to be almost as petite as her mistress, even blonder than Sophie and with a sweet little face. Sophie immediately wanted to give her a hug and then to see if her soft pale lips tasted as good as they looked.

She smiled warmly at her and was disappointed when the girl seemed to be flustered and confused, looking away and blushing.

She did however set about her appointed task of undressing Sophie efficiently enough – until she saw the nipple rings and went even paler. Then she gasped aloud when she took her trousers down and saw the weals on the naked cheeks of her bottom. Sophie was almost feeling sorry for her when the time came to crouch and take off her G-string. Sure enough, when she saw the glistening steel ring peeping proudly out from her tight slit, she cried out, her hands flying to her mouth as she stared with wide-open eyes. Lovely blue eyes, Sophie noticed as she smiled at Mistress Simone.

To her credit, Penny recovered quickly, proved to be a quick learner, and thanks to her assistance, Sophie's treatment was finished in good time, in spite of Simone's insistence on waxing her buttocks, saying that under a strong light she could clearly see some hairs, which were too fine for electrolysis.

The hot wax made her weals hurt quite a bit, which added to the enjoyment, and Simone made a point of reminding her new slave that Sophie had not even flinched under the treatment, which produced an encouragingly thoughtful look on Penny's pretty face.

With an unscheduled half-hour at their disposal, Mistress Simone asked Sophie if she would like to see Penny naked. Sophie said she would, Penny looked quite happy at the prospect and was soon stark naked, standing with her feet apart, her hands on her head and with her pink face tight with apprehension.

Remembering how awkward she had felt in the early days,

Sophie made suitable – and genuine – comments about her pert breasts, shapely thighs, hairless fanny and lovely complexion. She was glad to see Penny relax under the scrutiny, but puzzled by the deferential expression on her face, too self-effacing to understand that her poise had impressed the girl from the outset, as it had seemed so inappropriate in a slave. Her pierced nipples and clitoris, plus the vivid weals across her bottom, had only confused the inexperienced young girl and, as far as she was concerned at that moment, the approval of this exotic creature was almost as important as her new mistress's.

The significant element in what was otherwise a fairly unremarkable episode was when Penny was told to turn round. Sophie looked at her bare bottom – round, chubby, white, tense and beautifully proportioned – and began to feel distinctly sexy.

Touching it, revelling in the smooth warm skin and the elasticity of Penny's firm young flesh, had her fanny tingling away beautifully, and her feelings were strong enough to give her the nerve to ask Mistress Simone's permission to part the dimpled cheeks and look at her bottom-hole.

The heady atmosphere affected Mistress Simone as well, because she made Penny undress her and then lay on the couch with her sweet little bottom all ready to be kissed and licked by each slave in turn, before rolling onto her back, raising her legs, telling Penny to lick her bottom and Sophie to concentrate on her fanny.

On the way home, Sophie was very tempted to stimulate herself through her trousers, a pleasure made so much easier by her clitty ring, but was dissuaded by the sure knowledge that even if she restrained herself, the taxi driver would inevitably know what she had done.

Luckily Elspeth was in one of her especially receptive moods. Within three minutes Sophie was naked and eagerly undressing her mistress, feverishly taking her knickers off, realising her clitty had swollen so much that it pressed hard against the steel of the ring in its little hood. Happily accepting the inevitable price of a sound thrashing for being forward, she gave in to her surging desires, running her hands feverishly over her mistress's naked body, kissing and licking her tummy and thighs as she did so, instinctively avoiding the neat triangle of dark curls and, even more, the exciting slit below, knowing that to touch her there without express permission would incur severe displeasure.

Elspeth, who had been looking forward to an all-out sexual thrash with Daphne in Sophie's absence, and had been very disappointed when she cried off due to a heavy cold, was suffering from equal frustration. Not only did she enjoy Sophie's rather wild caresses, she also sympathised with the girl's feelings. As she surrendered to hers, she promised herself that she would really enjoy punishing Sophie for her uncharacteristic lack of discipline.

In the meantime, as the girl was obviously so desperate for sex, Elspeth made sure she got all she wanted. And a great deal more. In the process, she indulged most of her own tastes.

Sight. Sophie's naked body was forced into a series of increasingly revealing positions, culminating in having her lying on her back, her parted knees on the floor beside her head and her hands holding the lips of her fanny wide open, so she could peer into the glistening, bright pink convoluted folds surrounding the dark tunnel of her vagina.

Sound. Deep sighs, drawn-out moans, harsh panting, shrill cries, the occasional ringing noise of open palm on bare flesh, delicious squelchings as fingers delved into wet cunts.

Smell. The heady mixture of sweet hot flesh and the sharp scent of arousal.

Taste. Complimenting smell.

Touch. Arguably the most important of all and the only one which worked both ways, in that the feel of Sophie's hands on her flesh was equal to the more familiar feel of Sophie's flesh under her hands. And not just hands. Elspeth, a truly sensual woman, had learned a long time before that she could get almost equal and noticeably different pleasures by touching bare flesh with other parts of her body. Her feet, for example. She made Sophie lie face down on the floor and ran each sole in turn down her back, lingering on her squirming buttocks and pressing a big toe into the softer, warmer cleft until it nudged against the tight ring of her anus, slippery from the flowing juices, so she was able to force it into her rectum. Having done that, she squatted, lowered her own bare bottom onto Sophie's and squirmed it all around the rounded orbs, again revelling in the subtle differences in sensation.

Best of all was when she made her slavering slave crouch down, with her bottom thrust high in the air. She could indulge all five senses at once as she rammed the longest finger of her right hand up into her vagina and her left thumb into her bottom.

The sight of taut, wealed buttocks, quivering thighs, glistening cunt, that sweet little bottom-hole stretched round the base of her thumb.

The sound of Sophie's inarticulate cries as Elspeth ruthlessly drove her from one climax to a second and a third.

The lovely sharp scent of her sex.

The taste on her fingers when, from time to time, she withdrew them, licked them before plunging them back into their respective orifices, purely to sample again the pleasures of penetration. She was tempted to apply her tongue and taste the juices at first hand, but knew that Sophie would be confused by the gesture. As far as she was concerned, slaves licked mistress's bottoms, but not the other way round, and it was better to keep it that way.

Instead, she closed her eyes and wallowed in the feel. Primarily the considerable differences in back and front passages, with the extra thrill of pressing her invading fingers together through the thin membrane separating the two.

Then there was the even more blissful thrill of lying back

151

and letting Sophie get to work on her most sensitive parts, so that her climaxes matched her lucky slave's in both quantity and quality.

And, as a finale, she could indulge her taste for inflicting pain. Sophie had to be reminded that a slave's pleasures have to be paid for, and so was made to fetch the big paddle, assume the sorority position, and take two dozen fairly hard strokes. Then she had to stand in the corner with her crimson bottom on display until her tears had dried up.

Some time later Elspeth asked Daphne to come round, and the end result of a fairly torrid morning was a range of leatherwear which emphasised Sophie's status in a way she initially found rather shocking.

There was a black corset. It started just below her breasts and ended on the swell of her hips, leaving her breasts, bottom and fanny bare. Daphne and Elspeth laced it up with evident pleasure, until Sophie began to wonder if she would be able to breathe.

There were rings, back and front. Elspeth got out the gold chains reserved for special occasions, clipped them to the rings in her nipples and clitoris, and then fixed them to the corset, tightly enough to hurt. Not much, but enough.

Opaque, black, self-support stockings completed the main part of the new ensemble and Sophie was able to appreciate that the whiteness of her exposed flesh was thrown into even starker relief by the blackness of the minimal outfit.

There was one additional element. A triangular piece of soft leather, with a thin strip dangling from one point, which Daphne demonstrated with relish.

'You fix the top to the base of the corset with these press studs,' she explained to Elspeth. 'The main bit covers her cunt so you can have the fun of uncovering it when you want to. So far, nothing exceptional. But there are a couple of fiendish little extras.'

These consisted of two flexible rubber cylinders. The larger was slotted through a slit in the triangular part and into Sophie's vagina. The smaller one had a ring in the base, so the strip of leather could be passed through it before being inserted in her bottom. The last few inches of the strip were flattened, with several holes, enabling it to be buckled to the back of the corset, keeping the whole contraption firmly in place.

Both mistresses thoroughly enjoyed first fitting it, then watching Sophie do it herself, then making her walk up and down the room with it attached, smiling broadly at her tense expression as she tried to come to terms with the dual penetration.

Before long, Sophie had fully adjusted to the increased severity of the regime. The increasingly testing punishments, the bizarre costumes and the widening range of implements used on her, all combined to make submitting to pain even more challenging and exciting.

Elspeth's fears that increased intimacy would make her a less effective slave proved to be unfounded. Sophie was even more attentive than before. She tried her hardest to anticipate her mistress's desires, was quite prepared to accept punishment when she anticipated wrongly, and, best of all in Elspeth's eyes, still loved being put across her knee to have her knickers taken down and her bare bottom spanked with the palm of her hand. For all the heady pleasures of applying one of her implements to meekly proffered buttocks, Elspeth got just as big a thrill from having Sophie's soft weight on her thighs, her bottom right in front of her face, and the feel of her stiffened palm sinking into those deliciously yielding cheeks.

She continued to expand her slave's horizons. Once a month or so, she would ask four or five members of the Circle round for the day. Sophie would start off in her uniform, greeting the guests, serving coffee, generally acting as the perfect maid. But however perfect, the moment she had cleared away the coffee, each mistress would sit on the punishment chair, bend

153

the blushing girl over her lap, bare her bottom with varying degrees of impatience, and then spank her.

There was never a sense of urgency throughout the day, not only so that Sophie's buttocks were given some time to recover, but also to spin the enjoyment out. For example, by discussing the most recent punisher's technique.

After the warm up she would be made to parade in one of her more extreme costumes, all of which left the more exciting parts of her body exposed.

The guests would be allowed to beat her, using the implement of their choice.

After lunch, they would usually drift down to the cellar, where Sophie would be forced to demonstrate the equipment, bent into any number of revealing positions, so that Elspeth could give a practical demonstration of how various weapons could be directed accurately at varied targets, although her bottom was so attractive that virtually all their efforts were aimed there.

Sophie was encouraged to describe her feelings, both when she had been trussed up ready for punishment and afterwards, breathlessly describing the particular bite of whichever implement had been used.

In complete contrast, but equally arousing, were the pampering sessions. From time to time, Elspeth would come back tired and irritable from her occasional stints at the head office of the leading charity which had the benefit of her brains and energy.

Sophie would undress her, help her into the bath, wash her all over, dry her and then take her to their bed and massage her, taking her time to unravel the knots.

Gradually, the massage would move from the remedial to the openly sensual, with Elspeth's bottom becoming the centre of attention. Sophie would knead the pliant mounds with slowly increasing pressure until her mistress's breathing took on that urgent quality which showed quite clearly that she was ready for the climax. There was still no desire for haste and Sophie would concentrate on pulling Elspeth's buttocks apart, then pressing them together, sending the first really stimulating messages to her anus.

When the right moment came, she would bend down and kiss those beautiful cheeks, nibbling the pliant flesh before moving into the centre, holding them apart and applying her tongue, usually smiling at the distant memory of her distaste when she did it for the first time.

After a few minutes, a simmering Elspeth would turn over and open her legs, ready for her climax. Sophie would gaze lovingly at the vista of smooth white thighs and tummy, the lower part of a plumped-up bottom and, sexiest of all, her mistress's cunt, reddened by the flow of stimulated blood, the slit slackened by her arousal and the inner lips protruding. She knew to begin by stroking the insides of the thighs, then the buttocks. To run a finger up and down the exposed part of the cleft, then rest a thumb gently on each side of the glistening slit, open it up, lower her mouth and lick, delving deeper and deeper as Elspeth began to churn her hips and groan aloud.

Lastly, she would suck the scarlet clitty into her mouth and nibble gently until her mistress was completely satisfied. Only then was she allowed to lie back and reach down to her own slick centre and, with Elspeth watching with sympathetic interest, twiddle her clitty ring until she came.

Best of all, was that they spent several minutes in each other's arms, lost in their thoughts as they recovered. Sophie treasured the togetherness more than anything else.

It took Sophie some time to understand the reasoning behind Elspeth's next move. Had she been less preoccupied when the first hint was made, she may well have been less surprised by it. But she was, at the time, in the cellar, lying on her back on the whipping bench, doubled up with a leg spreader making sure she was so wide open that her anus was in full view of

Elspeth and their four guests. They were crowded round admiring the view, and Elspeth was explaining that she was going to use a single birch twig to whip her bottom-hole, perineum and cunt lips. 'But first, we'll let her stew for a bit.'

Mistress Daphne suggested that a butt plug would make her even more sensitive, and a quailing Sophie held her breath as one was found, lubricated, and thrust firmly into her helpless rectum.

As she was concentrating on her forthcoming torment, she vaguely heard Mistress Simone ask Elspeth if she had visited the Mansion recently.

'No, I haven't,' she admitted. 'Actually, that *is* a good idea. The change would do us both good, and the weather seems to be set fine for the next week or two. Yes, Simone, I'll do that. Are any of you free next week?'

The ensuing discussion went completely over Sophie's head as she lay there, sweating, and with the vast majority of her muscles beginning to protest. So she was actually relieved when silence fell, Elspeth approached the business end of her body, pulled out the plug and began to flick the whippy little switch against the most sensitive parts of her body.

Therefore, when Elspeth broke the news that they were going to have a long weekend in the country, the fact that other members of the Circle were involved escaped her.

As Elspeth's BMW hummed up the motorway to Leicestershire, her barely suppressed excitement communicated itself to Sophie and made the journey seem even longer. But at midday they turned off a winding lane and stopped in front of an impressive pair of tall iron gates, the only visible break in a well-maintained stone wall. Elspeth climbed out of the car, walked up to a small wooden panel on the left-hand pillar, opened it, and spoke briefly into a hidden microphone. The gates began to swing open, and she got back behind the wheel and drove on.

The drive curved to their right almost immediately they had

left the entrance behind them, and Sophie gasped at the size and elegance of the house that suddenly came into view. Elspeth grinned at her.

'Makes a bit of a change from crowded old London, doesn't it?'

'It certainly does,' Sophie agreed faintly, her eyes swivelling wildly around the extensive park surrounding the house.

More surprises followed. They parked near the front of the house. Elspeth waited for her to get the cases out of the boot and then led her up the steps to the open front door, with Sophie thinking Elspeth's light and beautifully tailored slacks clung rather too well to her bottom to be suitable for the country. Then she reckoned that her seductive walk would probably have universal appeal anyway. Then they were in the hall and she was gaping round at the largest single room she had ever seen and breathing in the heady scent of old stone, furniture polish and summer air.

Elspeth pressed a button by the door and Sophie put the cases down, stretching and thinking longingly of a shower before exploring the house and grounds.

A naked woman strolled in through a door ahead. Sophie gaped again.

Then she realised it was Mistress Devina, which only served to confuse her even more.

What was she doing there and how come she was able to follow her usual practice and take all her clothes off?

She did look nice though. Her hair was shining and her big breasts swayed as she walked across the hall towards a smiling Elspeth. Sophie's eyes drifted to her middle, watching the movements of her thighs and the shifting of the creases alongside her pubic triangle. In a subtle way it was very sexy, and Sophie's confusion was increased by the tingle in her fanny.

She stood quietly as Elspeth and Devina greeted each other, was both flattered and flustered when Devina turned to her with a warm smile, said how nice it was to see her again and then kissed her on the lips. She was, therefore grateful to move back to more familiar territory when the kiss was followed by an earnest plea to have her bottom massaged.

'I've been sitting in the sun and forgot to ask Carol to fetch a cushion for me. It was an awfully hard seat and my poor little buttocks are all numb and aching.'

'With pleasure, mistress,' Sophie replied briskly, and bent to her task.

She also remembered the strange atmosphere which characterised Devina's establishment and summoned up the courage to tick her off for her carelessness.

'Honestly, mistress, your bottom's all marked. Pink stripes from the top right down to your legs. You really must look after it better.'

Half expecting to be told to bare her bottom and bend over to have it soundly thrashed for her impertinence, she was relieved when she heard Devina confiding to Elspeth that she was very lucky to have such a considerate slave.

Elspeth agreed, Devina pronounced her buttocks were restored, and Elspeth signalled Sophie to pick up their cases and they eventually found their room.

Sophie was thrilled when Elspeth told her to strip naked before helping her take her clothes off, but was shocked into open-mouthed silence when, instead of testing the large four-poster bed that dominated the room, her mistress began to walk towards the door.

'Come on, Sophie,' she urged. 'Find some towels and follow me. We're going to have a swim.'

She followed nervously, her eyes glued to Elspeth's mobile and embarrassingly naked bottom, hoping that if there was anyone watching she wouldn't see them and so be spared the knowledge that their nudity was observed.

Her sigh of relief when they got to the pool was due to the simple fact that everyone else was naked. Even so, as she watched Elspeth throw her towel down near an empty chair and dive in, she felt her face burn at the thought of any number of strange eyes looking at her, and so walked firmly to the shallow end, jumped in, and set off for the far end in her usual slow breast stroke. She noted that her mistress could swim like a fish, scything through the water in a fast and economical crawl. The evidence that she was as good a swimmer as she was at most things filled her with pride, and she relaxed as the lovely cool water bathed away the stickiness left by their long hot journey.

It was not long before Sophie began to relax. By the end of the first day she had successfully defined her temporary status as a sort of subordinate companion rather than full-blooded slave. On that basis, she found it much easier to meet the other residents on more equal terms, with her deference to the known or obvious mistresses moving towards normal politeness rather than pure submission.

She also found the atmosphere increasingly sexy. Walking about openly naked, especially through the grounds, was a constant pleasure. Elspeth had insisted the rings remain and she soon discovered that, without any clothing to keep them in place, they shifted in time with the movements of her body and kept her breasts and fanny in a permanent state of soft arousal.

Then there were all the other bare bodies to look at. Mostly female, but she met up with a couple of male slaves and rediscovered the pleasures of flirting with members of the opposite sex, and for the first time in her life, able to look at their bodies without embarrassment or inhibition. Best of all, she found that Carol was even prettier naked than dressed and, now that she understood the nature of her relationship with Devina, was able to make friends with her, spending several happy hours gambolling in the pool with her.

The sultry weather, which lasted for the whole of their stay, was perfect. With the pool to cool down overheated skin during the day and with the evenings still warm enough to make clothes unnecessary, her confidence in her own body blossomed.

Her swimming improved.

Several times she and Elspeth made love, rather than fucked.

Sensible exposure to the sun turned her body a light brown, which suited her and made her look as healthy as she felt.

She learned a lot from talking to the other slaves.

Mary, a bouncy buxom blonde, took a shine to her and, fully clothed, they sneaked off into the woods, feeling deliciously naughty as they went.

Elspeth missed her and, before they went to bed, put her across her knee and gave her a lovely spanking, all the more appreciated after several days without a sore bottom.

Only one episode disturbed her. The master called in and the sight of his lithe body and naked prick made her shudder as the memories flooded back. He recognised her, summoned her over, and once again his warm friendliness completely failed to disguise the air of quiet and implacable menace that made him so terrifying.

He made her turn around so he could look at her bottom, and Sophie shuddered as she relived the last occasion he had made her bend over. When he restricted himself to making her reach back, part her buttocks and show him her anus, she felt very relieved, having half expected him to call for a cane and thrash her on the spot.

Later, however, she felt a twinge of regret that he had denied her the chance of showing her mettle.

As they set off for home, the heavens opened and they exchanged grins of relief at their good fortune. As they hummed down the motorway, Sophie felt totally refreshed and more than ready to face whatever other trials lay in store.

# Chapter Eight

Sophie didn't notice the slightly troubled look on Elspeth's face when she sent her off on her first assignment after their return, so set off with every confidence in her ability to cope with whatever lay ahead.

When she arrived at the house she was a little surprised that it was nowhere near as expensive as all the others she had visited, but immediately felt a sense of relief that she was in the sort of surroundings she was brought up in; a semi-detached in an unremarkable suburb, nothing luxurious but neat and well maintained.

Mistress Sarah fitted in perfectly. Middle-aged, permed brown hair, nicely plump, dressed in a simple summer frock and with a lovely shy smile. Sophie warmed to her immediately and, having already gathered that not all dominatrices fitted the fictional image of a leather-bound ogress, sat down in a comfortable chair and waited on events.

Mistress Sarah's slave did come as a surprise, and it was all Sophie could do to stop her jaw dropping into a cretinous gape when the exotic creature swept in with the wherewithal for a welcome cup of tea.

She was tall, wearing fishnet stockings, a tight white blouse which hugged a gorgeous pair of obviously unsupported breasts, a flared black mini skirt and very high heels.

Her shining black hair flowed down her back, her make-up was fairly lavish but applied with some skill, and her fingernails were long and scarlet.

Mistress Sarah looked at her adoringly as she came in and put the tray down carefully, then introduced her to Sophie with obvious pride.

'Chris, this is Slave Sophie.'

Chris turned to her with a tight little smile. 'Hello, Sophie. Nice to meet you.'

'And you,' Sophie replied weakly, still recovering from the impact of her appearance.

With cups of good traditional tea balanced on laps, biscuits within easy reach, the three of them refreshed themselves in silence, with Sophie very glad of the chance to try and work out their relationship.

Her first thought was that Sarah was a bit like Devina and dominated with polite requests rather than commands, but the underlying threat behind Devina's approach seemed to be missing.

She watched the ill-assorted pair surreptitiously, and it soon became even more obvious that Sarah's love for Chris was the predominant factor. Chris danced attendance dutifully and Sophie could find no fault with the standard of her service to both her mistress and their guest, but grew ever more certain that there was something not quite right about the girl. She just didn't seem at ease, and her deference was not really convincing. Sophie summed up her impressions by deciding that the thought of Sarah putting Chris across her knee and spanking her bare bottom seemed more than improbable.

Then with the first cup finished and a second one poured, Sarah began to ask Sophie about her life with Elspeth, and so brought an abrupt halt to her speculation.

Both of them listened intently to her general descriptions of the various and varied punishments Elspeth applied to her bottom and, every time she dried up, another keen question from Sarah set her going again.

She freely admitted to getting a tremendous kick from being spanked.

'Mistress Elspeth nearly always gives me due warning,' she said slowly, staring out of the window at the neat little garden as she tried to put her thoughts and feelings into words. 'So I have plenty of time to think about it. I know it's

162

going to hurt. That's the whole point. But even more important, it's my bottom that's going to feel the pain. My bare bottom.

'When she's ready, she'll call me through to the sitting room, I'll have to put our spanking chair in the right place. She'll sit down and move her legs apart so that her lap is a nice platform for me. We'll look at each other for a moment and, however naughty I've been, she'll smile at me. I know she's looking forward to smacking my bottom and that makes me happy.

'But apart from pleasing my mistress – even though that is the most important thing of all – the prospect really excites me. Physically, there is the feel of her lovely legs underneath me, her hands lifting up my skirt and then pulling my knickers down, sliding them slowly over my cheeks until they're halfway down my thighs and my bottom is all bare. That's a lovely feeling anyway, and even nicer when it's sticking up in the air. Mistress Elspeth always gives it a good feel and usually pulls my cheeks apart to have a look at my bottom-hole.

'I like her doing that. It's basically humiliating, but very nice.

'Then she spanks me. I love the feel of her hand on my skin. She doesn't hit me that hard. Each spank stings a bit but it's mainly a sort of warm feeling. I just lie there, my bottom wobbling as she smacks it, beginning to glow all over.

'After a while the pain builds up and I sort of move into a different phase. It turns into a challenge. Not to make a silly fuss. To keep my bottom reasonably still so she can aim her spanks properly.

'I feel very close to her, mentally and physically. I know she loves the feel of my bare bottom and the way it wobbles and goes bright red. I love being under her control. I've lost count of the number of spankings she's given me, but I still get a kick from being put across her knee.'

Sophie realised she was rambling and came to a stop, looking guiltily at her audience, expecting to see at least amusement on their faces, if not contempt at her girlish enthusiasm. Instead, she saw they were both staring at her, fascinated.

'Don't you feel the same way, Chris?' she stammered, blushing furiously.

They exchanged glances and Sophie again felt there was something mysterious about their relationship, but for the life of her she couldn't begin to identify it.

'We haven't actually got round to spanking yet,' Mistress Sarah said dryly, and Sophie gaped at her in genuine amazement. As far as she was concerned, a slave who wasn't at least spanked had no right to the title.

'Mistress Sarah, you must!' she cried, throwing all her natural caution to the winds. 'From what I could see from the seat of her skirt, Chris has got a terrific bottom. Perfect for spanking.' She looked from a thoughtful mistress to a startled slave. 'Honestly, Chris, offering your bottom to be bared and spanked is the perfect way of showing how much you love your mistress. Promise.' Then Sophie realised she may well have got it all wrong.

'Unless you don't like bottoms, mistress,' she said nervously.

'Of course I do,' Sarah snapped, and then turned and stared meaningfully at Chris, who looked rather uncomfortable.

Completely unaccustomed to taking charge, Sophie felt a surge of confidence and decided to carry on for a bit longer, hoping the other two wouldn't suddenly remember she was a slave and turn on her. On the other hand, she thought to herself, if they did, that would be fun as well.

In a flash of inspiration, she realised she could not only keep the upper hand but also get the spanking she was beginning to long for.

'Mistress, why don't you spank me?' she asked, with a perfect mixture of deference and decisiveness. 'So you can see how nice it is.'

Her suggestion was seized on with flattering enthusiasm, and she found herself across Mistress Sarah's lovely comfortable lap in very short order. Her skirt was wrenched up and her knickers yanked down with unseemly but forgivable speed, and she was just wondering how to break the news that haste was high on the list of things which ruined a decent spanking when she felt a nice soft hand squeezing her right buttock.

Heaving a sigh of relief, she settled down comfortably. Sarah helped herself to a lingering feel of both cheeks, cheerfully pointing out various salient features to Chris, and Sophie found that she really was very excited indeed. She had a momentary stab of panic as she felt her juices flow; with the source pressed fairly hard into Sarah's lap, the evidence would probably be horribly plain when she eventually got up. Then she felt the first spank and forgot all about it as she enjoyed the rare experience of directing her own spanking.

'Oh, that was a good one, mistress. I really felt it.'

'Perhaps some more on my left buttock?'

'Oww. Yes, hard and fast. Make my fat bottom wobble like a jelly.'

'Now give me six really hard ones but leave about five seconds between them... Oh that's lovely, mistress.'

By the end she was deliciously hot and sore. When Sarah helped her up she looked down at her flushed, happy face and couldn't resist giving her a grateful kiss, which was accepted in the spirit in which it had been offered, as there was no talk of further punishment for getting ideas above her station.

Then she sneaked a look at Chris and was pleased to see her eyes were shining, in contrast to their previous glazed and introspective look.

She begged Mistress Sarah to spank her slave. Chris looked doubtful, but then noticed a determined set to her mistress's mouth, so stood up and moved to stand to the right of the waiting lap, her face pale and her mouth tight.

Sophie was again puzzled by the lack of either the willing submission which came naturally to her, or of the playful protest which Mistress Devina seemed to enjoy from Carol. Instead, Chris laid herself across the waiting lap with a sort of weary resignation, whispering something to her mistress as she went. Sophie thought she had said 'not too far', but couldn't see the sense in that. Not at first. When Sarah lowered her old-fashioned frilly knickers very carefully and gently, leaving them only just below her bottom, Sophie realised she had heard correctly. But it made even less sense. Presumably Chris had seen Sophie's fanny while she was being spanked and was reluctant to offer the same view to her fellow slave.

Her initial feelings of slight contempt were soon dissipated by her genuine pleasure in the sight of Chris's naked buttocks, which fully lived up to the promise of the rest of her. Still relishing the rare opportunity to join in the action when she felt like it rather than when she was told to, Sophie not only made suitable – and perfectly genuine – remarks about the lovely smooth bottom waiting meekly to be spanked, she also felt brave enough to back up her comments with several hearty prods and pats. All of which confirmed that Chris's skin was satiny, that her flesh had that combination of firmness and softness that is unmistakably feminine.

It quivered prettily under the spanks and turned pink quite quickly, although Sarah's lack of experience was evident from the uneven blotchiness she finished up with.

Sophie told them both that she had thoroughly enjoyed watching, thanked them for letting her, and was just about to bring the conversation round to more extreme activities, when Sarah announced it was time for a drink and told a slightly dishevelled Chris to open a bottle of wine.

As they drank, Mistress Sarah encouraged Sophie to tell them more about her punishments, and she did her best to describe her feelings when she was beaten, explaining that she did not get sexual satisfaction from the more severe ordeals.

'It's really about the challenge of overcoming fear and pain,' she said thoughtfully. 'Plus, of course, pleasing my mistress.

She enjoys beating me and so I'm always pleased to offer her my bottom. However much she hurts me.

'The other important thing is that I trust her not to go beyond my limits. When I'm in position, sometimes tied up, at other times having the extra challenge of having to keep as still as I can, I know I'll survive the punishment. I won't be permanently marked. Mistress Elspeth likes me, likes my body, and will always bear in mind that she will want to beat me again before too long. And she prefers to start with a white and unmarked bottom.'

As the wine went down the interest in Sophie's conversation rose, and the atmosphere changed to the extent that she began to feel accepted. After lunch, and another bottle, they went back to the sitting room and Sophie felt she had broached their defences sufficiently to begin to try and probe a bit deeper, by then quite keen to get to the bottom of the vaguely mysterious relationship.

Mistress Sarah was both sober and bright enough to be able to read her thoughts and suddenly turned to her slave. 'Shall we show her?' she asked gently.

Chris looked a bit troubled as she stared hard at Sophie, who returned her gaze with a reassuring smile. Then her face cleared and she faced her mistress again.

'Why not? I think she'll be sympathetic.'

'I'm sure she will,' Sarah replied, and motioned Chris to stand up.

Sophie sat forward, her heart pounding with excitement, deliberately preventing herself from speculating on the nature of the mystery. Chris slipped off her blouse, undid her bra and, blushing prettily, pushed a pair of beautiful breasts towards her goggle-eyed fellow slave. Sophie's admiration was totally genuine, and the look on both faces when she asked permission to fondle them was eloquent testimony to the fact that she had done exactly the right thing.

As Elspeth was a committed bottom girl, breasts hadn't played a major role in Sophie's sex life and she enjoyed the firm, soft weight of Chris's, especially the way her big dark nipples puckered and grew under her touch. She was allowed a good five minutes before Mistress Sarah intervened.

'Would you like to see her bottom again?'

'Yes please, mistress.'

Chris turned, bared and posed, instinctively adopting that lovely stance with one leg forward and the other straight and rigid, her bottom changing shape as she did so, moving smoothly from a divided symmetrical hemisphere to two individual globes. As she stooped for a closer look, Sophie came to the inescapable conclusion that Elspeth was right – bottoms *were* tops!

She looked, stroked, patted and prodded until she sensed the other two were getting impatient, so she bent forward, kissed each cheek, stood up and pronounced her verdict.

'I love girls' bottoms, Chris, and yours is gorgeous.'

Again she caught Chris and Sarah exchanging glances, and again had an eerie sense that everything was not as it seemed.

'Why don't you sit down, Sophie,' Mistress Sarah suggested.

Sophie obeyed instantly, both from habit and a sense that something dramatic was about to happen.

As she said to Elspeth later, nothing could possibly have prepared her for what did. Chris shoved her knickers down to her knees, wriggled her legs until they slid down to her ankles, took a deep breath, and then turned round suddenly.

Her cock and balls swayed with the movements of her body and then settled into dangling prominence, while Sophie stared disbelievingly, her heart apparently coming to a virtual stop before racing madly. There was a roaring in her ears as she desperately tried to make sense of the patently impossible.

Chris had boobs. A narrow waist. Curvy hips. Smooth, hairless, fleshy buttocks. Rounded thighs – also smooth and hairless. Her face, hair and throat were totally female.

So how in hell's name could she have a willy?

Her totally scrambled brain kept Sophie not only silent but also rooted to her chair, whereas her basic instinct was to scream with horror and then run like hell.

Gradually the mists cleared and, as she stared, mesmerised, at the neat genitals, visibly shrinking before her eyes, she suddenly felt a bubble of pity, which welled up inside her and brought tears to her eyes. It all began to make some sense.

Poor Chris. By some vicious trick she was all woman, except in the one most vital area.

Sophie's near hysteria gave her even more insight than usual and she stood up, staggered a little, took the few paces across to the unhappy Chris, put her arms around her and kissed her. She heard Sarah sigh with relief and felt the tension drain away from Chris's shoulders. Their lips parted and their tongues clashed briefly and excitingly.

Sophie suddenly felt the wetness in the crotch of her knickers and desperately longed for release. For Chris. For her and for Mistress Sarah.

With all her inhibitions conquered by a combination of profound shock and deep sympathy, she took control.

She asked Chris if she could suck her cock. During her holiday in the Mansion, she had watched one of the girl slaves doing it to one of the boy slaves and had found it repellent to begin with, but had then been fascinated.

She had the wit to say she'd never been tempted to do it to a man. 'But I would love to do it to you.'

With her hands full of feminine bottom, she closed her lips round the soft shaft, licking and sucking and thrilling to its rapid enlargement, until she was having to stretch her jaw to accommodate it.

For the first time in her life, Sophie was completely dominated by lust, as though her subconscious mind had found the only way to cope with the incomprehensible.

She overcame her instinct to withdraw when she felt Chris jerk and managed to swallow the jets of salty sperm without gagging.

Turning to an anxious mistress, she softly suggested that it was her turn to be turned on.

A rapidly recovering Chris helped with the denuding of what turned out to be a surprisingly appealing body, with a big but round and firm bottom. Full breasts and firm thighs more than made up for the slightly rounded tummy and a waist too thick for perfection. Not that Sophie had any sort of ideal in mind. Her thoughts were totally occupied with her desire to do all she could to help both achieve contentment with each other, even though she was acting purely on reflex, because her limited experience made it impossible for her to work things out logically.

The two slaves were soon operating in harmony, turning the plump mistress this way and that, kissing, stroking and licking her all over, before urging her onto her back with her legs in the air. By mutual agreement, Sophie started at the bottom. She kissed the taut buttocks in turn, gradually working towards the gaping division between them, her eyes glued to the fully exposed anus.

Mistress Sarah began to moan and squirm as Sophie's educated tongue slithered tantalisingly down from her tailbone, pausing just as the tip reached the beginnings of the nice, pale brown surround. Then she looked down at the little raised circle of the ring, noticeably pinker than the rest, pursed her lips and blew into the twitching little hole.

Mistress Sarah cried out with surprise and begged Sophie to do it again. Sophie smiled into Chris's gleaming eyes and obeyed. Then she lowered her mouth and kissed where she had just blown, getting an even stronger reaction.

She then readied herself to lick Mistress Sarah's bottom-hole, convinced it would be a new experience for her and determined to make it a memorable one.

It was. At the first moist touch the shriek almost deafened her, and the convulsive straightening of those muscular thighs sent her sprawling. She knelt up, slightly stunned by the violence of the reaction and with a horrible feeling that she

170

had blown it completely. Blushing furiously, she looked up. Chris was wriggling excitedly and Mistress Sarah was staring at her, wide-eyed, dishevelled, her big breasts quivering spasmodically and looking deliciously wanton. Sophie, with the scent of her excitement still in her nostrils and the memory of her lovely softness still making her hands and lips tingle, was about to blurt out an apology when Mistress Sarah got in first.

'Was that your tongue?' she demanded. 'On my bottom-hole?' she added, rather unnecessarily.

'Yes, mistress.'

'But... that's dirty.'

'Not physically,' Sophie protested. 'Not when it's a lovely clean bottom like yours, mistress. Didn't you like it?'

Sarah blinked as she relived the novel sensations. 'Yes, it was... blissful. But are you sure that...' her voice trailed off uncertainly.

'Sure I want to do it again?'

'Well, yes.'

'Of course I do,' Sophie said firmly. 'And I'm a slave, so what I want doesn't matter, does it?'

'I suppose not. Chris, would you do it to me?'

'Yes, of course, mistress.'

Sarah's expression changed from confused to delighted in an instant. Then she lay back again, raising her legs, putting her hands on the backs of her knees for added support, and ordered her slaves to get on with it.

With a sigh of relief and a wink at a grinning Chris, Sophie applied herself.

With perfect timing Chris started kissing and licking her mistress's fanny, and the two of them slurped happily while the object of their affections seemed to make up for many years lost to her inhibitions.

It ended in tears – of happiness and exhaustion, as Chris slipped into Sarah's dripping fanny and Sophie knelt tactfully just out of reach, her eyes glued to Chris's pounding buttocks, marvelling again at the contrast between their femininity and the glistening shaft between them.

Their climax was even more exciting. Mistress Sarah told her slave to change places and she clambered on top, reaching back to guide that incongruous cock into the opening of her sex, before slowly lowering herself until it was right inside. Sophie crouched at Chris's feet, her own bottom thrust high and wide, so that her fingers had easy access to her own throbbing fanny and, with her eyes drinking in the sight of Mistress Sarah's big bare bottom shuddering and shaking as she bounced up and down on the fulcrum of Chris's shining cock, she reached yet another searing climax, this time restraining her cries, thoughtfully avoiding any distraction to the main participants.

They had time for a cup of tea before Sophie's car arrived, and once again she noticed the sad and withdrawn look in Mistress Sarah's eyes, although the warmth of her farewell slightly reassured her.

Elspeth had waited nervously for Sophie to get back, and one look at her slave's pale and drawn face was enough to confirm that her anxiety had been fully justified. And after she had broken the habit of a lifetime and actually bathed the silent girl, the look of gratitude she received made her realise that she needed to be handled carefully.

'Sarah isn't a full member of the Circle,' she explained over a glass of wine. 'Devina knows her vaguely, sensed there was something strange about her arrangements, and suggested that you would have the best chance of prising her secret out of her. Which you did. Well done, Sophie.'

The small answering smile showed clearly that Sophie, no longer in a state of sexual excitement, was still unable to come to terms with what she had seen. So Elspeth gently explained that Chris was a transsexual, who'd probably had hormone treatment to increase his femininity to the extent that he was a she except for that one area.

172

'There is an operation which would complete the process,' she continued, 'but it's very expensive, and I should imagine they're either saving up like mad or they've come to the conclusion that it's out of reach.

'If you think about it, things can't be easy for either of them. Chris obviously wants to be all woman but, from what you've told me, Sarah likes her the way she is. Girlish boobs and bottom, and at the same time a nice cock so she can enjoy the occasional fuck.'

Sophie's startled expression at her bluntness made her grin, and she reached over and squeezed her trembling hand. The girl blushed and smiled back.

'It would be nice if someone could help them,' she said wistfully.

'Perhaps we can,' Elspeth replied firmly. 'Now, let's think about supper and tomorrow we'll have a day out in the country. A complete change of scene.'

They set off early, drove to Tunbridge Wells, shopped, wandered through the Pantiles, found a nice wine bar for lunch, stretched their legs on the common below Mount Ephraim, then took the long way home.

It was a perfect antidote for Sophie, and a day that reinforced Elspeth's conviction that she had been amazingly lucky to have found her in the first place. They deliberately avoided any reference to sex in general and slavery in particular, and quite simply enjoyed the other's company.

Elspeth also confirmed another conviction, one which few, if any, of the other members of the Circle shared. Basically, she felt strongly that even the best slaves need an occasional break. Physically and mentally. Perhaps Sophie was a cut above other slaves and was able to make the transition from slave to companion and back again without any trouble – and was equally rewarding in both roles – but Elspeth still felt that some R&R should be provided.

Admittedly, whenever she was away at meetings of the

Circle, Sophie was alone and therefore had plenty of opportunity to unwind, but their days out nearly always benefited them both.

Sarah's problem exercised them the following day and Elspeth had the inspired thought of bringing Daphne into the discussion, who listened with unexpected sympathy, thought hard for several moments, excused herself and dashed out, saying she would be back within an hour.

In fact, she was twenty minutes late and Elspeth was sorely tempted to put her across her knee for a sound spanking in front of Sophie, but then decided against it.

Such thoughts vanished as soon as Daphne opened her capacious bag and produced what she triumphantly announced would probably solve the problem.

Elspeth greeted her contribution with a cry of delight. Sophie with a puzzled stare.

It was quite simply a double vibrator, the base of each joined flexibly and one of them to several thin cords.

'The joy of this one, Elspeth, is that you can change the vibrators. If, for example, you wanted to fuck your partner up her bottom and she didn't feel up to taking a full size one, you simply take this one out... like this... and fit a smaller one. And, of course, you can either have them switched on or off. As far as Sarah and Chris are concerned, Sarah can be dominant and still feel as though she's being fucked. They can go ahead with the operation without losing too much of what they have at the moment.'

Naturally, both mistresses wanted to try it out. In less than two minutes a nervously excited Sophie was naked, and about three minutes after that she had helped both the others to the same state. There was a brief pause while naked charms were examined and felt, then Elspeth took charge.

'I'll try it out on Sophie first,' she decided, as she fondled the strange equipment. 'How do you put it on, Daphne?'

'Easy. Put this one up inside... no. I'll do it for you. Spread your legs. That's it. I'll get you juiced up with the tip, shall

I…? How's that? Gosh, you smell gorgeous... Now, dip your knees. Lovely. And in we go. Right, this strip goes round your waist, holding it all secure at the front, and this thin one goes up between the cheeks of your bottom and hooks onto the waist bit. Hang on, before I fix it would you like to have your bottom-hole licked?'

'Oh yes please,' Elspeth beamed, looking down at the amazingly life-like cock thrusting up from between her legs, bobbing gently as she wriggled at the sensations its twin was giving to her insides.

'Come on, Sophie. Lick your mistress's anus for her.'

Sophie hurried forward to obey, and enjoyed the feeling of Elspeth's smooth buttocks yielding under the pressure of her fingers, the sight of that delicately wrinkled orifice, and then the taste and smell of the woman she loved, more than she could ever remember doing before.

Elspeth was too impatient to want the bottom treatment for longer than a couple of minutes and so, once she and Daphne had decided that doggie fashion was the most appropriate pose, she was soon on her hands and knees, with her bottom in the air and her glistening fanny on full view and easily accessible.

Daphne found watching almost as enjoyable as participating. She moved contentedly around, viewing the action from a number of different viewpoints. At one extreme there was the very sexy sight of Elspeth's perfect bottom, opening and closing as she thrust with growing confidence and enthusiasm. At the other there was Sophie's flushed face, her eyes dreamily half-closed as the smooth hard prick reamed her.

Reckoning it quite all right to kiss a slave as long as it was for your pleasure not hers, Daphne did just that, gnawing Sophie's soft lips and breathing in her gusty sighs as her climax approached.

Then it was her turn. Knowing the mistress half was sleek and slippery with Elspeth's come made the insertion even more exciting, and then the sight of Sophie's lovely full bottom in front of her as she carefully guided the tip of the vibrator into her seething cunt was literally an eye-opener.

After that she lay on her back with her legs up and was gloriously fucked by an insatiable Elspeth. She reach down as soon as her cunt was filled, gripped those glorious buttocks, feeling the play of her muscles as she thrust and withdrew.

Stiff muscles and aching orifices were rested while they enjoyed one of Elspeth's delicious lunches, accompanied by a celebratory bottle of champagne and served by a naked Sophie, whose wiggling buttocks, bobbing breasts and gleaming rings in nipples and cunt added further spice to the occasion.

Suitably refreshed, both mistresses decided to renew their assault on a far from unwilling Sophie, but using her bottom. Again Daphne watched happily, enjoying Sophie's screwed up face, the view of her anus stretched so tightly round the vibrator that it looked like a piece of white elastic and, by no means least, a sideways view of the action, with the passive partner's dangling breasts a delightful contrast to the bobbing thrust of Elspeth's.

She did find, however, that fucking Sophie's bottom was more restricting than using her cunt and slightly less fun, although the thought of her pain and degradation as she was comprehensively buggered did make the sensations provided by her vibrator somewhat more intense.

A totally exhausted slave was eventually sent up to an early bed and the two mistresses finished a memorable session by making slow and sensual love to each other. As they lay in each other's arms they both agreed the equipment had passed all tests with flying colours, and that a similar set would make it possible for Sarah to let Chris have the operation and still enjoy being fucked afterwards.

In due course, Sarah and Chris were invited to Elspeth's house and she and Daphne conducted an intensive training session, which Sophie watched with growing satisfaction. Especially the finale, with Chris lying back, legs drawn right back and Sarah screwing her in the bottom. Their rapt faces were almost enough to distract her from the sight of Mistress Sarah's soft, matronly buttocks, tensing, relaxing, dimpling and, as her thrusts lost their stately rhythm with the approach of her climax, wobbling deliciously.

Although Mistress Sarah's problem was satisfactorily solved – in the short term at least – the experience had an adverse effect on Sophie. Elspeth was patience personified for several weeks, but the girl's introspection began to pall. She still presented her bottom for punishment with as much courage as ever, but the inner spark that made her rather special was noticeably dimmer than before.

Elspeth came to the conclusion that she should go easier on her slave for a while, and concentrate more on the joys of CP rather than domination and submission.

She left more copies of her favourite spanking magazines lying around for Sophie to find and, when she caught her reading them, did not get angry but sat down with her and discussed the photographs and articles.

It was then perfectly logical to re-enact the better scenes, spanking purely for fun.

Picking up where she had left off several months before, Elspeth told Sophie far more about the history of some of the more traditional implements, often referring to some relevant books from her extensive library.

Sophie was especially fascinated by stories of punishments given to nuns in a few notorious eighteenth century convents. She would listen dreamily as Elspeth vividly described imaginary scenes, with pretty noviciates presenting their bared bottoms to the whip, administered by an eagle-eyed Mother Superior, while the choir accompanied the sound of the whip on quivering flesh and the cries of the victims, their sweet voices combining with the heady, incense-filled atmosphere to ensure that the girls' minds were as receptive to the correction as the soft flesh of their bottoms.

At Sophie's suggestion, they did their best to recreate the scene Elspeth had described so graphically, lighting the cellar with candles, taped music and eau de cologne providing adequate substitutes for the choir and incense.

Sophie found a black dressing gown which passed as a habit and knelt humbly on the whipping bench, whimpering softly as Elspeth grimly ordered her to bare her sinful flesh for castigation and then applied the martinet to her rounded buttocks in a stately rhythm which fitted the occasion perfectly.

It was Sophie's idea to invite other mistresses to formal dinners and between them, they established a routine which delighted all those who came.

Sophie would greet the guests and serve the first drinks stark naked. Then she would have to put on the corset – with one of the guests helping her with the final lacing – and finally insert the central strap herself, bending right over to lubricate her anus before inserting the butt-plug and dildo.

She would serve dinner like that, then strip again and eat her food like a dog, from a bowl on the floor, with her bare bottom in the air and open for all to view her most private parts.

The climax was a little entertainment. She and her mistress would put on a short play, always with a punishment theme. With Daphne's skill as a dressmaker to help them, they would take a variety of roles. Schoolgirl and mistress; boss and secretary; eighteenth century prison inmate being whipped by a wardress; American college girl wanting to join a prestigious sorority and being 'hazed', i.e. submitting to the paddle as part of her initiation; Mother Superior and noviciate.

Sophie proved to be a competent little actress, and the popularity of their soirées grew.

She soon rediscovered her enthusiasm and her intelligent interest in history and methodology made life equally rewarding for Elspeth.

But, and only very occasionally, Sophie withdrew into her shell again. Even Elspeth's skilled but gentle interrogation could not persuade her slave to come up with the reason, until Devina brought Carol round for a day. Once or twice, Elspeth saw that Sophie was especially vivacious and self-confident when she was mildly dominating Carol, and the penny dropped.

After her first visit to Sarah and Chris, she had admitted that she had rather enjoyed taking charge of the proceedings, and Elspeth had not taken enough notice of her comment. Her pleasure when she was asked if she liked the thought of giving Carol a sound spanking was so evident that there could no longer be any doubt in Elspeth's mind, and she watched the wailing visitor go across Sophie's lap with mixed feelings. Especially when she saw the broad smile on her slave's face and the gleam in her eyes as she happily flailed away at the wriggling bare bottom filling her sight.

Sophie had expanded to the point where being a slave, pure and simple, was no longer enough to satisfy all her desires.

It was time to move her on.

But first, she had to be subjected to an even more rigorous regime.

The first stage in that was to prepare her for another visit from the master.

Elspeth noted her growing nervousness and did her best to encourage her, but she still trembled like a leaf when she led him into the sitting room. And she was still shaking slightly when he ordered her to strip naked and show him her anus, although Elspeth did notice that her cunt was glistening as she bent and parted her own cheeks.

She took sixteen hard strokes of the cane, and then six with the master's favourite tawse with encouraging bravery and afterwards, even sank to her knees with her ravaged bottom high and open, offering that delicious little anus to him.

He accepted her offer solemnly, let her suck and lick his cock until it was hard, and then penetrated her firmly.

Even in severe pain, made worse by the way he drove his hard stomach against the crests of her crimson buttocks, she still did her very best to keep her groans to herself and generally behaved extraordinarily well.

Until he withdrew before he had come, tucked his shiny cock away, and brusquely ordered Elspeth to move to the middle of the room and touch her toes.

For several moments all three of them were totally still.

The master, delighted by the way Sophie had taken her severe beating, gazed contentedly at the tightened seat of Elspeth's light skirt, happily looking forward to the rare treat of applying his cane to those very shapely buttocks, the memory of Sophie's clinging rectum around his cock still tingling fresh.

Elspeth, bending gracefully, the tips of her fingers resting on her toes, the taste of fear sharp in her mouth and the skin on her bottom crawling in anticipation, patiently waited for further orders.

Sophie, her buttocks blazing and her anus aching, stared at her mistress's rear in stunned disbelief. The thought of her beloved Elspeth presenting her bottom so meekly for the master's wicked cane was so far beyond her comprehension that she began to reassure herself with the thought that it was all a bad dream.

And things *did* get worse!

'Please bare your mistress's bottom, Sophie.'

As ever, his voice was low and unemotional, and made his order sound more of a polite request than anything else. And, as usual, the thought of doing anything else but obey immediately was impossible. His power may have been expressed subtly, but Sophie hadn't the slightest doubt that it was absolute.

'Yes, sir,' she whispered as she moved forward, her strength all but spent by the combination of her thrashing, being thoroughly buggered, total confusion and utter dismay. She had not cried while she was being punished, but fat oily tears rolled down her ashen cheeks as she crouched painfully behind her mistress and her trembling hands eased the skirt up over her protruding buttocks and onto the small of her back.

She blinked them away as she reached for the waistband of the taut, virginally white silk knickers, instinctively wanting to see her bare bottom, even under those harrowing circumstances. Even in that unusual pose, it was beautiful. Too beautiful to be marked by that evil rattan.

'This is all wrong,' she whispered, not really caring if the master overheard.

'Shh!' hissed Elspeth.

The master told her to move back and sit down. She did, and was grateful for the surge of pain as her bottom sank into the carpet.

The view of Elspeth's bottom was even better from below. She could see the lightly furred fig of her fanny peeping out between her tensed thighs, the lips plump and the slit tight.

Her head began to swim as the master carefully rested the cane across the top of her Mistress's bottom, shifting his feet for the perfect stance.

Mesmerised, she watched the pliant, pale brown cane move slowly up until it was above the wielder's broad right shoulder. It hovered for a second, the tip vibrating as though impatient to sink into that firm white flesh.

It blurred down. She saw Elspeth's bottom shiver as the loud crack of the impact echoed through her seething brain.

She was sure she saw a white line flare up, even though she would have thought it impossible for anything to be whiter than Mistress Elspeth's skin.

Then, exactly where the white had been, there was a pink

line. Sophie gasped in amazement as it swelled and darkened, until it stood proud, right across both buttocks.

Sophie whimpered softly and again her senses reeled as the person she loved, respected and admired more than anything or anybody was methodically caned on her naked bottom.

Each crack made her feel quite sick.

Each muffled groan wrenched at her guts.

Each vivid weal hurt far more than the purple ones on her own bottom.

Only her entrenched sense of discipline prevented her from hurling her body between the master and his new and completely inappropriate victim.

Sophie's relief when the master gently told Elspeth that the sixth stroke was the last was so intense she almost toppled over. But the view of her mistress's bottom as she slowly straightened up, carefully holding her skirt well above her waist as she did so, provided enough of a distraction to keep her in place.

The master moved in front of Sophie for a thorough inspection and then, to her surprise, bent forward and gently kissed each quivering cheek.

'Beautiful, my dear,' he said with real warmth.

'Thank you, master,' Elspeth replied, and Sophie was too far gone to note the steadiness of her voice.

And things *did* get worse!

The master asked Elspeth to kneel on the footstool and stick her bottom out so he could bugger her.

A dazed Sophie was told to lubricate her anus. It was the last straw.

'Please, master,' she sobbed, 'take my bottom. Not my mistress's. Please.'

The master smiled warmly at her, then ordered her to touch her toes for six of the best across the tops of her thighs.

Desperately hoping that her extra ordeal would replace the one planned for Elspeth, Sophie bent with a surge of joy and took the six agonising strokes in silence.

But her hopes were in vain. Elspeth got up on the stool, thrust her bottom out and offered her dear little anus, first to her slave's shaking and clumsy finger and then to the master's nine inches of guided muscle, taking every inch with no more than a bit of heavy breathing.

Sophie was forced to kneel beside Elspeth's jutting bottom, with her bleary eyes glued to the steady pistoning of the master's cock as he indulged himself to the full. Sophie had to fight down the urge to be sick at the sight of that impressive penis sliding in and out between Elspeth's taut, wealed cheeks.

It took them both several days to recover, during which time Sophie slowly began to appreciate that things would never be quite the same again. She shied away from trying to analyse it too deeply, but her suspicions were confirmed the first time she was paddled, as soon as the marks left by the master's cane had disappeared.

The thrill of presenting her bare bottom to the expanse of polished wood was no less than it had been before.

It still hurt. The afterglow was just as excitingly sexy. She just hadn't felt quite so deliciously submissive.

Elspeth took her out for a day in lovely Hampshire the following day and, as they walked through woods and fields, she gently broke the news that it was time for Sophie to move on to another stage in her training.

'The Circle runs a very secret establishment,' she explained. 'Where slaves and mistresses can put all sorts of ideas and fantasies into practice. A sort of university or college, if you like. You're going there for an extended course. Starting on Sunday.'

Sophie stopped and gazed into the distance, her mind in a whirl. Her first thought was a fear of being sent away from Elspeth.

'Does that mean I won't see you again?' she whispered.

'Don't be silly.' Elspeth laughed and hugged her.

'All right then.' Sophie agreed softly, and as their mouths met she suddenly felt a surge of excitement.

# Chapter Nine

As the car that had brought her to the remote house in the depths of the Kent countryside disappeared back down the drive, Sophie drew a deep breath and decided to risk punishment by allowing herself a brief pause to collect her thoughts.

The journey had been interesting to say the least. She had been sitting quietly in the back while the male driver and his female companion, both in the sort of discreet uniform typical of a chauffeur to some tycoon, chatted quietly in the front. She had recognised part of the scenery from that day in Tunbridge Wells with Elspeth, and the memories flooded back, making her feel sad and alone again, overcoming the anticipation of pastures new.

Some time later they had driven carefully down a narrow lane, slowing down as they passed some woods.

'In there,' the girl had said and Sophie perked up, assuming they had arrived, only to frown as she saw no sign of anything but a rough track leading into the trees. After a few bumps, they stopped. The man turned the engine off and they sat for a few moments, Sophie wondering and the other two clearly listening.

'This'll do fine,' the man said to the girl before turning to Sophie and ordering her out of the car.

She had obeyed, looked around, stretched, and then suddenly felt afraid. There was something slightly eerie about the woods. Apart from the occasional rustle as the gentle breeze stirred a branch, there was complete silence. No birds sang and there was not even the distant hum of traffic on a main road to reassure her. Her palms began to sweat, and she swung round to her strange companions, a demand to know what the hell was going on dying before it reached her lips as she saw they were both getting undressed.

Her first thought had been that they wanted to beat her, or at least give her a spanking, and she found that almost reassuringly normal, before realising that they were hardly going to deliver her with a marked bottom.

'What are you going to do to me?'

'Have some fun,' the girl replied cryptically as she folded her trousers.

'Oh,' replied Sophie feebly, gazing at a nicely rounded pair of thighs. Soon they were both naked and her face burned as her gaze flickered from one to the other, looking at the man for interest and the girl for preference.

'Strip.'

'All right.' Sophie began to obey, her hands moving to the waist button of her much loved leather trousers, and beginning to feel less frightened and more excited at the prospect of being at their mercy.

It had been even better than she'd expected, especially after she worked out that the two had to be slaves, although given that they had been made responsible for seeing her safely to her destination, presumably quite a bit senior to her.

They spent some time looking at her body, walking around to see her from all angles. And then moved smoothly in for the kill, fondling and nibbling as she stood with her hands on her head, eyes closed and her teeth bared in a grimace of humiliation and bliss as the four hands roved at will.

Then the girl fetched a rug from the car, spread it, and Sophie automatically lay down on her back. Almost before she had been able to draw breath, the girl's neat little bottom loomed above her, opening as she squatted to make first her anus and then her hairless fanny accessible to Sophie's willing tongue.

The man urged the girl to hurry, pointing out that time was getting on. She ground her bottom painfully against Sophie's face, while her juices flowed and her groans echoed through the silent woods.

There had been time to take the man's stiff cock in her mouth and she swallowed his come with something approaching pleasure, turned on by the unexpected turn of events and unusual surroundings.

Finally the girl brought her off, twiddling her clitoral ring with one hand and with the other busy in her vagina.

Then they considerately – but in total silence – cleaned her up, using a damp cloth thoughtfully concealed in the boot. She had bent over so they could refresh her anus.

'I bet it's ages since you had your bum wiped,' the girl laughed, and the sudden memory of her mistress, lifting her bottom from the seat and smilingly waiting for Sophie to wipe it, had brought a pang of homesickness.

Sophie had a quick look around the house and its surroundings before ringing the bell. A rambling old farmhouse rather than a mansion; lots of woods all around; a few neat flowerbeds and a surprisingly small lawn; some paddocks; an orchard. The trees were just about in full leaf and she realised it was only a year ago when she first knocked on Elspeth's front door. It felt far longer. With similar feelings of nervous expectation, she reached out and pressed the bell and, as she waited, it struck her that far less than a year ago she wouldn't have been able to take her ravishment by the driving slaves without some degree of both panic and conscience.

The door opened and a pretty girl looked at her cautiously.

'Slave Sophie?' she asked.

'That's right.'

'Oh good, come on in.'

Sophie took a deep breath, crossed the threshold and waited, looking around at the spacious hall, furnished very much as one would expect, with some large pieces of furniture, dark with age and gleaming sensuously, polished floors, ancestral portraits and several vases of daffodils adding

187

splashes of colour.

The girl appeared in front of her and Sophie transferred her attention. She was sweet. Her short hair was golden, her eyes wide, blue and serious, her full mouth seemed to invite lascivious kisses and her skin was pure peaches and cream. Sophie felt her fanny tingle as they surveyed each other, and her nervousness ebbed away slightly at the prospect of having this delicious creature around.

'Leave your bag there, Slave Sophie, and follow me. Sister Philippa wants to see you immediately. Oh, my name's Slave Jenny, by the way.'

'Yes, of course.' Sophie put her small bag tidily out of the way in the nearest corner, straightened her shoulders and, inwardly smiling at her new companion's air of uncertain authority, followed her up the main staircase.

If Jenny's face had aroused Sophie's interest, her rear view almost stopped her dead in her tracks. Below her tight, short-sleeved white blouse, her black skirt was so short the chubby bits at the base of her bottom were completely exposed, so there was a delicious twinkling movement under the sway of the scrap of material as she walked. A second look confirmed she was not completely bare-bottomed, as Sophie caught sight of a flash of white covering the soft bulge of her fanny, and then another further up the cleft between her cheeks. She was wearing a pair of panties only one step up from a thong, and Sophie decided the effect was devastating. Pert, slave-like, but well on the right side of total exposure.

She was just hoping that she would be wearing a similar uniform, when Jenny stopped by a solid looking wooden door, knocked firmly, listened, opened it and then ushered Sophie in. The deep breath she had taken in readiness for her interview gusted out explosively at the sight that greeted her. She stood still, gaping and her heart hammering.

A tall woman was standing with her back to the door, looking out of the window, dressed in a long, black, hooded robe. There was an air of understated menace about her, partly due to the severity of her costume, with its undertones of the power exercised by the mediaeval clergy, and partly due to the almost unnatural stillness of the figure. What, bizarrely, both increased and, at the same time, diminished her air of authority, was the extraordinary fact that her bottom was quite bare. The back of the robe was cut away so that there was an inverted V of nothing from waist to feet.

Sophie felt a chill run up and down her spine as she gazed spellbound at what was undeniably a very beautiful bottom, focusing intently on the smooth white curves and the dark line of the tight cleft in an attempt to keep her fear within reasonable limits.

Then Sister Philippa turned round and all Sophie could take in was a pair of dark, fathomless eyes appraising her thoughtfully from the depths of the hood. It seemed perfectly natural to acknowledge her superior with a deep curtsey, so she did, keeping her head up and meeting the implacable stare with a surprising degree of confidence.

She had obviously done the right thing, because a lovely warm smile transformed the shadowy face, and Sophie breathed out silently and felt her legs go weak. In the few moments before Sister Philippa spoke, Sophie collected her scattered thoughts and tried to clarify her first impressions of the woman who was obviously going to have a major influence on her fate over the next few weeks.

A seriously beautiful bottom. Full and womanly but firmly rounded.

Long, elegant legs.

Pure white skin. Not a sun worshipper.

Penetrating eyes.

A friendly and very attractive smile.

An air of quiet authority. Even more striking than Elspeth's.

Not to be trifled with. There was no mistaking the presence of the iron fist in the velvet glove.

Very like Elspeth. Which was reassuring.

After that brief appraisal, Sophie was not able to do much

more than take in as much information as she could. Sister Philippa enlarged on the reason why the Circle ran the establishment, and reminded her that only the most promising slaves were allowed in for any length of time.

'We do occasionally run day courses,' she explained, 'mainly for slaves who have slipped up in their general performance and whose mistresses decide that a short sharp shock will do them good.

'In your case, Mistress Elspeth thinks your skills need more polish than she can provide and that you also need a tougher, more resilient attitude. I would also like to mention that Elspeth has given you an excellent reference. She has also asked me to tell you that she loves you very much and has every confidence that you will benefit from our attentions.'

Sister Philippa smiled warmly as she passed on Elspeth's message, and Sophie felt her eyes prickle at the reminder of all she had left behind. But then she was told to strip and give her clothes to Slave Jenny, and the instant reminder of her true status brought her sharply back to the present.

Soon, Jenny had trotted out with her clothes and she was standing naked, in the prescribed position – feet apart and hands on head – and with her pulse slowing as she relaxed.

She was examined at leisure. With enough confidence in her figure to feel reasonably proud of what she was displaying, and having had any silly modesty knocked out of her by Elspeth very early on in her training, she was able to appreciate the muttered compliments, to be gratified when Sister Philippa joined the growing number who found her bottom-hole especially pretty and, at the same time, to control her arousal as palms stroked and fingers probed.

After a detailed explanation of the day to day activities and routines, Jenny was summoned and told to escort Sophie to Sister Helga for her medical. Sophie curtsied again, turned to follow Jenny, and was then stopped in her tracks.

'Just a moment, Sophie. I would like to put you across my knee and give your nice bottom a good spanking before you go. Come here, please.'

'Yes, sister,' Sophie stammered, and turned back to find her punisher already sitting down behind her large and beautifully polished desk. As she walked across the room, she felt all the usual pre-spanking symptoms, only even more vividly. Apart from the prospect of the familiar pain and the still faintly embarrassing position, there was the added interest of different circumstances; a new lap to rest on, a different hand and possibly, a change in technique and application.

Certainly Sister Philippa's thighs were broader than Elspeth's, and her hand felt bigger and slightly rougher. She also spent far longer feeling her bottom than Elspeth did, although Sophie put that down more to lack of familiarity with the target than special interest in her buttocks.

The one element most noticeably lacking was the feeling of affection Elspeth always communicated, even when Sophie had really annoyed her. She very soon realised that as far as Sister Philippa was concerned, she was not a great deal more than a bottom, however much she liked its shape and feel.

Not that Sophie was upset by this revelation. She was far too well trained by then to expect anything else, and had long since learnt that a lack of emotional involvement made even the tolerable pain of a spanking on her bare bottom that much more of a challenge.

And Sister Philippa certainly did challenge her. She spanked hard and fast, the slaps echoing hollowly through the old room, and her wobbling cheeks were soon blazing merrily. Once again she felt a pang of longing for Elspeth and her more methodical and leisurely approach. But after a while she began to fall in with the new rhythm, digging her toes into the floor and pressing down with her hands to keep herself stable and her bottom still, concentrating hard on the growing pain and keeping her breathing as steady as she could.

The eventual warm smile and compliments on both the quality of her buttocks and her behaviour were music to her ears, and she followed Jenny's bottom on the way to her medical with growing confidence in her ability to be a credit to her beloved Elspeth.

Sister Helga presented a totally new, and in many ways, even more exciting ordeal. Her room was at the other end of the house from Sister Philippa's, which entailed a potentially embarrassing walk for Sophie, made even worse by Jenny's insistence on following her, pointing out quite reasonably that she wanted to have a good look at Sophie's bottom.

Relieved that they had not met anyone on the way, Sophie let Jenny knock on a less imposing door and usher her in. The room was well equipped as an examination room, with the couch in the middle and a cluttered desk under the window. Appropriate medical charts were scattered haphazardly around the walls and a faint smell of antiseptic added to the air of authenticity.

Sister Helga's Scandinavian origins were unmistakable; very blonde, blue-eyed, a lovely clear complexion and, judging from the prominent bulges in the front of her white coat, splendid breasts. A complete contrast to Sister Philippa, but equally attractive.

It came as no surprise to Sophie when, after some fairly routine questions about her medical history, she was told to lie face down on the couch. She waited for Jenny to lower the upper portion so she could lie flat, clambered up, settled down and waited, hoping her examiner would have the decency to make sure both hands and stethoscope were warm.

'I'll start by taking your temperature,' Sister Helga announced, and Sophie began to turn over and sit up.

'No, stay where you are,' Sister Helga ordered.

Sophie rested her chin on her folded hands and opened her mouth in readiness.

Her mouth snapped shut and her eyes flew open when she felt fingers on the cheeks of her bottom, near the cleft, pressing in and then moving slowly apart. She felt cool air touch the inner surface of her bottom as it was opened up until a faint

192

prickling sensation invaded her anus and she knew it was in full view. Then she felt something brush against the opening itself and gasped as it slid inside her and into her rectum. Initially cool, thin and hard.

She recalled a distant memory of a girlfriend who had been staying with a family in France, and had said that the worst bit had been a dose of the flu, as madame had strange ideas where to put the thermometer. Sophie's curiosity at the time had not been strong enough to press for the gory details and, as she lay there feeling rather ridiculous, she was glad she hadn't.

Helga stroked her buttocks as she waited, admired the fading blush, then declared her temperature normal and got on with the examination, with Sophie not in the least surprised at the way her ruder parts came in for most attention. Nor was she taken aback when her first sight of Sister Helga's rear revealed that the back of her white coat had been cut away and that her broad and slightly flat bottom was on full display. She pondered over the strange fact that the dominant members of the establishment seemed to be bare-bottomed all the time, while the submissives had at least some covering, but could only guess that the sisters wanted to taunt the slaves by showing off permanently white and unmarked behinds, whereas the slaves' costumes were designed to require a deliberate baring of their buttocks and were short enough to show off the results of any punishments.

As she lay with her feet up in the stirrups while Sister Helga poked and prodded away in the depths of her vagina, Sophie reassured herself with the thought that, judging by the two sisters she had met so far, being able to see their bare bottoms was hardly a penance. Especially Sister Philippa's, which was even lovelier in retrospect than it had been on first sighting.

If having her temperature taken rectally had come as something of a shock, the last part of her check-up represented a considerable escalation.

When her vagina had been pronounced healthy, she was

told to kneel on the end of the couch with her bottom stuck up in the air. Any lingering doubts as to what Sister Helga planned were quickly dispelled when she moved to stand by her head, ostentatiously put a surgical glove on her right hand, picked a large tube of lubricating jelly, extended her middle finger and spread the jelly liberally from tip to base before disappearing.

Sophie just had time to shuffle her knees even further apart and press her breasts into the top of the couch before she felt a bare hand on her left cheek and then that familiar invasive feeling as the finger was thrust remorselessly into her rectum, too quickly for her to relax her sphincter. She held her breath while it wriggled around in her, and then let it out when she felt it withdraw, leaving a rather nice tingling ache in its wake.

'What a neat, pretty little anus,' Sister Helga said unexpectedly.

'Thank you, sister,' Sophie replied instinctively, and was not in the least surprised to receive six ringing spanks on each taut buttock for talking without permission. She very nearly fell into the obvious trap by apologising for her error, but managed to stay perfectly still, her stinging bottom still thrust obscenely in the air.

'You may now say that you are sorry and thank me for punishing you.' There was definitely a hint of regret in Sister Helga's voice, but Sophie complied hastily anyway. Sister Helga may have been looking for a reason to give her more spanks, but Sophie had a firm suspicion that she would be well advised to keep something in reserve for the immediate future.

There was definitely a hint of relish in the voice which announced that Sophie needed an enema.

This was yet another new experience for Sophie and not one she viewed with any great pleasure. She had to stay put while the preparations were made, and her gorge rose when she felt the tube slither up her bottom, gasping when it seemed to go about half a mile up her.

The jet of warm water took her by surprise and was almost pleasurable to begin with, although after a few minutes her bowels felt full to bursting and she couldn't stop herself from hunching her bottom inwards in an attempt to stop the cramps which gripped her. Two slaps on the tops of her thighs soon taught her the error of her ways and, forearmed, she was able to take the rest of the dose without incurring further penalties.

And things *did* get worse!

After a horrible few moments crouching, grunting softly as she fought the urge to let go, she was allowed to stagger to the lavatory behind a screen in the far corner of the room. She was just about to explode when Sister Helga's gloating voice penetrated.

'You will not relieve yourself until I give you permission,' she said.

Sophie was far too preoccupied to see the gleam in her tormentor's eyes. She closed hers and remembered everything she had been taught about controlling pain in general and her anal muscles in particular, sitting on the hard seat, trembling and sweating.

At last she was given permission, and so great was the relief as the water flooded out of her bottom that it wasn't until the end that she realised Sister Helga was still watching her.

Her burning embarrassment at having to do something so essentially private in front of another woman was not made any less when she had to wipe herself and then move across to the bidet to wash her bottom, still under observation.

Even that was not the end of it. Sister Helga made her touch her toes, then crouched behind her, parted her quivering buttocks and examined her closely, finishing off with a loud sniff, as though making absolutely sure that she had cleaned herself properly. Sophie wanted to curl up and die. The thought of any lack of thoroughness being discovered was too awful to contemplate and the relief when a friendly slap told her she had passed the inspection was almost as intense as getting rid of the liquid had been.

As she moved back to sister's desk for the expected spanking, she began to realise that the enema had made her feel really good inside, to the extent that she didn't concentrate on looking for differences in technique until halfway through her punishment.

After a very welcome shower, Jenny was summoned again and led her to a nearby room where Sister Maureen had her new clothes ready. Apparently, Elspeth had thoughtfully faxed through her measurements and, apart from minor adjustments to the length of the skirts, everything fitted like a glove and she was soon standing proudly in a tight white blouse, pelmet-length skirt, virtually backless white knickers, and comfortable slip-on shoes.

As she was inspected, she reflected that for all the charms of total nudity, her uniform was notably sexier and had the added bonus of making her feel part of the establishment. With that thought to comfort her, she looked at Sister Maureen properly.

Less striking than the other two sisters. Perhaps in her early forties. Petite. Dressed in a long dark robe, like Sister Philippa's. Rather beady little eyes behind plain spectacles. A tiny bottom which wobbled surprisingly as she trotted across the room to fetch something. A precise, schoolmistress-like way of talking.

And as enthusiastic a spanker as the other two.

Even better at it, Sophie realised less than a minute after she first felt her firm thighs under her tummy. Elspeth had once explained that, like ball games, timing is as important as pure strength when it comes to spanking effectively. And there was no doubt in Sophie's overloaded mind that Sister Maureen's timing was spot-on, even allowing for the fact that her bottom was already quite sore before the first spank.

To her relief, Jenny led her to a little sitting room on the ground floor where a steaming pot of tea, a plate of biscuits and a large slice of obviously home made fruit cake provided a welcome sight.

'Have a bit of a rest, Slave Sophie,' Jenny told her in a markedly more friendly tone of voice. 'I'll be back to take you to see Sister Tanya in half an hour.'

'Thank you, Slave Jenny,' Sophie replied gravely. Jenny smiled at her, and Sophie's spirits lifted at the first sign of warmth.

As she sipped blissfully, she mulled over her impressions to date. On the plus side, all three sisters showed every sign of being superb dominants, with the sort of quiet authority which brought out the best in her. Their openly displayed bottoms did nothing to reduce their power but made them even more exciting. Sophie reflected briefly that in the past year, her awareness of the almost infinite variety of the female rear had increased enormously.

Secondly, all three clearly loved spanking. Sophie realised that one of her buried concerns had been that the new regime would regard a smacked bottom as too trivial for serious consideration, and she was hugely relieved that she was not going to be denied that lovely sense of intimacy only really achieved when across a woman's knee.

As she poured herself a second cup, she turned her mind to the inevitability of being thrashed properly, and the hot flush of fear made her catch her breath. She was in no doubt that the sisters would be expert and enthusiastic, and the thought of being at their mercy both thrilled and frightened her.

Then Jenny reappeared, her dear little face tense, and Sophie guessed she was about to face a sterner test. Leaving the tea tray on the table, she followed Jenny along a narrow corridor leading towards the back of the house, butterflies filling her tummy and her breathing shallow and uneven.

Sister Tanya's appearance did absolutely nothing to still

her fears. Nor did the room. It was a punishment chamber, fitted out with a bewildering array of benches, stools, bars and chains, some hanging from the ceiling, others draped casually around the walls. An amazing variety of canes, paddles and whips provided the main decoration for all four walls, with the occasional graphic painting of red striped bottoms to drive home the real purpose of the room.

As the blood drained from her face, Sophie turned her attentions to Sister Tanya. She shuddered. Tall and slender. Jet-black hair, short and glossy. Startling make up, especially her lipstick. Bright red. Dark, glittering eyes. The corners of her full mouth turned up in amusement at the sight of the trembling slave staring at her like a rabbit facing a hungry stoat.

Dressed in a black catsuit. Leather. Gleaming in the soft light. A leather choker. Studded. The studs twinkled with every little movement.

Knee length boots with high heels.

A gleam of white curve below her hip made it clear that her bottom was also bare.

Poised.

Controlled.

Terrifying.

Sophie felt her racing pulse pound in her head as she waited numbly for the severe whipping which seemed completely inevitable. But for once things didn't get worse. The idea behind Sister Tanya's induction was simply to familiarise her with the apparatus, and the combination of relief and growing interest in the mechanics of punishment resulted in a session which Sophie found both educational and enjoyable.

She was made to strip and then taken to a traditional whipping bench, lying flat on her face, legs together and strapped down at ankle, mid-thigh, waist and wrist. Then her buttocks were stroked and prodded while Sister Tanya pointed out what a compact and rounded target they made.

Her wrists were cuffed, two chains pulled down from the

ceiling, clipped to the cuffs and then pulled up tight so that only her toes touched the floor. Once again her bottom was pinched and prodded and the consistency of the flesh described.

As they moved from one piece of apparatus to the next, Sophie found herself increasingly interested in the various ways of presenting her bottom for punishment and, by the time they reached the last and most elaborate, was actually turned on.

This was the birching block, standing ominously near the furthest wall, and Sophie had cast several nervous glances in its direction, trying to work out exactly how it was used. Sister Tanya enlightened her.

'The traditional block, as used mainly in boys' schools, was a simple affair, consisting of a bit to kneel on and a higher part to support the upper body,' she explained. 'The naughty boy – and as girls' schools became more common – girl, would kneel down, thighs resting against the front of the upper part, lean forward and present his or her bare bottom to be whipped. Ours is much more flexible. Let me show you.'

It took nearly half an hour to demonstrate the main features of the ingenious and beautifully crafted piece of furniture. The torso support could be moved through about thirty degrees, varying the angle of Sophie's upper body and therefore the jut of her bottom. Her legs could also be arranged in a variety of positions, from together and slanting more or less straight to the floor, to widely parted and brought right forward, doubling her up and stretching her bottom wide open.

As she moved her willing subject around, Sister Tanya explained that the differences in presentation allowed the sisters to cater for an infinite variety of bottoms.

'With nice fleshy buttocks like yours, Slave Sophie, I would probably have it like this,' she said as she tightened the strap round her waist. 'Your cleft is open, I can see your anus... very pretty... you've had an enema, haven't you? Yes, your rectum is still a bit slippery. Where was I? Oh yes, but it is still fairly well protected by the inner curves of your cheeks. On the other hand, your flesh isn't drum-tight, which would make it far easier to break the skin during a decent whipping. We wouldn't want that, would we?'

'No, sister,' Sophie agreed fervently, while reflecting that her pose was extreme enough to make any whipping far from decent.

Sister Tanya obviously agreed, because she spent several minutes toying with her horribly vulnerable rear end, ending up by forcibly reminding Sophie that her fanny was as exposed as her buttocks by fingering it expertly until she was on the verge of coming. And the inevitable writhings as the waves built up also served as a potent reminder that she was so helplessly bound to the block that she was almost totally immobile.

The session had evidently aroused Sister Tanya as well, as she unstrapped her quickly, sat down on the end of the whipping bench and ordered Sophie to kneel at her feet and lick her boots clean.

Then to take them off and suck her toes.

Then to kiss her buttocks all over before getting her tongue as far up her bottom as she could.

Finally to kiss and lick her cunt until she came.

Eventually, with her head swimming from a combination of trepidation and lust, and with a heady mixture of tastes and scents in her mouth and nostrils, Sophie plodded off with Jenny to be introduced to the other element in her new life. Her fellow slaves.

As far as Sophie was concerned, these had been more of an unknown quantity than the sisters. After all her training submission was second nature to her, and her essentially shy nature had always made it hard for her to form casual relationships easily, so she was not surprised when she was welcomed rather coolly.

Not that it bothered her unduly. She was quite happy to be

the 'new girl', to sit quietly on the sidelines and either listen or to drift off into her own little secret world. Not that any of the other three slaves were especially unpleasant, although the self-appointed senior one, Brenda, showed early signs of being something of a bully. Generally, and especially Jenny, they helped her whenever it occurred to them to do so.

They were kept busy, which helped. There was the big house to keep clean, meals to be prepared and served, gardening fatigues, washing and ironing and any other tasks the sisters wanted carried out.

Sophie had every cause to be grateful to Elspeth's tuition in the less common techniques. She was the only slave who knew how to use old-fashioned beeswax furniture polish, which meant that care of all the antique pieces was soon her sole responsibility, so that she spent most of the time working on her own.

It was the free time which was the problem. Their quarters were in a converted stable, separate from the main house, where they could relax unsupervised. Each had a small bedroom, there were two well-equipped bathrooms, a kitchen and laundry facilities, so that there was no excuse for having either a dirty uniform or body, and a fairly basic sitting room.

Reminders of the outside world were banned, so there was neither television nor radio. Just a collection of relevant books and magazines, all dealing with domination, submission and punishments. As the slaves saw their quarters as a welcome haven from these subjects, they were not read often.

For the first couple of evenings, Sophie was only too happy to go to bed early. But as she began to settle, she found it increasingly difficult to avoid accusations of stand-offishness, and so had to spend more time with the others. She alone found the books and magazines of interest, and so tended to sit quietly reading while the others chatted desultorily about the events of the day.

Brenda showed her true colours on the third night. She and Jenny argued heatedly about the best way of mixing salad dressing and, as soon as she saw she was losing, Brenda pulled rank.

'I'm not taking any more lip from you, Jenny. You've earned a punishment. Stand up and take your dressing gown off. Now!'

As usual, their uniforms had been washed, dried and ironed ready for the following day, so all were in their night clothes. A sulky Jenny rose to her feet, took her gown off, tossed it onto her chair and stood for a moment facing Brenda.

Sophie put her book down and paid attention, suddenly intrigued. Brenda, a big girl in every way, was glaring down at her victim, her close-set eyes gleaming lustfully, while the far prettier Jenny was red in the face and with an expression which somehow managed to combine both resentment and pleading simultaneously.

'You know what to do, darling,' Brenda snarled. 'On your knees, arse up in the air and pyjamas down. Move!'

Sophie couldn't believe that Brenda was going to spank Jenny. Surely even she wouldn't dare leave marks on her bottom. She watched breathlessly as the smaller girl turned, got down on her knees, stuck her bottom up, reached back, tugged her pyjama bottoms down, and then settled herself. With an unpleasantly gloating expression on her heavy face, Brenda moved round to her victim's head, extended the middle finger of her right hand and pushed it into the already open mouth. As Jenny reluctantly licked it, Sophie realised what a Brenda punishment entailed, and her own anus tingled in sympathy. With growing revulsion at the thought of having to submit to another slave, she watched poor Jenny's face screw up in humiliation as Brenda pushed her wet finger firmly up the reluctantly offered bottom, pumping her hand in and out and obviously wriggling her finger around in the tight confines of Jenny's rectum.

She stole a quick glance at the fourth slave, Lavinia. In some ways she was the least pretty of them all, but there was something indefinably attractive about her which rather intrigued Sophie. Their eyes met and Lavinia winked at her before looking back at the action. From her viewpoint, facing Jenny's bottom, she would arguably have had a more interesting view, and Sophie had just decided to join her when Brenda announced that the punishment was over, and a still blushing Jenny clambered to her feet, pulled up her pyjamas and sat down again sulkily.

Brenda then stared at Sophie. 'Now you know what to expect if you upset me,' she said.

'I'll do my best not to,' Sophie replied evenly.

In bed, she mulled over the strange incident and realised that, while she despised Brenda's bullying, there had been an exciting frisson about her punishment. Although she wryly admitted to herself that she would have liked to have had a full view of Jenny's bottom, what she had been able to see had been stirring. The crouched body, with the white curves of her naked flank and thigh in view. Her bared teeth as Brenda rammed her finger up into her rectum. Brenda's cruel face looking smugly down at her victim's taut nakedness and those gleaming eyes focused on her tender bottom-hole, so reluctantly proffered.

Sophie shuddered, thrust the disturbing image from her mind, and fell into a disturbed sleep.

By the end of her first week, Sophie felt reasonably confident that she had got to grips with the routine as far as the sisters were concerned. She was enjoying it. The work was satisfying, the uniform – with the hem of the skirt constantly brushing against the lower curves of her buttocks and the thong pressing into the depths of her cleft – was sexy to wear, and the frequent glimpses of the other slaves made it as nice to observe.

The sisters wore their backless robes most of the time, and seeing their completely bare bottoms was always a pleasure.

The food was simple but good.

She was spanked often enough to keep her up to the mark,

but neither frequently nor hard enough for it to be in any way excessive.

She began to wonder when she was going to be whipped, and the desire to show what she could take made her almost long for it.

Before her wish was granted, she had to face up to a far less painful ordeal. Inevitably, she clashed with Brenda. She saw the gleam in the bigger girl's eyes and could not fail to notice the extended finger waved in front of her face.

'I've been dying for a chance to get up your fat bum, Sophie. Now on your knees and get it all bare for me.'

Sophie felt her face burn as they locked glances, and she realised it was her best chance, not just to stick up for herself but also to try and get the other two on her side. 'No,' she said defiantly.

Before she could even blink she was enveloped in a painful bear hug, squeezing first her breath and then all resistance from her body. She was trying to gasp out a convincing surrender when she was flung to the floor, winding her completely, and Brenda's big, thinly clad bottom was pressing down on her breasts while two strong hands pinned her thighs. The bitter taste of total defeat added to her pain and discomfort as the nerves in her tight anus began to crawl.

Her legs were pulled up and tucked under Brenda's arms, her nightie pushed out of the way and, as she licked the finger which had been thrust back in her face, she reflected that she would have been far better off biding her time before making a stand.

The penetration was painful, drawn out and, because it was being done by a slave not a mistress, indescribably humiliating.

The only good thing which emerged from the whole sorry episode was that Lavinia was much friendlier towards her.

The next day she was whipped. So were the other three. Sister Philippa broke the news to them after breakfast, with the unwelcome addition that they would have to wait until after dinner.

Not surprisingly, the day crawled past, with Sophie having a great deal of trouble concentrating on her work, with the inevitable result that she earned three quite sound spankings before lunch, each one hard enough to make her mend her ways but not so severe that she had marks on her bottom when the time came to be whipped.

As all four made their slow and silent way to the Punishment Room, Sophie was more nervous than she had been for ages. She assumed that Sister Tanya would be carrying out the punishment, and even the spankings she'd dished out had been enough to give her a profound respect for her abilities. She helped calm herself by looking at the other slaves' bottoms at every opportunity, finding extra comfort in the reasonable expectation that she would be allowed to watch Brenda's big bare bottom writhing under punishment.

As the lovely old grandfather clock in the hall struck the hour, the four pale, tight-lipped slaves shuffled nervously into the Punishment Room, and Sophie duly followed the others as they took up their positions behind three chairs set in a row at one end of the room, each already occupied by a smiling sister.

Brenda, as the senior, was to be whipped first and Sisters Maureen and Helga, the former in her usual robes and the latter in her white coat, were in charge of tying the slaves to the apparatus Sister Tanya had selected. Sophie watched keenly as Brenda stepped forward, stripped down to her knickers and walked steadily across to a beam bolted to the floor and set about a metre away from the far wall. She stood patiently while Sister Maureen took her knickers right off, pressed her groin against the polished wood and leant forward with her arms extended to head level.

In a trice, her wrists had been cuffed and clipped to a chain fixed to the wall, which was then drawn tight and clamped. Finally, each ankle was tied to the feet supporting the beam, so her legs were nicely parted.

The sisters stepped back, looked at Brenda's bottom thoughtfully, pinched and patted both buttocks, nodded at each other and returned to their seats. As she gazed at Brenda's bare bottom, Sophie suddenly felt a wild exhilaration. She did not like the trussed up slave patiently waiting for her whipping, but had to admit that the girl had a surprisingly exciting body. She had not seen her completely naked before and had not particularly wanted to. Obviously she had seen enough of her bottom in her uniform to know it was proportionately big, with a pronounced overhang. But what surprised her was that the rest of Brenda was, in an earthy way, very sexy.

Her dangling breasts were big but lovely and firm, her waist remarkably narrow, her back well muscled and her tummy flat. Not surprisingly, Sophie's gaze returned to that rounded bottom and had to admit that it was much more beautiful than she had realised, especially as Brenda was quite relaxed, so that her rump was pushed out towards her audience.

Then Sister Tanya appeared and the atmosphere was immediately even more electric. She sauntered up to Brenda, startlingly dressed in only a black corset, tight, knee-length boots, studded wristbands and choker. Her black hair was neatly pinned, her heavily made-up eyes and red mouth exaggerated the pallor of her face, and the shining black leather showed off her pure white skin.

Sophie stared at her, her breath reduced to shallow pants as she walked slowly round her victim. Pert, firm breasts, bobbing gently above the corset; the neat triangle of black pubic hair; the smooth firm thighs and arms; tight little bottom, with neat folds and perfectly rounded cheeks.

Very beautiful, terribly threatening, and utterly dominant.

In a daze, Sophie watched as Sister Tanya selected a four-foot long whip, tapering from the thick handle to about twelve inches of plaited cord. She ran the full length through her left hand, her dark eyes glittering and the tip of her tongue emerging to lick her lips in a gesture of such lascivious cruelty that Sophie shuddered.

Then she made her preparations, all of which were deliberately designed to make Brenda feel even worse. She trailed the cord down her spine. Then she pressed the end into the deep cleft between her twitching buttocks and Sophie heard a faint hiss from the sweating slave when she felt the pressure against her anus.

The whip was transferred to the left hand while the right one gave both cheeks a lingering feel. The hand rose and hovered. Elegant fingers, ending in bright red nails, poised over those twin mounds of soft, helpless, feminine flesh. A blur. The ringing sound of hand on bottom. A rippling wobble, which reached both plump thighs. A faint pink patch. The same on the other buttock, the small pain a tormenting reminder of the far greater agony to come.

Then Sister Tanya moved to Brenda's left, extending her arm to rest the business end of the whip on Brenda's bottom, shuffled her feet slightly for perfect range and balance, raised it and let fly.

Sophie's pent up breath came out in a shuddering sigh as her fascinated eyes drank in the startling effects. The loud crack of the impact; the way the relaxed flesh of Brenda's big buttocks rippled frantically; a brief glimpse of a thin white line, which magically became a thicker one, going from pink to a deep mauve/red amazingly quickly. She winced and gulped at the evidence of frightening effectiveness and it was only when the whip was on its way back down again that she realised Brenda had not made a sound.

Sister Tanya whipped Brenda with remorseless precision. Her first stroke had landed dead centre and she moved from above it to below it with every succeeding lash, spreading the area of reddened flesh evenly over the full and generous area available to her, and Sophie found herself increasingly entranced by the strange beauty of the spectacle.

There was the undeniable attraction of both bodies, the one naked and the other exposing just the more interesting areas, and Sister Tanya's languid, economical grace as she wielded the elegant whip.

Brenda's bottom was steadily being transformed into a colour which few, if any, artists could have captured in oils, ranging from a delicate salmon pink to near purple.

The movement of the various areas of naked flesh had beauty. Sister Tanya's breasts bobbed gently as the impact of the whip travelled up her arm. Brenda's much bigger and softer one's, dangling heavily below her straining torso, swung and swayed at both the impact and the inevitable muscular contractions as the boiling waves of pain surged inwards, outwards, upwards and downwards from the narrow stripe left in the lash's wake. Most striking of all was the rippling wobble of her bottom at every hissing stroke.

And still she made no sound – apart from an occasional hiss.

Sophie did not like Brenda, but respect for her adversary grew by the minute.

Then it was Jenny's turn. Brenda was untied quickly, given a drink of water and, on amazingly steady legs, walked back and took her place in the line of slaves behind the chairs. Jenny walked over to the middle of the room, her nervousness making her take short steps, so that her little bottom jiggled and bounced under her tiny skirt. She removed it, then took off her blouse and stood while Sister Maureen pulled her G-string down and off.

Sister Helga examined her bottom, pronounced it fit to be whipped, and Sister Tanya asked her two colleagues to place her on the bench.

Variety is the spice of life, Sophie thought as she watched Jenny being helped to lie flat on the selected apparatus and then have her wrists and ankles tied to the legs and broad leather straps buckled tightly round her waist and knees. She had a neat and quite chubby bottom and, in her prone position, it swelled up prettily from her thighs, the clean-cut gluteal folds very visible. 'The bottom's smile,' Elspeth had said once when studying Sophie's in a similar pose, and she could see exactly what she had meant.

Sister Tanya chose a broad, long, split strap for Jenny. Rather like an outsize tawse, and wielded it with the same expert grace she had shown with the whip. Sophie rather liked Jenny, and so didn't feel the same desire to see her suffer. But even so, the loud thwacks as leather sank into flesh, the springy quivering and spreading redness, were still exciting enough to keep her interested. And when Sister Tanya wanted her to touch her toes for a dozen with the cane as a finale, the very different shape of her bottom, with her fanny stretched open to show the complex inner lips, she certainly found the sight quite arousing.

Unlike Brenda, Jenny gasped moaned and cried out during her punishment, although never enough to arouse contempt.

Sophie's interest quickened even more when Lavinia stepped forward and undressed. She felt increasingly drawn to the shy, self-contained girl, with her clipped upper-class accent, and had already planned to try and get close to her. Not that she was a beauty. A nice face, with gorgeous big grey eyes, classical cheekbones and a perfect complexion, but her hair was a mass of unruly brown curls and her mouth and chin too small. She had a sweet smile and very shapely legs, so offered more plusses than minuses in terms of her appearance, but it was her bottom which fascinated most.

Again, Sophie hadn't seen it completely bare but the sight of it in her uniform literally made her mouth water. Her buttocks jostled, bounced and twinkled beautifully under the hem of her skirt, and the prospect of seeing it in all its naked glory was enough to take her mind off her own imminent ordeal.

It proved to be as spectacular as it had promised, curving as dramatically down from her very narrow waist as it did up from her thighs. The flawless skin, tight cleft and sweeping folds had Sophie sighing with pleasure, and the fact that it was so big in proportion to her generally slender body made its lovely shape and texture even more spectacular.

She was laid across a trestle, her legs widely parted, her plump fanny in full view, and lashed hard and fast with a riding crop. Her buttocks were obviously splendidly firm, as they bounced, shook and quivered rather than wobbled, and her fine skin showed the effects of her whipping quickly and dramatically.

Like Jenny, she was not able to restrain her cries, but did manage to keep her suffering bottom acceptably still.

She was untied, let up, her dark red bottom checked, and then she was walking stiffly back into line, her face tight with pain.

Sophie watched the trestle being folded up and put way, then the birching block was carried to the middle. With a jolt she realised it was her turn. Her mouth was suddenly parched. And her palms wet. Sweat ran down from under her arms as she fought to control her breathing.

Not that any of the whippings she had witnessed were beyond her experience. It was just that Elspeth wasn't there and so there was no comforting presence to give her extra strength. As she tottered unsteadily to the complex bench, she just managed to transfer her affections to Sister Philippa and to keep her lovely face in mind, proving to her rather than her own mistress that her bottom was both nice and capable of absorbing punishment.

It worked. Her fingers were quite steady as she took off her blouse and skirt, and her legs and buttocks hardly trembled as Sister Maureen took her knickers off. She mentally thanked Sister Tanya for introducing her to the block before being bent over it in earnest, as she could be suitably pliant when the sisters moved her limbs into position before tying her tight, torso sloping down, parted knees brought up and held while a bar was slid into one of the holes running through the base until the ends projected on each side and, when her knees were released, supported them and held her legs virtually immobile.

With the last buckle fastened, they stood back, obviously

surveying the results of their labours. She was vaguely tempted to crane her head round and see what sort of reaction her beautifully presented bottom was getting from the sisters but decided that she would be ill-advised to try.

She wondered if Lavinia had recovered sufficiently to be able to focus on it.

It felt even more vulnerable than the first time. Probably because there were seven pairs of eyes on it, not just one.

She wondered if her anus was visible. Her fanny undoubtedly was and she was sure that she could feel cooler air wafted into the open division.

She wondered what implement Sister Tanya planned to use on her.

She knew that whatever it was, she was going to end up with a ferociously sore bottom.

She began to anticipate the pain, getting herself ready for the challenge of accepting it as a slave should. Gracefully and gratefully.

'An excellent bottom,' Sister Philippa announced unexpectedly. 'And very nicely presented.'

There was warmth and excitement in her voice, and Sophie felt a surge of affection for her.

Her hands had been cuffed to another bar through the base and she was able to turn her wrists and grip hard. She knew it would help.

'You are going to birch her, Sister Tanya?' That was Sister Maureen.'

'I think so,' Tanya replied, her affected drawl just failing to disguise her arousal.

After an interminable wait, Sophie felt the cool, damp, slightly prickly caress of the birch resting against the roundest part of her bottom as Sister Tanya adjusted her aim. Her heart raced and she closed her eyes, concentrating fully on her yawning, vulnerable, naked bottom.

That unmistakable *thwick* reached her ears as about a thousand sharp little pinpricks assaulted her taut skin. She let out her breath slowly and silently, gripped the bar even more tightly and forced the rest of her body to relax.

Only her bottom mattered. To her, the three watching sisters and the other slaves. She no longer counted as a person. Just a biggish, rounded bottom. A bare bottom. Soft flesh and sensitive skin. An open cleft. Even more sensitive skin. Already suffused with that maddeningly persistent hot sting which she remembered so clearly from the only other birching she had suffered.

Stroke upon stroke. A dozen across the full width of her bottom. Then a different phase. Short sharp ones aimed at the less accessible parts. The inner curves of her cheeks. Around her cringing bottom-hole. Skirting her fanny. Around her tailbone. the sides of her buttocks. Her bottom getting hotter and hotter.

Sweat poured off her as she gritted her teeth in a desperate but futile attempt to stop herself crying out.

In spite of the fact that she was so tightly fastened, her hips still jerked a little at every stroke. She tried to resist but couldn't.

She sobbed quietly, more from her despair at her lack of control than from the pain, although that was bad enough in all conscience.

And getting worse. Burning, throbbing, stinging.

Her hands slipped off the bar and hung loose.

Red mists filled her brain.

She moaned continually.

Then it was over. She became aware of busy hands by her sides as the waist belt was undone. A blissful release of the pressure. Then her knees and ankles were freed and she groaned as her cramped legs were straightened.

They helped her to her feet and gave her drink of cold water, which refreshed her so effectively that the pain in her bottom almost overwhelmed her. She staggered a little, then. gritting her teeth, she walked back into line with her head held high.

Then they had to kneel at Tanya's feet, kiss her hand and thank her for the whipping.

After that, a painful procession of naked, crimson-bottomed slaves to Sister Helga's treatment room, where, nursing the glow of contentment in her heart, she watched the others lie on the couch, to have cream gently applied.

Then it was her turn and the relief was indescribable as the magic potion cooled and soothed.

Then, after a drink of warm milk, it was bed and blissful oblivion.

# Chapter Ten

A week after her birching Sophie woke up, realised it was Sunday, that she and Lavinia were off duty, it was still quite early and so she lay back with that delicious and rare feeling that she had no need to get up until she felt like it. Judging by the light penetrating the curtains the weather was fine, which made the prospect even more pleasing.

The calm, contented mood which had made its presence felt after she had survived her first whipping with some credit, had grown stronger.

She was beginning to enjoy the Establishment far more than she had thought possible. The sisters were proving skilled and imaginative at the complex arts of domination and, at the same time, displayed occasional flashes of humanity, so that while her essential submissiveness was encouraged and nourished, she was never seriously degraded. She still mattered. Only as a slave but like Elspeth, Sister Philippa and her colleagues respected the status of slave and gave full credit to those who performed well.

Sister Philippa had made that plain the day before. She had been crossing the main hall, had seen Sophie at work and had stopped. Sophie had carried on with her polishing, alert for the first word from her superior, which would be the signal to drop her cloth, stand up, curtsey and wait for instructions. She waited for what seemed an age. Then a soft chuckle brought a puzzled frown.

'You disappoint me, Slave Sophie.' The sorrowful tones were so theatrical that Sophie nearly smiled as she sensed something different in the air. 'Yes, I had hoped that you would stop working and give me an excuse to put you across my knee. It's far too long since I had your lovely buttocks at my mercy. Oh well, better luck next time.'

Sophie's sudden urge to feel those lovely thighs under her tummy; to sense those warm, laughing eyes gazing at her bare bottom; to feel that elegant, soft hand on her skin, inspired her to risk severe punishment by speaking out of turn. 'I would love you to spank me, Sister Philippa,' she said quietly.

Which is precisely what a smiling sister administered. Hard, loud and long. To a lovingly bared bottom only just recovered from the birching.

It had been sheer bliss, Sophie reflected as she snuggled luxuriantly under her duvet and the memory sent her hand drifting between her parted thighs, stroking the soft lips of her fanny, before twiddling her clitty ring with one finger while another stole into the slippery tunnel. As she recovered, she thought about the one fly in the otherwise smooth ointment of her existence. Brenda. While Jenny and Lavinia had shown much more warmth towards her since she had stood up for herself, Brenda had clearly reckoned that winning their all-too-brief fight had been nowhere near enough. She took every opportunity to put Sophie down and the slightest show of resentment had the inevitable result – on her knees, bare bottom thrust up in the air, anus tingling in anticipation of the always uncomfortable penetration and busily working as much saliva into her mouth as possible before opening it to wet Brenda's finger. As ever, with a different person doing the penetrating and in a better atmosphere, she would have got a kick out of it. She had even learnt to enjoy her weekly enemas.

'Oh, well,' Sophie comforted herself as she heard Brenda and Jenny getting ready to go on duty, 'something will turn up.'

She heard their fading footsteps across the yard and decided that it was too nice a day to lie frowsting in her bed, so got up, stripped off her nightie to have a shower and then decided that a cup of tea would be an even better start. She was about to make herself decent again and then remembered the simple pleasure she had found in walking about naked during the holiday at the Mansion, so ambled into the kitchen, enjoying the fresh air on her skin, the free movements of her bottom and the nice feeling of freedom. She was initially a bit concerned about Lavinia but complete silence from her room suggested that she was still fast asleep.

She put the kettle on, found a mug, the teabags and a spoon. She dropped the spoon, cursing as she saw it bounce and slither towards the little alcove containing the washing-up machine. Down on to her knees she went, only to find that she had to stretch right to the back to reach it, with the inevitable result that her naked rump assumed a position which would have pleased Brenda immensely.

'Now there's a sight for sore eyes!' said Lavinia, with a relish which was totally lost on a flustered Sophie, who grabbed the spoon and scrambled apologetically to her feet.

Lavinia was grinning warmly and Sophie decided that the least said about her nudity the soonest mended, so simply offered to make another cup.

As they sipped appreciatively, her embarrassment faded to the extent that she felt rather ashamed at her reaction and began to wish that Lavinia was in the same state.

'Any plans for the day?' Lavinia asked as she washed up the mugs.

Sophie gazed at the beautifully filled and gently quivering seat of her companion's pyjamas, hastily put the obvious thought out of her mind and said something about sitting outside with a book. She had noticed a well-used and interestingly illustrated one on the History of Corporal Punishment and was looking forward to broadening her mind. 'What had you got in mind?' she said innocently.

Lavinia then told her that they were allowed to wander round the grounds, including the woods, as long as they took all their clothes off, presumably to make escape even less tempting.

216

'Why don't we take advantage of a lovely day, take a rug, some sandwiches, something to drink and be on our own,' she suggested tentatively.

Sophie felt her face burn with pleasure and agreed with barely restrained enthusiasm.

They soon found a suitably hidden glade, left the rug and their picnic and decided to enjoy their freedom by just ambling around the woods. Sophie's desire for friendship outweighed her interest in bodies and sex, so she hardly took any notice of Lavinia's nudity as they chatted with growing intimacy about the sisters, their chores, the food – deliberately avoiding any reference to bottoms and punishment.

Until they wandered back to the glade, sat down, opened the cool bag and opened the bottle of Chablis which was their Sunday treat from Sister Philippa. They sipped in silence and Sophie felt a warm glow of contentment steal through her. The soft sighing of the wind in the trees; the dappled sunlight; the perfect temperature; the intermittent bird song. And the growing conviction that there was a potential rapport between her and Lavinia.

She looked at her out of the corner of her eye and realised that first impressions could be very deceptive – she was really very attractive.

Their eyes met and one of them must have swayed slightly, because their shoulders brushed and Sophie gasped as what felt like an electric shock surged through her from the point of contact.

It was as though both lost all their inhibitions simultaneously. Subjects which they had avoided until that moment were suddenly of consuming interest. Lavinia asked Sophie how she had got into slavery and Sophie held virtually nothing back, telling her new friend far more than the basic circumstances of her introduction to Elspeth. She poured out her feelings, from her terror of rejection, to the deep pleasure she got from being put across her knee to have her bare bottom spanked. She even confessed to having to wipe her mistress's bottom and, to her relief, Lavinia reacted enviously rather than with horror.

Then Lavinia told Sophie of her first experiences. The unloved daughter of an Earl, after she had left school, she had been encouraged to go and work for a friend of her mother's, who ran a riding stables in Leicestershire.

'Jane soon had me completely under her thumb,' Lavinia said, staring dreamily into the distance. She used to make me muck out the stables in the nude, to save laundry! Then hose me down in the yard, even when the two lads were about.'

Sophie sat enthralled as Lavinia's sad tale unfolded. Clumsiness rewarded with sound spankings. Across the knee, bottom bare. Even in front of the lads, if she sinned in the stables rather than the house. Then progressing to being bent over for a leathering with any handy piece of harness.

She had got used to that and was beginning to get a thrill from taking her britches and panties down, feeling the fresh air cooling her upthrust rump before the whistling lash heated her flesh up to boiling point.

She had even got used to being buggered by the lads. It had started when they caught her having a sneaky cigarette in one of the loose boxes, had angrily pointed out that straw burns easily and had threatened to tell the Boss, leeringly anticipating the pleasure of watching her bare arse thrashed scarlet.

Her pleas for an alternative had been met with the threat of another way of hurting her bottom and she had reluctantly pulled down her jeans and knelt down for each in turn to penetrate her virgin back passage. She had managed to avoid throwing up but the feeling of complete degradation had lasted far longer than the ache in her bottom-hole.

Naturally, the lads wanted a repeat performance and Jane had caught them in the act. To Lavinia's horror, she had hooted with laughter and encouraged them to continue. After that, her punished bottom was always made available to both men.

'I was nineteen,' Lavinia reminisced, 'and even then my

bottom was really big. It was difficult to get my anus fully exposed, so Jane would straddle my back and hold my cheeks apart, so that they could see what they were doing. She even greased it for them.'

Such entertainments were too exciting to be restricted to mere stable lads and Jane was soon asking like-minded friends to come and watch. One of them had been a member of the Circle and, when Jane's stable went bankrupt, found Lavinia a permanent place at the Establishment.

As her voice died away, Sophie impulsively put her arms round Lavinia's shoulders, hugging her sympathetically. Once again, the feel of her warm, satiny skin galvanised her and, in a trice they were lying on the rug, kissing with rapidly increasing passion.

All Sophie's pent up desires to make love on an equal basis surged up to the surface, with the result that her first climax came in a bewildering blur of Lavinia's soft skin and questing hands and mouth.

The second one was more as it should be. She was able to enjoy the novel sensation of exploring another girl's body at her own pace, knowing that her new lover was perfectly happy to lie back and revel in the equally novel sensation of being stroked and kissed as much for her pleasure as for her partner's.

Sophie toyed with Lavinia's small breasts and big dark nipples.

She spent minutes on end studying her far from small bottom, marvelling at the firmness of the flesh, the amazing curves, the warm softness of her incredibly deep cleft. Parting her cheeks to peep at her anus was pure pleasure, unspoilt by the complete lack of compulsion or duty. She buried her face in the division, gently kissing and licking, slowly moving her tongue towards first the pale brown surround and then to the pink opening itself. Lavinia's moans were music to her ears.

She turned her over so that she could devote the same degree of enthusiastic attention to her plump little fanny, cooing over the smooth lips and smiling happily as the tight slit slackened to expose the coral pink inside, glistening with excitement and filling her nostrils with the heady scent of very turned on girl as she applied lips and tongue.

Lavinia asked her to turn round, so that Sophie's bottom was in view and reach and Sophie's climax built up inexorably as her nose, eyes and mouth were filled with the sight, feel and scent of intimate flesh, while her lover palmed her equivalent part, shifting her clitty ring around before slipping what must have been two fingers inside her.

Her third came after lunch, when they changed places and Sophie learnt what it was like to be thoroughly pampered. The feel of Lavinia's tongue on her bottom-hole was a revelation and she understood immediately why all the mistresses she had met were so insistent on having it done to them – apart from the obvious element of enforced debasement when it was part of the submission/domination equation, it was an amazing thrill.

After that, both were completely spent, so lay happily beside each other, talking with growing confidence in their friendship.

Soon afterwards, Sophie sorted Brenda out. The two of them were on weekend duty and the big, gawky girl started off in a pretty foul mood and got even less agreeable as the morning wore on. She even took advantage of a temporary lull in the kitchen to make Sophie present her bottom for a fingering, which the younger girl only did after her hissed protest was overcome with the threat of two fingers up her bum if Brenda had to wait until they got back to their quarters.

Seething, Sophie whipped down her G-string, stuck her bottom out and groaned with both anger and pain when Brenda decided to thrust two fingers up her anyway. As she clambered to her feet, her tormentor made her suck her fingers clean and the sick feeling in her stomach turned to hatred.

Under the circumstances, the sisters were lucky to get lunch at all. In spite of all Sophie's efforts to turn Brenda's slapdash preparations into something at least presentable, both were sentenced to an extra whipping, to be administered after an early supper.

When the time came, Sophie was determined to show that she could take punishment as well as Brenda.

They were made to strip naked in the Hall and lead the procession through to the Punishment Room. Sister Philippa sat down in the middle chair, Sophie stood behind her with a sympathetic Lavinia and an excited Jenny on each side, watching Sisters Helga and Maureen carry the birching block forward until it was only a few feet in front of Sister Philippa and then strap a sullen Brenda firmly in position. Sophie's hopes that she would see Brenda's fat bare bottom in the distended position which she had been made to adopt were dashed. Her torso was parallel to the ground, she was kneeling with her legs together and straight, so that not even her fanny peeked out at the base of her softly rounded cheeks.

'Very pretty,' Lavinia whispered. 'And her bottom will wobble very nicely.'

It did.

A naked Sister Tanya selected a thick short cane and began to flick it rapidly against Brenda's bottom, starting at the top and working steadily down to the well-defined gluteal folds, each sharp tap hard enough to please Lavinia, to leave a pink line and yet obviously cause little pain.

Sophie suddenly remembered her session with the sweet little Chinese mistress – Mae Wong? – and her challenging demonstration of the oriental approach to causing pain in an erring bottom. Little, often and for a long time.

Once they had got over their initial disappointment over the lack of dramatic sound and fury, all the spectators settled down to enjoy the spreading redness, the sexy quivering of naked flesh, Sister Tanya's nudity and Brenda's noticeable confusion.

Then Sister Tanya handed the cane to Sister Helga, who slipped off her robe and carried on the good work. As she had only seen Helga's bottom, Sophie found that her attention was divided between the rounded whiteness of her splendid breasts and Brenda's even more rounded, and by then bright pink, buttocks.

The whipping went on and on. All four sisters had a turn and Brenda's bottom moved steadily through the full spectrum of shades of red until it was nearer purple. Clearly the remorselessly slow increase in the pain both confused and troubled her, as she showed few signs of her usual stoicism. She began to tuck her bottom in, wiggle it from side to side as the burning, aching torment spread deep into her ample cheeks. Every so often, little moans and cries escaped. The slaves exchanged surprised glances and the sisters triumphant smiles.

After well over thirty minutes, a tired Sister Philippa tossed the cane aside, examined the trembling rump and nodded to Sister Tanya, who got up, swayed elegantly across to the display of canes, selected a much longer and whippier one, strolled back, measured it against the centre of the crimson, swollen target and let fly.

Brenda screamed as the weal swelled up and clenched as tightly as she could.

'Relax your buttocks, Slave Brenda,' Sister Tanya snapped.

She did, but each one of the remaining five strokes produced the same surprising result and, after the sixth and last had landed, she was sobbing brokenly, only managing to pull herself together after Sophie had been tied down in the same position and was forcing herself to relax and welcome the pain, not to fight it like Brenda had done.

She took the first part very well. The final six did test her but she sensed that she would not harm her reputation by acknowledging the fact that each one hurt like hell. She cried out, squeezed her blazing buttocks together, shook them from side to side but always had her bottom properly presented before Sister Tanya had to order her to relax.

Afterwards Sister Helga gave her a jar of the special cream

and suggested that she should get one of the other slaves to apply it.

As they walked slowly back to their quarters, she felt a surge of contentment as the pain in her bottom faded into that addictive afterglow. She sensed an opportunity to change Brenda from petty tyrant to acceptable colleague and resolved to seize it with both hands.

She began by offering to apply the cream to her bottom, did it gently and sympathetically and, as her hand soothed the hot, ridged flesh, she softly told the weeping girl that there was no harm in accepting that a whipping was painful.

'In fact,' she added, 'if you think about it, Sister Tanya puts a lot of skill and effort into whipping us and it's only fair to her to show that she's hurting. As long as you don't act like a silly little baby, it's okay to cry out and wiggle your bottom a bit. Honestly.'

'I suppose so,' Brenda mumbled.

Sophie smiled as she dabbed a blob of cream on the most swollen part of the last weal, smoothed it around and then straightened up – rather painfully.

'There you are, Brenda. All done. Sleep well.' Then she bent down again and lightly kissed the crest of each cheek. That inspired her to move up to Brenda's head and kiss her swollen, red eyes. She was rewarded with a smile and a whispered, 'Thank you, Sophie.'

From that moment, the atmosphere improved significantly. Lavinia and Jenny blossomed under Sophie's intelligent and subtle direction and she soon managed to get lure a subdued Brenda from inside the shell she had hidden behind since she lost her tenuous hold on the other slaves. She did this by turning the tables on her, making her present her bare bottom to have a finger up it and then by doing it in a way which was blatantly sexual rather than punitive. Afterwards, she even kissed the blatantly exposed orifice and then reached underneath, playing with her clitty ring until Brenda was

223

gasping and weaving. She gilded the lily by asking Jenny to kiss the stunned ex-bully's mouth and Lavinia to play with her softly dangling breasts until she came.

In a flash of inspiration, she let a bemused Brenda recover and then suggested that they should strip Lavinia naked and take it in turns to nibble her bare bottom. Lavinia caught on immediately, shrieked in maidenly outrage and took to her heels. A laughing trio caught her by the edge of the woods, wrestled her to the ground, stripped her and helped themselves to mouthfuls of delicious buttock flesh.

The evening rapidly degenerated into a prolonged bout of childish horseplay which proved to be the perfect antidote to the repressions of slavery and the bond between the four of them was sealed.


The sisters soon noticed the change. The slaves worked with more enthusiasm and efficiency, the food was improved and all four began to anticipate needs and desires, rather than simply wait for orders.

Sister Philippa, not the oldest but easily the wisest, immediately guessed the reason and began to watch Sophie with growing interest.

Apparently casual questioning produced some interesting ideas. For example, Sophie suggested that, while she fully understood the pleasure of spotting slack work and administering a spanking on the spot, it was a bit disruptive. Therefore why not have the slaves take it in turns to be a sort of whipping girl and be given light duties in exchange for being spanked whenever one of the sisters felt like warming their right hands?

They soon worked out a Duty Bottom rota.

The same thought process led Sister Tanya to propose a Duty Mouth rota, so that the sisters always had a slave on call to attend to their bottoms and fannies whenever they felt in need of a quick climax or two.

Sister Maureen wistfully confided to Sophie that she would

have loved to have been a Victorian schoolmistress, in charge of a group of high spirited mature girls, in an institution where corporal punishment was actively encouraged.

A week later, after Sister Philippa had remembered the existence of a trunk full of varied and appropriate costumes, the four slaves, in gym slips and strangely constricting blue knickers, trooped into a room with a row of authentic desks and a blackboard. A bit diffident to begin with, they soon got into their roles, were noisily disobedient and, quite properly were put across a happy Sister Maureen's knee for spanking after spanking, which got increasingly involved and severe as the evening wore on, ending up with all four kneeling up on Teacher's desk, red cheeks well parted to expose four little bottom-holes while she slapped merrily away with a wooden ruler.

Sophie's whippings increased in severity and ingenuity. One especially memorable one had her with her back to the wall, her arms stretched out parallel to the floor and her wrists tied tightly to a couple of rings, her feet also apart and tied to rings set in the floor. Her front, from neck to feet, was methodically whipped by all four sisters, each equipped with a horsehair fly whisk, which although not bitingly painful, produced a maddening itchy sting which had Sophie praying for something more traditional across her bottom.

She thought that her wish had been granted when she was untied and turned round to face the wall. To her dismay, the same implements were then used on her back and legs, avoiding her bottom completely. By the time her ankles had been dealt with, she had the extraordinary feeling that she had been lying on a bed of nettles in the hot sun. She prickled, itched, burnt and tingled all over. Except for her bottom, which positively longed to be hurt.

To her relief, she was then led to the block, tied to it with her torso straight but her knees drawn slightly up, and a light but shiny and very stingy paddle expertly applied to her yearning bottom. As a finale, her knees were refastened much higher,

her top half lowered and her open bottom cleft set on fire with what she guessed was a strip of hard leather.

All four were introduced to a new piece of apparatus sent with the master's compliments. The punishment chair. They were stripped, led into the sisters' drawing room and stared in fascinated horror at the strange looking object placed in front of the big sofa.

It consisted of two shallow steel bowls, oval rather than round, supported by gracefully curved columns which came together at the base. The bowls were separated by a gap about two inches wide, except for a steel bar across the middle.

In the bar was a hole.

Filling the hole was a vibrator, accurately modelled on a medium sized penis.

As the slaves stared, the object of the chair struck them almost simultaneously. They were going to be made to sit down, with the vibrator lodged deep inside them. Presumably in their bottoms.

Lavinia looked excited, Sophie intrigued, Jenny resigned and Brenda rather sick – in spite of Sophie's gentle fingering, she still had not learnt to like having her bottom-hole penetrated.

And things *did* get worse!

Sophie was told to go first and, before she was impaled, to bend over, touch her toes and keep her legs straight. Six ringing spanks from Sister Maureen, six strokes of a leather paddle from Sister Philippa, six from a birch wielded with Sister Helga's customary Nordic skill and then six stingers from Sister Tanya's favourite cane reduced her plump buttocks to twin mounds of molten lava.

The reason for the beating was obvious as she was guided down on to the waiting prick, her seething cheeks held apart to make the penetration of her cringing anus even easier. She bore down at the first touch on her sphincter, the cold, greased plastic slid up easily and then the cool touch of steel on her hot buttocks reignited the flames.

Her cheeks plumped into the welcoming curves of the bowl, the soft flesh moulding itself to the hard contours. Her rectum was full of vibrator, the pressure from sitting hurt the cheeks of her bottom and, when her feet were pulled forward and placed on a footstool so that almost her full weight was on her base, the combination of painful sensations was sensational.

She had to stay for five whole minutes, wondering of they were going to turn the vibrator on and, on balance, hoping that they wouldn't. Sweat poured out of her, as she panted hard through gritted teeth and tried to count the seconds.

Eventually she was helped to her feet, unable to suppress a deep groan as the prick plopped out and stumbled to her appointed place behind the sisters' sofa with burning buttocks, an aching anus and a profound respect for whoever had thought up such a devious and vicious contraption.

Watching the other girls' bottoms being beaten and then spread as they were lowered into place made her feel much better.

Some gentle hints to Sister Helga brought about a change in the weekly enema administration. Sophie had come to enjoy the sensations involved, especially the preparations and it occurred to her that if they could all watch the others presenting their bottoms, see the sinister black tube sliding past their glistening bottom-holes into the sensitive depths, they may well learn to get similar pleasure – as well as the benefits. She would certainly enjoy the spectacle. Sister Helga agreed, occasionally asked Sophie to lend a hand, notably to hold Lavinia's unusually deep cleft open for easier access. All four slaves changed their minds about what they had previously regarded as a humiliating and faintly disgusting ordeal.

Sophie's relationship with Lavinia blossomed. The increasingly sexual atmosphere in the Establishment inspired them both to make love with matching fervour and also to enjoy and appreciate simply lying in each other's arms, the silence only broken by the occasional juicy kiss. Sophie grew to love her gentle soul as much as her opulent bottom, exploring both with equal enthusiasm and satisfaction.

Other mistresses spent the odd day as honorary sisters, properly robed, so that the slaves had new bottoms to admire and service, different laps to rest on and other hands cracking into the naked flesh of their bare bottoms. Sophie recognised Mistress Devina's jiggling buttocks immediately but respected her anonymity by giving no sign of recognition, other than licking her anus with extra pleasure and crying out far more vociferously than usual when she was spanked and beaten.

Life was varied, challenging, never boring and filled with happiness and contentment until she saw a visiting Mistress in the background, whose overall shape seemed disturbingly familiar. Until she turned and walked away – Sophie felt as though an invisible fist had gripped her insides as she recognised the elegant, firmly mobile sway of the round, white, bare and perfect buttocks briefly glimpsed before their owner disappeared.

It was Elspeth. Sophie tried to concentrate on polishing the brass candlesticks which she had been happily engaged with but her trembling hands and beating heart made it almost impossible. She was, therefore, very relieved when Sister Maureen softly told her that they were not up to standard and so she should report immediately to Sister Philippa for punishment.

Concentrating on the imminent physical pain took her mind off the mental anguish of her sudden longing to see her mistress and she plonked herself across the back of the armchair without having to be told and without looking at the robed figure behind the desk. Hands folded her skirt up, eased her G-string down her waist, tugging the cord sensuously out of her cleft.

She bent her knees in to thrust her bare bottom out with

proper prominence, her thoughts wildly shifting from yearning for the onset of the hot sting to wondering why Sister Maureen always emphasised the phrase 'bare bottom' when announcing a punishment.

The hand got to work in earnest making her relaxed cheeks shudder and wobble deliciously. She settled down to benefit from her punishment and then it dawned on her that there was something different. The hand did not feel like Sister Philippa's. It wasn't her usual rhythm.

It was Elspeth. Vaguely wondering why she hadn't seen her when she had come into the room, Sophie felt tears prickle her eyes as she pushed her bottom out even more, wanting Elspeth to know that her touch had been recognised.

It was a happy reunion. Sister Philippa gave her permission for Sophie to have the rest of the day off and she regaled her first true love with all the details of her new existence, lurid and otherwise.

She talked about Lavinia and Elspeth said that she would love to meet her. She was summoned.

Sophie bared her friend's bottom and showed Elspeth how nice it was.

Elspeth asked Lavinia to strip naked and walk up and down so that she could see it in relation to the rest of her body and pleased both slaves with her genuine compliments. Lavinia asked tentatively for a spanking and was patently happy when Elspeth obliged her.

Sophie wanted another one. And got it.

Then Elspeth dropped a bombshell. Lavinia had to get back to her duties and after she had got dressed, Sophie was told to spank her.

She gaped at her mistress, open-mouthed. She couldn't be serious. Could she? Surely it was dangerous to give a slave the chance to develop a taste for administering punishment? Even to another slave.

Dreamily, she found a suitable chair, sat down, guided Lavinia over her lap, tucked her little skirt up, gazed down on her bare buttocks as though she had never seen them before and then, with her hands seeming to act separately from her brain, pulled down her minimal panties, exposing that stupendous bottom completely.

Her hand rose, paused, then fell. Her palm, ears and eyes all combined to tell her that it had been the feeblest of spanks, making little sound, hardly making the afflicted buttock even quiver, let alone wobble, and not leaving a trace of pink in its wake.

She gritted her teeth, forced the fact that she loved Lavinia out of her mind and spanked again, with proper effect.

Then the sheer, sensual pleasure of it took over. The soft yielding weight of Lavinia's body on her thighs; the way her bare bottom filled her vision; the heady feel of silky skin and pliant flesh under her palm; the spreading pink glow; the sighs of pain and pleasure coming from below and to her left.

A laughing Elspeth had to call a halt, because Lavinia's buttocks were a deep crimson, yet the wild-eyed Sophie showed no sign of having had enough.

A red-faced Lavinia, scrambled to her feet, frantically rubbing her bottom, before bending for her knickers and scampering out of the room, looking back at a remorseful Sophie, eloquently conveying respect, surprise and forgiveness in one glance.

Later that evening, Elspeth took Sophie for a walk in the grounds, both pleasing and embarrassing her by insisting that they should both be nude. Once she had come to terms with the rise in status, Sophie began to look at Elspeth's body more openly than she had ever dared to before and was thrilled not to be rebuffed – and even more thrilled at the confirmation that her mistress's figure easily bore comparison with any other she had seen.

Then Elspeth dropped an even bigger bombshell.

'You really have done well, darling. And Sister Philippa has had an idea. I think it's brilliant but the decision is yours.

Would you like to be promoted from my slave to be a junior member of the Circle. You can still live with me – and I'll still spank and beat you whenever you want – but you'll come here on a regular basis, firstly to help the sisters with the general running of the place and secondly to learn how to dominate. What do you say?'

Sophie shuddered, took a deep breath, looked Elspeth straight in the eye, hesitated and then made her reply. 'I'd love to... Elspeth.'

Elspeth smiled broadly, flung her arms round Sophie's trembling body, hugged her tightly, then stepped back, looking thoughtful.

Sophie looked a bit puzzled and then totally confused when Elspeth turned her back and slowly, sensuously bent over and gripped her ankles, dipping her knees and pushing her naked bottom in unspoken invitation.

Sophie felt the blood rush to her face as the penny dropped. As excited as she had ever been, she smoothed her palm over the satiny cheeks, pressed her fingertips into the cleft, tickled the tight little rosebud, then rested her left arm on the small of Elspeth's back and spanked her.

When she had spanked Lavinia, she had been carried away with lust and surprise. She spanked Elspeth with a calm but loving deliberation which still had the beautiful woman gasping with pain by the end.

When she decided that the meekly offered bottom was red enough, she bent down kissed both cheeks all over and then gently eased her tongue into the cleft until the tip brushed the twitching little ring. She realised immediately that licking Elspeth's bottom-hole from choice was far more satisfying than doing it out of duty.

Then, as they ambled back arm in arm, Sophie had a bleak thought. What about Lavinia? She eventually plucked up enough courage to raise the subject and when Elspeth said that there was room in her house for another girl, her happiness was complete.

Before Sophie left, she had to undergo a ceremonial farewell to slavery. After discussion with the sisters, she agreed on the details and, a week after Elspeth's visit, wearing only a studded collar and calf length boots, she walked slowly down the corridor to the Punishment Room, head held high and in a strange state of nervous exultation.

Mistresses known and strange had gathered. So had the master. The other three slaves waited patiently outside the door and returned her nervous smile. She made her entrance, curtsied to the front row of the master and the four robed sisters and stood, head held high as Sister Philippa explained the reason for the gathering.

She then put her carefully worked out plan into action.

A chair was handily placed with its right side to the audience. She sat down, the leather cool against her naked skin and then asked Sister Maureen to step forward and bend over her lap. Her neat little bottom provided an ideal starting point as Sophie first of all deliberately parted her cheeks to show everyone her anus, then spanked her crisply until her cheeks glowed brightly.

Then Sister Tanya, grim-faced, as Sophie expected from the most truly dominant of the sisters, presented her lovely round behind, hissing softly when her anus was exposed but otherwise taking her spanking without a murmur.

Next, Sister Helga trotted up and flung herself across Sophie's thighs with surprising enthusiasm and her spectacularly white skin reddened beautifully as Sophie spanked her with growing skill.

Finally, Sister Philippa's lovely bottom was filling her vision, displaying a rare combination of mature breadth and pert youthfulness.

The slaves were summoned and Sophie strapped each one to the birching block and, with Sister Tanya's help, demonstrated the full range of its possibilities, taking into account the significant differences in the three bottoms.

Jenny was neat and pert in every respect. Buttocks, anus

and fanny. Sophie arranged her in the most extreme position, with torso sloping down and knees doubled up and widely parted, so that the audience had an unobstructed view of the lot while Sophie applied paddle, strap and then birch, having previously agreed with Sister Tanya that these implements needed less practice to master than canes and whips.

Brenda's bottom presented a complete contrast. Big, soft, rather wobbly buttocks but divided by a surprisingly shallow cleft so that her bottom-hole popped into view quite easily. Unlike Jenny's neat, pinky-brown orifice, Brenda's was big, dark and bold, to the extent that Sophie reckoned that it formed such a focal point to her splayed bottom that it rather detracted from the view of punished buttocks. Kneeling on the block with ninety degree angles at pelvis and knees presented her bottom moer appropriately for the main part of her whipping, although Sophie decided that she was being unfair to both the audience and Jenny by not putting Brenda's anus on display, so finally asked Sister Maureen help her adjust her crimson-bottomed victim into the most extreme pose so that she could have her open cleft, anus and fanny tickled up with the tips of the birch.

On the old principle that the best should be saved until last, Lavinia stepped forward after Brenda's rump had been anointed with the magic healing cream. Sophie, by then in a state of heady excitement, took full advantage of her in-between status – neither slave nor dominatrix – to make their relationship quite plain. She undressed her completely, turned her back to the audience and firmly invited them to admire her rear. She patted the plumpest part of each cheek to show off the delicious springy quiver; she made her bend over and part her buttocks to display the delicate, pale brown anus she had come to love so much. Then she helped her on to the block, carefully arranging her, knees slightly parted and bent in, torso gently sloping, straps at mid thigh and waist, their shiny blackness emphasising the gentle girl's flawless complexion.

She whipped her dear friend and lover hard, revelling in the sense of power but always fully conscious of her reactions and concentrating on the parts of her bottom which she knew Lavinia found most receptive. As she had done with Brenda, she finished off by flicking the frayed ends of her rod into her open division, making her adorable little bottom-hole twitch with pain and pleasure.

When it was over and before she applied the cream, she felt no embarrassment at bending and kissing both hot, corrugated cheeks all over.

The slaves left and Sophie faced her approving audience, slowly removed her boots and collar and stood, with her twinkling rings drawing their eyes to her shapely breasts and tight, plump, compact fanny.

Sisters Tanya and Maureen carried over the rectangular whipping frame and bolted the feet to the floor. She stood in between the uprights, moved her feet apart so that they could be tied fast. Her arms were pulled out to the sides and tied tightly to rings in the wooden uprights.

She was ready, naked, spreadeagled, only able to move her head and hips. Her mind drifted as everyone enjoyed a last look at her white, unmarked body.

Her right palm still held various impressions – the softness of the sisters' bare buttocks; the handles of the implements she had used on the slaves.

Sister Helga had given her en enema just before the ceremony and her insides felt clean and clear. And her anus tingled slightly as she recalled the moment when the slim, hard tube had slid past it and into her rectum.

She caught Elspeth's eye and her dazzling, happy smile sent a surge of pure happiness through her. She knew that she would offer even this experienced and sophisticated group a memorable spectacle.

Sister Tanya moved into view, startling in her black catsuit, her little pink bottom peeking cheekily out of the hole in the back. Studs twinkled in the strong light.

Sophie took a deep breath, thrust her trembling breasts out to receive the first, maddening sting of the horsehair whisk and mentally prepared herself for pain and nothing but pain.

For ten minutes, her entire front was lashed. Arms, sides, tummy, thighs and legs. Breasts and fanny. Especially her breasts and fanny. 'Stick your cunt out,' Tanya whispered.

She did and held it out, even though the coarse hair stung like mad.

She could relax as her legs were whipped all the way down to her feet.

Then she was untied, turned round and tied up again.

Her back and legs were set on tingling fire.

But not her bottom. As agreed.

At the end she slumped against the ropes, breathing hoarsely, calling on her deep reserves of strength to handle the treatment of her unmarked bottom with even more than her usual fortitude.

Maureen and Helga slotted a horizontal beam into the apparatus, level with her pelvis, the thickly padded centre making her bottom jut out nicely.

Philippa paddled her. A big, heavy hardwood paddle, which jerked her against the beam with every stroke and made her bottom wobble frantically.

Helga whipped with a heavy martinet, first rearranging her body so that her hands were tied to her ankles and she was doubled over the beam like a hairpin. The pointed crests of her buttocks bore the brunt of the punishment but her cleft was obviously too tempting a target to be ignored and the bite of the lashes' tips had her crying out in pain. But not in protest.

Maureen had her feet tied together and gave her twelve of the very best with her favourite school cane, concentrating on the lower parts of her bottom.

Then the finale. On the block. Knees right up, head well down. Blazingly sore bottom thrust up. Everything on view.

An added refinement. The padded section under her

squashed breasts was removed, revealing a panel covered with fairly sharp little studs. Her breasts were still a bit sore from the fly whisk and the only way to ease the additional pain was to press down with her hands and try to lift the softness clear.

Which was difficult.

And which added greater prominence to her bottom.

Tanya applied the birch with loving skill. Her love of that magnificent implement, her love of Sophie's bottom and her affection for its owner all seemed to communicate themselves to the helpless girl.

She appreciated the way that the birch stung only her skin. The other, heavier implements had hurt flesh more than skin.

Her purple bottom gyrated in the confines of her bonds, eloquently describing the joy of suffering.

The red mists spread through her head and her strength faded completely, so that the only reaction from the final six was the barely noticeable quivering of her buttocks.

Then it was over.

The icy feel of the first blob of cream began to bring her round but it was still ten minutes before she felt able to stand unaided and acknowledge the congratulations of her audience.

Elspeth's open mouthed kiss made her blush with pleasure and speeded up her recovery more than a little.

Then she was ready for the final act. She knelt on a footstool and offered her exposed bottom-hole to the master, who accepted with grave courtesy and reamed her rectum with considerate gentleness until his climax approached and his hard belly slammed against her buttocks.

Lastly, and totally unexpectedly, her rings were removed.

She looked down at her unadorned nipples, still puckered and standing proud of the pink flesh around them, and felt a pang of regret.

Then it struck her.

She was free.

# More exciting titles available from Chimera

****

All **Chimera** titles are available from your local bookshop or newsagent, or direct from our mail order department. Please send your order with your credit card details, a cheque or postal order (made payable to *Chimera Publishing Ltd*) to: **Chimera Publishing Ltd., Readers' Services, PO Box 152, Waterlooville, Hants, PO8 9FS**. Or call our **24 hour telephone/fax credit card hotline: +44 (0)23 92 646062** (Visa, Mastercard, Switch, JCB and Solo only).

**UK & BFPO -** Aimed delivery within three working days.
- A delivery charge of £3.00.
- An item charge of £0.20 per item, up to a maximum of five items.

For example, a customer ordering two items for delivery within the UK will be charged £3.00 delivery + £0.40 items charge, totalling a delivery charge of £3.40. The maximum delivery cost for a UK customer is £4.00. Therefore if you order more than five items for delivery within the UK you will not be charged more than a total of £4.00 for delivery.

**Western Europe -** Aimed delivery within five to ten working days.
- A delivery charge of £3.00.
- An item charge of £1.25 per item.

For example, a customer ordering two items for delivery to W. Europe, will be charged £3.00 delivery + £2.50 items charge, totalling a delivery charge of £5.50.

**USA -** Aimed delivery within twelve to fifteen working days.
- A delivery charge of £3.00.
- An item charge of £2.00 per item.

For example, a customer ordering two items for delivery to the USA, will be charged £3.00 delivery + £4.00 item charge, totalling a delivery charge of £7.00.

**Rest of the World -** Aimed delivery within fifteen to twenty-two working days.
- A delivery charge of £3.00.
- An item charge of £2.75 per item.

For example, a customer ordering two items for delivery to the ROW, will be charged £3.00 delivery + £5.50 item charge, totalling a delivery charge of £8.50.